Harvest of Bones: A Thanksgiving Horror Anthology

S.B. Fates

Published by Sean Benoit, 2023.

This is a work of fiction. Similarities to real people, places, or events are entirely coincidental.

HARVEST OF BONES: A THANKSGIVING HORROR ANTHOLOGY

First edition. November 7, 2023.

ISBN: 979-8223681762

Written by S.B. Fates.

Also by S.B. Fates

Dark Corners: Tales from the Shadow Realms
The Shadows We Cast: Tales of the Uncanny
Shadows of the Multiverse
Echoes in the Void
Shadows of Malice: Chilling Chronicles of All Hallows' Eve
Eclipsed Virtues: Tales of the Damned Superhuman
Harvest of Bones: A Thanksgiving Horror Anthology

Table of Contents

Prelude by S.B. Fates

Welcome, dear reader, to our grotesque banquet of tales—a veritable cornucopia of nightmares that I have carefully cultivated for you. "Harvest of Bones" is not merely a collection; it is an invitation to glance into the abyss that gapes wide beneath the November frost, under the golden leaves and the scent of spices and roasted meat.

Each story you are about to devour, like a dish passed around a table heavy with bounty, has been prepared with the darkest ingredients harvested from the human psyche. These tales are not merely to frighten but to provoke the taste of dread on your tongue, a lingering aftertaste that no amount of sweet pie can dispel.

You might find yourself at home among the familial chaos of "Giblets of Wrath," feeling the prickle of recognition as old wounds are laid bare. Or perhaps you will walk the "Threshing Floor," your footsteps echoing against a silence that is far from peaceful. You may lose yourself in "Pilgrim's Regress," where the past and present entwine in a macabre dance, or you might flip the pages to the rhythm of the oars of "The Gravy Boatman," where every stroke takes you further from the light.

With "Stuffing the Void," I invite you to taste the desperation of a grief that feeds on the soul, and in the "Feast of the Wicker Man," you will feel the heat of the flames that consume more than just straw and twine. And finally, "Thanks-taking" will offer you a seat at a table where to dine is to despair.

This anthology is a tribute to the shadows that lie in wait in the heart of tradition, the specters that haunt our festive celebrations. For within the embrace of Thanksgiving, where we gather to give thanks for our blessings, we might forget that darkness is most potent when contrasted with light, and that evil often festers in places of joy.

So, come. Take your place at this table I have set for you. Pick up your fork and sharpen your knife. It's time to carve into the "Harvest of Bones." And remember, in the feast of fear, it is not the body but the mind that is consumed. Bon appétit.

~ S.B. Fates

Giblets of Wrath

The Whitley estate, with its towering gables and sprawling grounds, stood as a stoic guardian over the town of Harrowgate. Its shadow stretched long and thin as the sun dipped low in the sky, casting an amber glow over the fading splendor of the once grand manor. The air was heavy with the scent of decay, leaves rotting beneath the skeletal embrace of ancient trees, their gnarled fingers scratching at a leaden sky.

As the remaining light bled from the day, a procession of vehicles whispered up the long drive, tires crunching on gravel that had seen better days. One by one, the Whitleys returned to their ancestral roost, drawn back by blood and tradition to a home that felt less welcoming with each passing year.

Eleanor Whitley stood at the window, her piercing blue eyes tracking the arrivals with the scrutiny of a hawk. The tight pull of her hair only served to accentuate the sharpness of her features, her gaze unsettlingly intense. The mansion, with its dark wood and faded tapestries, seemed to mirror her—a testament to bygone grandeur, shrouded in an aura of suppressed dread.

The first to step out was George, his form stooped, as if carrying the weight of the estate's crumbling façade on his shoulders. His brown, grey-flecked hair caught in the wind, flapping about like the weathered shutters hanging loosely on their hinges. George's hands, shoved into the pockets of his worn jacket, trembled slightly—not from the cold, but from a familiar anxiety that clawed at his chest every time he crossed the threshold of his childhood home.

"Still standing, I see," he muttered, more to himself than to the house.

Marlene hurried to his side, her thin frame wrapped tightly in a coat that seemed to swallow her whole. Her eyes, quick and darting, took in the ominous presence of the manor before fixing on George with an intensity that belied her nervous disposition.

"It's like it's waiting for us," she whispered, a shiver tracing the length of her spine, "as if the house knows we're here."

George offered a grunt that might've been agreement, his gaze never quite meeting hers. They made their way to the door, hand in hand, a united front against an unseen enemy.

Next came Sarah, her car pulling up with a purr that seemed too lively for the somber surroundings. She stepped out with a grace that defied the mood, her untamed curls bouncing freely. A smile played on her lips, but her eyes, so much like her grandmother's, betrayed a strength and solemnity that clashed with her carefree demeanor.

"Home for the holidays," she sang out, a tinge of irony to her voice. "Can't wait to see what's on the menu this year."

The final arrival was Thomas, who emerged from his taxi like a shadow detaching itself from the encroaching night. His slow, deliberate movements were a stark contrast to the taxi driver's hurried unloading of his bags, eager to leave the oppressive atmosphere of the Whitley grounds.

"Thanks," Thomas said dryly, his voice as dark as the humor that always seemed to dance around the edges of his words. "Don't wait up."

As the doors of the Whitley estate opened with a mournful creak, the family assembled in the foyer, a space that felt too large, too cold. The walls, lined with portraits of stern ancestors, seemed to watch them with silent judgment. Eleanor descended the grand staircase, each step deliberate, the whisper of her dress against the marble the only sound in a heavy silence.

"My darlings," she began, her voice cutting through the air, "welcome home."

As the last rays of sun vanished behind the horizon, the estate was swallowed by the gathering gloom. The Thanksgiving reunion had begun, and with it, the slow peeling away of the family's genteel façade, revealing the fragile web of tension that bound them together—a web that was destined to be shattered before the weekend was through.

The house seemed to exhale as the door closed, swallowing the last of the day's dying light. Eleanor stood framed by the dim glow of the foyer, her silhouette rigid and commanding. Yet as the eyes of her family met hers, a flicker of something unsteady danced in their depths, a flame struggling against a cold wind. It was gone in a heartbeat, replaced by the stern matriarch the Whitleys knew—or thought they knew.

"Eleanor," George's voice was barely above a whisper, but it filled the cavernous space as effectively as a shout.

She offered a nod, her response devoid of warmth. "George. Marlene." Her gaze shifted to Sarah and Thomas, lingering just a moment too long, as if searching their faces for something she dreaded to find. "Sarah. Thomas. You've all grown so thin. City life doesn't feed you like the country does."

Her words hung heavy, each one weighed down by an unseen burden.

Thomas chuckled, a sound devoid of any real humor. "Or maybe it's this place that's eating at us, not the other way around."

Eleanor's eyes narrowed, but she let the comment pass, her fingers tightening imperceptibly around the balustrade. "Dinner will be at seven. Be punctual." Her command was a dismissal, and she turned, ascending the stairs as though she carried the weight of the house on her own shoulders.

As the family dispersed, the silence was oppressive, filled with unspoken words and unease that clung to the air like cobwebs. In her room, Eleanor closed the door with a soft click. She leaned back against it, allowing herself a moment of vulnerability. Her breath came out in a shuddering sigh, the façade of the indomitable matriarch crumbling away in the privacy of her sanctum.

The room was frozen in time, with Victorian wallpaper clinging to the walls and heavy drapes that blotted out the encroaching night. She approached the dresser, her hands trembling as she pulled open a drawer. Beneath layers of linen, her fingers found the leather-bound journal she had hidden away decades ago. The binding creaked as she opened it, the pages yellowed with age.

The words within were written in a hand she knew as well as her own, the looping script of her late husband, confessions that were never meant for her eyes—nor anyone else's. Her breath hitched as she read, each word a nail driven into the coffin of her sanity.

There was a stir in the air, a whisper of movement that had her snapping the journal shut. She turned, eyes scanning the room for any sign of an intruder. But she was alone—or so it seemed. The feeling of being watched was palpable, a gaze she could almost feel on her skin. It was a sensation she had become familiar with, one she had hoped would be buried with her husband.

The dinner bell's chime crept up the stairs, a harbinger of the night to come. Eleanor tucked the journal away, her composure once again an impenetrable mask. She could not afford to be shaken, not when her grip on the family was held by so delicate a thread.

Descending to the dining room, she found the family assembled, a tableau of tension and false smiles.

"Ah, there she is," Marlene said, her voice brittle. "The queen descends from her throne."

Eleanor chose to ignore the barb, taking her place at the head of the table. "I trust the rooms are to your satisfaction?"

"They're just as I remember them," Sarah replied, "though I could do without the dust and..." Her voice trailed off as she caught Eleanor's gaze, the warning in it clear as glass.

Thomas was staring into his wine glass, the crimson liquid reflecting in his dark eyes. "To family," he said, raising his glass. The toast was more obligation than sentiment.

Glasses clinked hollowly as they echoed the sentiment, drinking to a family unity that felt as fragile as the crystal in their hands.

The meal passed with clinking cutlery and stilted conversation, the undercurrent of something sinister threading between words left unsaid. Eleanor's control was a vise, but as the evening wore on, a cold draft swept through the room, causing candles to flicker.

Marlene caught her breath, looking up. "Is there a window open?"

But it was Eleanor who felt the chill settle deep in her bones, a coldness that came from within the walls of the house itself. The whispers of the past were growing louder, and as the shadows played upon the walls, she knew that the secrets she held close were clawing their way to the surface, threatening to tear everything asunder.

Her grip tightened around her knife, the silver glinting ominously. The matriarch's fear had taken root, and as the evening unfolded, Eleanor Whitley realized that this Thanksgiving was merely the beginning of an unraveling that could not be stopped.

George stood outside on the veranda, the cold air gnawing at his bones. The ember of his cigarette glowed bright in the darkness, a beacon of his isolation. Smoke curled up into the night sky, disappearing into the void as if carrying away pieces of his thoughts. He drew in a lungful of the sharp, wintry air mixed with the bitter tobacco, his mind churning with unrest.

The door behind him creaked open, and the light from inside spilled out, casting long shadows across the lawn. "George," came Eleanor's stern voice, laced with an edge that cut through the stillness. "What are you doing out here? You're missing dessert."

George didn't turn to face her. "I'm not hungry," he said, his voice a low rasp.

"You never were one for sweets," she said, her tone softening just enough to seem out of character. "But this isn't about food, is it?"

"It never is," he muttered, finally facing her. The orange light painted her features in a harsh contrast, highlighting the lines time had etched into her face.

They stood in silence, the distance between them filled with years of words left unsaid, until George's voice broke the quiet. "We need to talk about him, mother. About dad."

Eleanor stiffened, her eyes flitting away for an instant before regaining their usual resolve. "There's nothing to say. He's gone, and that's the end of it."

But George shook his head, his eyes hardening. "No. It's not the end. You know it as well as I do. There's something about this house, about our family..." He paused, the last word tasting like poison.

Eleanor's hand flew to her throat, where a necklace – a simple gold chain – lay against her skin. "I will not let you unravel everything we have built because of some baseless suspicions."

"They're not baseless and you know it!" George snapped, the embers of his anger fanned by the chill. "The journal, mother. I found the journal."

Her façade cracked, her hand dropping from her necklace. "What are you talking about?"

"In the ashes," he said, his eyes burning not from the smoke but from the revelation. "You didn't burn it all. I found a piece, enough to know that there's more to dad's death than the story we've been fed."

A tremor passed through Eleanor's body, her breath visible in the air as if her soul was attempting to escape the confines of its fleshly prison. "You shouldn't have read that," she whispered, her voice almost inaudible.

"But I did," George countered, stepping closer. "And it's time we stop pretending. It's time we face what this family truly is."

There was a dangerous silence before Eleanor spoke again. "You don't understand what you're asking for, George. The past... it's better left buried."

"Lies are what should be buried, not the truth," George said, his tone resolute. "How many more Thanksgivings are we going to sit through, pretending we're a family, when all we have is a house full of ghosts?"

Eleanor's gaze met his, and for a moment, he saw the terror in her eyes—the fear of a woman haunted by specters he could not begin to understand. She took a step back, as if the weight of his words was a physical force.

"I need to protect this family," she said, but the commanding tone she was known for had vanished, replaced by a frailty that George had never heard before.

"By hiding the truth?" he asked.

The door to the veranda opened again, and Sarah's voice floated out to them. "Mom? Dad? Are you coming in? It's freezing out here."

They both turned to look at her, and in that brief exchange of glances, an unspoken agreement passed between mother and son. Not now. Not in front of the others.

"Give us a minute, Sarah," George said, managing a smile that felt like it might crack his face.

Sarah nodded, casting a curious glance between them before retreating inside, the warmth of the house swallowing her up.

Eleanor looked back at George, her expression hardened once more. "We will discuss this," she said, her voice low. "But not tonight. Enjoy the rest of the evening, for your sister's sake."

With that, she turned and walked back into the house, leaving George alone with the cold and his thoughts. He flicked the remainder of his cigarette into the night, watching as the red tip faded into ashes.

Tonight, the ghosts of the past had been stirred, and as he followed his mother's footsteps back into the Whitley estate, George knew that there was no turning back. The whispers and the ashes had spoken, and by dawn, nothing would ever be the same again.

Marlene Whitley's hands trembled as she folded the linen napkin on her lap, her movements sharp and erratic like the crackling of thin ice. The dining room, with its high-backed chairs and elongated table, had become a theater of unease, every glance and gesture imbued with silent accusation. The crystal chandelier above cast fragmented light, throwing distorted shadows that seemed to mock her distress.

"Isn't this just lovely?" she chirped, the edges of her voice frayed as she tried to pierce the growing tension. "Eleanor, the pecan pie is divine."

Eleanor nodded with a tight-lipped smile, her attention momentarily diverted from the hushed conversations at the far end of the table. "Thank you, Marlene. It's an old family recipe."

Marlene attempted to return the smile but felt her face contort into a grimace as her eyes caught sight of something peculiar—a series of jagged symbols crudely carved into the underside of the table. Her heart pounded against her ribs, a caged bird desperate to escape, as she traced her fingers over the markings, their significance eluding her.

"What are those?" she whispered, more to herself than to anyone else.

"What was that, dear?" George's voice carried from across the table, his eyes narrowing.

"Nothing," Marlene said too quickly, recoiling as if the carvings had scorched her fingertips. "Just admiring the craftsmanship."

As the evening dragged on, the walls of the Whitley estate seemed to close in, suffocating in their antiquity. Marlene excused herself, her laugh a shrill soundtrack to her retreat as she fled to the sanctuary of the kitchen. The clamor of the family's voices faded behind her, replaced by the ticking of the grandfather clock in the hall, each tock a thunderous proclamation of her growing hysteria.

The kitchen was dim, the only light emanating from the oven's digital display and the pale moonlight that filtered through the windows. Marlene moved towards the refrigerator, the soft hum of its motor a comforting reminder of normalcy. She reached for a bottle of water, her hand shaking so violently that the plastic crinkled loudly in her grasp.

Then she heard it—the faintest whisper, like the hiss of a serpent, coming from the pantry. "Not real," she murmured, pressing a hand to her chest as if to hold her fraying nerves together. Her eyes darted around the room, landing on the block of kitchen knives, their blades glinting ominously.

"Get a grip, Marlene," she scolded herself, a giggle bubbling up and spilling over into a cascade of crazed laughter.

Taking a deep breath, she crept toward the pantry, the whispering growing louder, more insistent. She flung the door open, the light from the kitchen slicing through the darkness. But there was nothing—just cans and dry goods lined neatly on the shelves.

A draft of cold air brushed against her neck, sending shivers down her spine. Marlene spun around, her eyes wide, the eerie sensation of not being alone clinging to her like a second skin.

She was about to leave when a glint caught her eye—a knife missing from the block, its absence a silent scream in the quiet kitchen. Her gaze slowly swept the room, landing on the swinging door that led back to the dining room.

The whispering ceased abruptly, as if aware of her discovery, and Marlene's laugh fractured into hysterics. She stumbled backward, her back pressing against the cold metal of the refrigerator, and as her laughter echoed through the Whitley estate, it carried with it the chilling realization that the horrors of the past were not content to lie dormant.

They were awake, hungry, and hidden within the very walls that had promised to keep her safe.

Sarah Whitley's boots clicked against the ancient wood of the Whitley estate's floors as she moved with purpose towards the head of the table, her mother's hysterical laughter still echoing from the kitchen like the mad cackling of a witch over a bubbling cauldron. The eyes of her family followed her every step, a mixture of bewilderment and dread in their gazes. The oppressive weight of tradition hung heavily in the room, a noose around the neck of progress.

"Grandmother," Sarah began, her voice steady but tinged with an undercurrent of defiance. "Why do we continue these farcical traditions? This charade of familial bliss?" She gestured broadly at the opulent dining room, her eyes blazing. "We're suffocating under the weight of this so-called heritage!"

Eleanor's piercing blue eyes locked onto Sarah, unblinking, statuesque. "Our traditions are the threads that weave the fabric of this family, my dear," she said, her voice low but ironclad. "You do well to remember that."

Sarah leaned in, her voice dropping to a conspiratorial whisper that nonetheless carried to every ear in the room. "But what about the secrets, Grandmother? The whispers that hide behind the smiles? Are those traditions too?"

A sudden gust of wind rattled the windows, as if in answer to her challenge, and with a crackle and a hiss, the lights flickered and died, plunging the room into darkness. A collective gasp rose from the table, the sound tinged with a primal fear that darkness so often invites.

"Stay seated!" George's voice cut through the blackness, his attempt at authority barely veiling his own alarm.

But Sarah was already moving, her eyes adjusting quickly to the dim moonlight that bathed the room in a ghostly hue. "A power outage," she stated matter-of-factly, as though she hadn't just railed against the family's darkest secrets. "I'll find some candles."

Her footsteps retreated, and in the void she left behind, the family sat frozen, a tableau vivant underscored by the ever-present ticking of the grandfather clock. In the dark, the space seemed to contract and expand in unpredictable waves, as if the house itself were breathing.

The hunt for illumination soon turned into a game of hide and seek, though none had voiced the rules. Sarah, her heart pounding not from fear but from the thrill of confrontation, moved through the familiar rooms with ease. She could feel the house revealing its hidden passageways and alcoves to her, as it always had since her childhood.

Her hand brushed against the velvety surface of an old photograph, and she paused. With a flicker of her lighter, she illuminated a disturbing collection of family portraits. The faces, once stern and proud, had been scratched out, leaving hollow voids where eyes should have been. A shiver ran down Sarah's spine—not from the chill in the air, but from the realization that the house was sharing its secrets with her, revealing its history of darkness and madness.

She traced a finger over the jagged lines obscuring her ancestors' faces, a silent communion with the past. Every scratch seemed to whisper tales of malice and retribution, and Sarah knew, deep in her rebel heart, that she was the one meant to bring these secrets into the light.

"Sarah?" Thomas's voice came from the doorway, a hint of trepidation bleeding through. "What are you doing?"

Sarah snapped the lighter shut, plunging them back into obscurity. "Playing the game, Tommy," she replied, her voice a singsong murmur. "Don't you hear it? The house wants us to find it. To seek out the truth hidden in the shadows."

Thomas moved closer, his own lighter flickering to life, casting an eerie glow on his face. "Or maybe it's just a power outage. Nothing more sinister than that."

But Sarah's laugh, soft and haunting, belied the skepticism in his voice. "Oh, Tommy, when has it ever been that simple with the Whitleys?"

The wind howled outside, a banshee's wail that seemed to mock their search for answers. The house creaked and groaned, alive with the stirrings of a restless past. And in the dark, the game continued, each seeker blind to the fact that they were also the hunted, the past reaching out with ghostly fingers to draw them into its embrace.

The storm had been brooding on the horizon since morning, but it was only as dusk fell that its first tendrils swept across Harrowgate, creeping like wraiths amongst the bared trees of the Whitley estate. The weather seemed to mirror the darkening mood within the house, as if the very heavens were privy to the undercurrents of malcontent amongst the family.

Thomas stood at a window, watching the storm approach. He seemed part of the shadowy room, barely distinguishable from the furnishings save for the occasional glint of light off his eyes. The murmuring conversation had lulled to a pensive silence, but Thomas's quiet was of a different nature; it had depth, as if he was not truly with them but conversing with the phantoms that the storm had disturbed.

Sarah, candles now in hand, cast a warm glow as she reentered the room, her earlier fervor replaced by a sisterly concern. She paused, noting Thomas's silhouette against the windowpane. "Tommy?" she called softly, not wanting to startle him.

He turned, and there was something in his gaze that gave her pause—an intensity that seemed out of place, even in the context of their bizarre family gathering.

"I found something," Thomas said, his voice low, almost lost beneath the growl of thunder. He moved away from the window, his form becoming more solid as he stepped into the candlelight.

Sarah's eyes followed him as he reached into his pocket and produced a fragment of aged paper, creased and yellowed with time. The journal fragment trembled slightly in his hand.

"What is it?" she asked, her curiosity piqued.

"It belonged to him," Thomas said, a hint of reverence lacing his tone as he referred to the original patriarch. "It speaks of things... Things that have been long buried."

The house seemed to lean in closer, its creaks and sighs a chorus of anticipation.

"Let's hear it, then," Sarah urged, a part of her regretting the prompt as she spoke it.

Thomas cleared his throat and began to read, his voice taking on a timbre that seemed to conjure the very essence of their forebear.

"'November's breath is cold on my neck as I write this. The curse of '29 has laid heavy on our kin. The earth hath no fury like a promise scorned. And so it shall be, as the leaves wither and die, so too shall the Whitley line feel the grip of penance...'"

A chilling silence followed, the last word hanging in the air like the afterimage of a lightning strike.

"What curse?" Sarah whispered, though she wasn't sure she wanted the answer.

"The legend says," Thomas began, his voice now a grave melody, "that our great-great-grandfather made a vow to the land here, a vow he broke. And so, each generation must pay the tithe. A Thanksgiving curse, they called it. A reckoning that comes with the harvest moon."

Lightning flashed, a jagged scar across the sky, illuminating Thomas's face in stark relief. "They say the land remembers, Sarah. It remembers and it calls out for what it's owed."

Sarah felt a shudder course through her—not from the cold, but from the realization of what lay in his words. Thomas wasn't just speaking of old tales; he was weaving them into the present, into the very walls that surrounded them.

"The land is just land, Tommy," she said, trying to convince herself as much as him. "It doesn't remember. It doesn't demand."

But Thomas shook his head slowly, his eyes never leaving the window, where the storm had begun to batter the glass with rain. "You haven't heard the whispers, sis. The voices on the wind. They're not happy with whispers and secrets anymore. They're hungry for more."

As if on cue, a crash echoed from the other side of the house, the sound of something heavy and solid hitting the floor—something, or someone. The family's collective breath caught, a symphony of dread.

"We should check on the others," Sarah said, her voice barely concealing the tremor of fear.

They moved together, Sarah leading with her candles, casting long, dancing shadows on the walls. As they left the room, the fragment of journal slipped from Thomas's hand, settling on the floor as the storm outside raged with increasing ferocity, an unseen spectator to the unfolding drama within the Whitley estate.

The crash had drawn them all to the library, a sanctum of dark wood and leather-bound spines that seemed to smell of secrets. Eleanor stood in the doorway, her silhouette rigid, the matriarchal mask betraying no emotion. George and Marlene, close behind, clutched at each other with a frail desperation, as if their touch could ward off the encroaching darkness.

It was the bookshelf that had fallen, a monolith of mahogany that now lay sprawled across the Persian rug, its contents spilled like the entrails of some great beast. Dust motes danced in the air, stirred into life by the disturbance. And amidst the chaos, a narrow void in the wall revealed itself—a hidden compartment laid bare.

"God in Heaven," Marlene gasped, her voice a fragile thing, fluttering against the onslaught of the storm outside.

"Be still," Eleanor commanded, her voice slicing through the din of the tempest and the pounding of their collective hearts. "This was no accident. This house... It speaks when it's time to listen."

Sarah's hand was the first to move towards the void, her fingers brushing against the cool edge of the hidden alcove. Her touch seemed to ignite a silent symphony, a resonance with the secrets of old. And there it was, nestled in the dark, a journal bound in leather cracked with age, its clasp a tarnished silver that spoke of a time long gone.

As she drew it forth, the whispers seemed to grow louder, the hiss of history joining the howl of the wind. The family circled, an unwitting coven, as Sarah laid the journal on the only table untouched by the collapse.

"The patriarch's journal," Thomas said, the timbre of his voice a dark thread weaving through the tense air. "The whole thing. Not just fragments."

Eleanor's hands trembled as she reached for it, the stern façade giving way to something more human, more vulnerable. "Let me," she whispered, the words almost a plea. They all watched, a collective breath held, as she opened the journal with reverence, the crackle of the binding a sound like bone snapping.

The first page was a scrawl, the ink faded but the message clear enough to chill the blood.

"'Blood will have blood,' it began. 'The soil of the Whitley estate is steeped in sin, and I have sown it with my deeds.'"

Eleanor's voice wavered, and for a moment, she seemed not the imposing matriarch but an old woman burdened with the weight of years.

The passage continued, Eleanor narrating the horrific account, the patriarch's own words describing a heinous act so vile it seemed to draw the shadows closer, as if they wished to drink in the tale.

It spoke of betrayal, of a blood oath broken, and the wrath of something that the patriarch referred to only as 'The Custodian of the Land'. An entity or force, it seemed, that demanded a terrible price for the Whitley's prosperity.

As the tale unfolded, so too did the room seem to constrict, walls pressing in, the storm outside echoing the chaos that once reigned over the very ground on which they stood.

George broke the silence that followed. "This is madness," he spat, his voice harsh with scorn. "Our wealth is born of hard work, not some... some faustian pact."

Sarah watched her father, the skepticism in his eyes a fortress against the fear that threatened to dismantle his composure.

But Thomas, he reacted differently. A nod, slow, almost imperceptible, as if some piece of a puzzle had fallen into place for him. "It explains so much," he muttered, mostly to himself. "The accidents, the disappearances over the years. We've been blind."

Marlene's laughter sliced through the tension, a sound that bordered on hysteria. "Curses? Blood oaths? We are not some gothic novel characters. This is reality!"

Eleanor closed the journal with a snap, the sound final, like the closing of a coffin lid. "Reality is what we have chosen to ignore," she said, her gaze sweeping over them all. "But no longer. This... entity, this Custodian... it has come to collect."

The candles flickered as a draught found its way through the crevices of the old room, and with it came a smell, earthy and rotten, like the decay of autumn leaves. Eleanor's voice was a whisper, but it carried, heavy with the gravity of truth.

"We must prepare. The storm is not just weather; it is a herald. And by morning, our family will have to face the reckoning it brings."

Outside, the lightning cracked the sky once more, a spine of light that illuminated their faces in flashes of stark white. Fear, doubt, resolve—a spectrum of humanity brought to the fore by the revelation of their bloodline's secrets.

The wind gnawed at the corners of the Whitley estate as if hungry for the secrets that lay within its walls. Inside, the air was thick with the musk of old books and the metallic tang of fear. The lightning was no longer just a light show to the Whitleys; it was a harbinger of the night's horrors, carving shadows into every corner, making the familiar seem grotesque.

Thomas was the first to hear it—a muffled thump from the depths of the house, a sound out of place in the nocturnal symphony. "Did you hear that?" he whispered, the edges of his words tinged with an urgency that sent a shiver through the room.

Sarah met his gaze, her own nerves taut. "It came from the cellar."

Without another word, they moved as one entity, a chain of trepidation that slithered down the creaking steps to the wine cellar, the darkness enveloping them like a shroud.

Eleanor led the way, her hand barely trembling as it found the switch, the bulbs overhead flickering to life with a reluctant hum. The light did little to dispel the dread; the shadows seemed to recoil and then gather anew, more defiant.

The wine cellar, usually a place of vintage spirits and whispered secrets, had transformed into a scene from a gothic nightmare. At the far end, the mock dinner table had been set, but it was not wine that filled the crystal goblets—it was blood, dark and congealed.

And there, seated at the head of the table, was the body of a distant cousin, Margaret Whitley, her sightless eyes staring into the void, her mouth agape in a silent scream of terror. Her body was arranged with a macabre dignity, her hands resting on the linen as if she had simply paused in thought, save for the crimson that stained her throat.

A collective gasp tore through the family, a sound so broken it seemed to carry the weight of their dynasty's sins.

George's words cut through the horror. "What in God's name..."

"No God presides here," Eleanor stated, her voice resolute but a hand creeping to her mouth, a crack in her stoic armor.

Marlene's form was shaking, her face pale as death. "Who would do this?" Her voice was barely audible, a thread of sound that seemed as fragile as their sanity.

"We must call the police," Sarah said, practicality veiling her trembling hands.

"No!" The word was a gunshot, explosive and jarring from Eleanor. "Not yet. We don't know if... if whatever did this is still here."

The suggestion hung there, a more terrifying prospect than the body. The idea that the killer could be among them, listening, perhaps even taking pleasure in their fear.

Thomas's eyes were scanning the room, alight with a macabre curiosity. "There's no sign of a struggle," he observed, a detached note in his voice that did little to calm the nerves of the others.

Sarah, the strength of the family in times of stress, took control. "We need to secure the house. Make sure no one else can get in—or out."

"Are you suggesting one of us is a murderer?" Marlene's voice was a whiplash, her eyes wild, darting from face to face as if searching for a hint of the monster among them.

George, the weary storm-chaser, found his voice. "We can't trust anyone—not even each other. Not now."

Eleanor, with a fortitude that belied her years, approached Margaret's body. "She was chosen for a reason," she said, her fingers brushing the cold hands of the deceased. "This is a message."

"But what does it mean?" Sarah's eyes were brimming with tears that she refused to shed.

"It means," Eleanor began, turning back to face her kin, her blue eyes the color of ice, "that the sins of our past have come to feast, and Margaret... Margaret was the first course."

A silence fell, dense as the darkness beyond the cellar door, a silence filled with the unspoken acknowledgment that their Thanksgiving had turned into a funeral. The Whitleys were no longer just a family; they were suspects in a crime that transcended murder, a crime against their own blood.

Outside, the storm raged on, indifferent to the plight within the house, a storm that seemed destined to rage until it had claimed what it came for. And the Whitleys, bound by blood and terror, could only wait for the next revelation, the next horror.

The feast of Thanksgiving had begun, and before the night was through, the Giblets of Wrath would demand more than any of them were prepared to give.

As the last echo of Eleanor's ominous words died away, the Whitley estate seemed to respond, groaning as if in pain. The walls creaked louder, windows slammed shut, and the lights flickered like the final beats of a dying heart. It happened in the span of a few breaths—the house plunged into darkness, the storm outside raging against the barricaded windows, the sound muffled as if submerged underwater.

George was the first to react, his voice a rasp in the dark. "Stay calm. I'll check the fuse box." His words were a futile attempt to inject normalcy into the insanity that had become their reunion.

Marlene clung to his sleeve. "Don't leave us," her words fractured by fear, the tremor in her grasp betraying the terror that threatened to overwhelm her.

"I won't be long," he said, peeling away her fingers gently, a false promise lingering in the air.

Sarah fumbled in her pocket, the beam of her phone's flashlight cutting through the pitch black. The others followed suit, small islands of light in a sea of shadows. Eleanor remained still, her eyes closed, as if in prayer or recollection.

Thomas, armed with the glow of his phone, peered at the corners of the cellar, where the darkness seemed too dense, too intentional. "There's something about the shadows," he murmured, more to himself than to the others.

Sarah's light found her brother's face, his features drawn tight. "What do you mean?"

"They're moving... unnaturally. As if they have a life of their own." His voice was calm, but it held an edge of fascination that was as disturbing as the observation itself.

It was then they heard it—the unmistakable click of a lock engaging from the other side of the cellar door. Panic erupted like a firestorm.

"We're locked in!" Marlene's voice escalated into a scream that fought against the stonework.

Eleanor's eyes snapped open, her voice cutting through the hysteria. "Silence!" The commandment carried the weight of her years and the certainty of authority. "We will not succumb to panic."

The beam of Sarah's light caught the solemn set of her grandmother's face, a portrait of resolve. She nodded, swallowing her fear. "Let's find another way out," she suggested, her voice steady, her flashlight leading the way as they navigated the gauntlet of shadows back to the stairs.

They ascended in a close huddle, stepping out into the main hallway where the absence of George was immediately palpable. The air seemed colder, emptier.

"George?" Marlene's call was met with silence.

Eleanor took charge. "Thomas, Sarah, search the ground floor. Marlene, with me. We'll take the upstairs."

Their movements were methodical, each step deliberate as they scoured the darkened corridors, calling out for George. But it wasn't his name that brought the hunt to a standstill—it was the symbols.

Sarah found the first one, etched into the wooden floor just outside the parlor—a series of lines and curves that mirrored the cryptic insignias from the journal. Its presence was a silent scream in the void.

"Over here," Thomas's voice drew Sarah to another symbol, this one carved into the wall, the plaster around it crumbling.

The marks told a story, a narrative that danced perilously on the edge of understanding. Each one was a breadcrumb leading them through the house, a morbid trail woven through the tapestry of their home.

As they followed the symbols, a sense of being hunted seeped into their bones. The house had become a predator, its halls and rooms the digestive tract of some eldritch creature. The darkness was no longer just an absence of light—it was a presence, watching, waiting.

Their search led them to the library, where the musty smell of books was now laced with something coppery, something wrong. And there, in the center of the room, illuminated by the unreliable beam of Sarah's phone, was George.

He was seated in his favorite armchair, his body slumped, his head bowed as if he had simply dozed off. But the pool of darkness beneath him told the true tale. His hands rested on his lap, palms up, offering up his lifeblood to the pages of an open book, his final story written in the only ink that mattered in that cursed place.

Marlene's wail was a piercing counterpoint to the thunder outside, a raw sound that held no sanity. Eleanor's hand went to her mouth, her composure fracturing.

"We need to leave," Sarah said, the conviction in her voice a stark contrast to the scene before them.

"No," Eleanor whispered, her gaze locked on her son's still form. "The house won't let us. Not until it's finished with us."

The air was heavy with an unspoken truth, a realization that dawned in their eyes one by one.

They were not merely inheritors of the Whitley legacy.

They were its sacrifice.

Marlene's breath came in sharp gasps, her mind a swirl of chaos as she navigated the twisting corridors of the Whitley estate. The shadows seemed to press in on her, each one an accusatory finger, each creak a whisper of her name. She reached her room, the one sanctuary left, and with trembling hands, she locked the door behind her.

The click of the lock was a small comfort, a flimsy shield against the siege of darkness that gripped the house. She leaned against the door, her heart drumming a frantic rhythm in her chest. Outside, the storm wailed like a banshee, its cries the soundtrack to her unraveling sanity.

The room was a tomb of memories, of better days before the shadows took over. Her eyes darted around, seeking out the familiar—pictures of Sarah and Thomas, their smiles frozen in time. But comfort evaded her. The faces in the photos seemed to watch her, their expressions twisted into silent judgments.

It was then she saw it—the shadow. It flitted across the room, a darker patch against the gloom, a void that sucked in the weak light. A scream clawed at her throat, but it was smothered by fear. She stumbled away, knocking over a lamp that shattered with a violence that matched her panic.

Her hands found the cold surface of the desk, and her fingers scraped across the wood, searching for something, anything, that could serve as a weapon. But what she found instead was a sliver of space where the wood didn't quite meet—the seam of a hidden drawer.

With a combination of dread and compulsion, she tugged at it. The drawer gave way with a sigh, revealing its secrets in the pale light of her trembling phone. There, nestled within the velvet lining, was a diary—the cover worn, its edges tinged with the stain of age.

Eleanor's name was inscribed on the inside cover, the handwriting a delicate script that belied the strength of the woman who bore the name. Marlene's breath caught as she flipped through the pages, the words a cascading torrent of paranoia and fear.

November 22, 1955. It watches me. The shadow at the corner of my eye, a flicker of something foul. I feel its hunger...

The entries detailed rituals, protection spells scrawled in a frantic hand, incantations meant to ward off an unseen menace. As she read, the words began to dance before her eyes, blurring into a singular message that seemed to bore into her mind.

It knows you. It knows all the Whitleys...

Marlene's laugh bubbled up, a sound that was part hysteria, part revelation. The book fell from her hands, landing open on the floor as she backed away, her eyes wide and unseeing. Her laughter echoed through the room, a counter melody to the storm's dirge.

She was a Whitley. The shadow knew her, had always known her. And it had been waiting.

The room began to close in on her, the walls a contracting esophagus, the shadows a net cast by a hunter. She needed to hide, to disappear within the bowels of the estate where not even the shadows could find her.

But first, she had to see. She had to understand.

Her fingers traced the lines of the symbols, the same that had been etched into the house's flesh. They held power, a promise of something beyond the veil of sanity she clung to. She repeated the words, the incantations, her voice a raspy whisper that fought to rise above the madness that claimed her.

Outside her barricaded sanctuary, the house waited, its bones creaking in anticipation. And Marlene descended further into the depths, where the line between reality and nightmare blurred beyond recognition. Her fate, like the house itself, had become a thing of shadows and whispers, of giblets and wrath.

The dining room of the Whitley estate had been set with an opulent array of gleaming silver and fine china, crystal goblets catching the quivering light from the candles that flickered like captive spirits. Eleanor, a visage of stoic beauty, presided over the table, her eyes betraying a glint of the storm that raged within Marlene's mind.

George sat, a statue of a man, his features set in stone, the lines of his face etched with the fatigue of a life too long lived in the shadow of the Whitley legacy. His eyes were hollow, reflecting the dance of candle flames, yet seeing nothing of the here and now.

Sarah's chair scraped against the hardwood as she took her place, her demeanor that of a warrior in a garden party dress, ready to face whatever specters this feast might summon. Her usual lighthearted banter was absent, replaced by a grim determination.

Thomas had not yet appeared, and the empty space where he should have been was a silent scream that echoed through Marlene's fractured consciousness.

The dinner began with Eleanor's aged, yet firm voice cutting through the tension. "Let us give thanks for the bounty we are about to receive," she intoned, but the words seemed like a mockery, an incantation of a far different sort.

As the plates were filled with steaming turkey, vibrant cranberry sauce, and an array of side dishes, there was a palpable sense of unease. The food seemed too vibrant, too alive, as if mocking the deadness that had settled in each of their hearts.

It was Sarah who first noticed the peculiar undulation of the gravy, a subtle shift that one's eyes could barely grasp. "Do you see—" she began, but her words were cut off by a sudden sharp yelp from Marlene.

Marlene's fork clattered against her plate, her hand retreating as if bitten. The turkey on her plate, carved into generous slices, seemed to knit itself back together, the skin stretching over the reformed breast in a grotesque mimicry of rebirth. "It's moving," she gasped, her voice a thin thread of sanity about to snap.

Eleanor's piercing gaze swept over the table, a hint of something indefinable in her eyes. "Eat," she commanded. But her authority was a brittle thing, frayed by the chaos that had begun to bloom like a poison flower.

Sarah, brave and unflinching, pierced a slice of turkey with her fork, her other hand gripping her knife with white-knuckled force. "It's just our minds," she declared, but even as she spoke, her slice of meat curled around her fork like a serpent preparing to strike.

George remained motionless, his gaze fixed on the undulating cranberry sauce that was beginning to resemble a pool of blood, thick and congealing. A shiver ran through him, but whether it was fear or something darker, no one could tell.

Eleanor rose abruptly, her chair scraping against the floor with a sound like a death rattle. "Enough of this," she announced, her voice steady even as the room began to breathe around them, the walls pulsing in rhythm with their mounting terror.

As if on cue, the lights flickered, the candles sputtering as though choking on the thickening air. The shadows at the corners of the room grew bold, stretching towards the table with hungry anticipation.

"Thomas," Sarah whispered, her eyes suddenly wide. "Where is Thomas?"

The question was a catalyst, fracturing the last vestige of composure. Marlene's eyes darted around, her breath coming in shallow bursts. "His shirt..." she choked out, "Bloodied... in the garden."

And there, like a specter from a forgotten grave, Thomas's chair remained empty, the fine fabric of his napkin stained with droplets of red that spread like blooming roses.

The family stood, a collective gasp rising from them as they turned towards the door, expecting, fearing. But the hallway beyond offered no salvation, no answers, only the echo of their own dread footsteps in a house that had become a mausoleum for their sanity.

The feast lay before them, untouched yet violated, a mockery of a celebration, a gathering of souls who no longer knew if they were the hunters or the hunted in this grotesque play that unwound within the Whitley estate.

Eleanor's voice, once the commanding force of order, now seemed lost, a mere whisper against the crescendo of terror. "We must find him," she uttered, her words almost a prayer, "before it's too late."

But too late for what, none dared to say. The Feast of the Damned had begun, and its courses were yet to be fully served.

The room lay still in the wake of Eleanor's words, as if the house itself held its breath. The air was thick with the scent of the uneaten feast, yet a chill settled over the room that no fire could warm.

Eleanor's gaze swept across her family, each face reflecting a growing horror at the evening's eerie turn. "There's more at play here than mere superstition," she began, her voice a tremble wrapped in the steel of resolve. The family drew closer, a uniting of spirits in the face of the unknown. "The sacrifices," she continued, "were not just tradition. They were protection."

Sarah's mind reeled. "Protection? From what?" The question hung in the air, a specter itself, awaiting the dreadful acknowledgment of what lurked beneath the surface of their family's legacy.

Eleanor's eyes, those clear blue orbs, flickered with the weight of hidden knowledge. "From the curse that has plagued our bloodline." She turned then, her fingers trembling as they retrieved an ancient leather-bound journal from the cabinet—a tome as old as the house itself.

With a solemn gesture, she laid the book on the table, breaking the seal that had kept it closed for decades. The pages whispered as she turned them, revealing faded ink and a tale so sinister it seemed to leech the warmth from the room.

"Our founder," Eleanor spoke, her voice quavering, "was no mere pilgrim seeking religious freedom, but a man fleeing from his own dark deeds. He made a pact with something... unholy... to protect his line. But such protection required a sacrifice. Every year, on this day, to sate the darkness that would otherwise consume us."

George, his raspy voice barely audible, interjected, "Are you saying we've been... party to this?" Disbelief warred with the evidence of his own eyes—the unnatural movement of the feast before them.

Eleanor's nod was barely perceptible but irrevocable. "It has been... necessary."

Marlene, her eyes wide, whispered with a horror that clawed at her throat, "And Thomas?"

No one spoke. The answer lay in the unsaid, in the fear that gripped them all, that perhaps this year's sacrifice had been chosen—and had fled.

Sarah's chair fell back with a crash as she stood, her face pale but her voice steady with rising fury. "You orchestrated this? You've been choosing who—" She couldn't finish, her heart pounding with the implication of her own words.

The room seemed to close in around them, the shadows deepening. Eleanor's next words were spoken into a silence that seemed to stifle even the beat of their hearts. "I did what I must to protect us all. But the pact... it's been breaking. The soil of our lands has been soured by the blood spilled upon it, and the evil we bargained with now demands more."

It was then that the truth became a blade hanging over them all—no single psychopath had been behind the strange occurrences and the terror that haunted the Whitley lineage. It was a collective madness, an ancestral evil that had seeped into their very bones.

As if to confirm their darkest fears, a guttural scream echoed from the upper floors, a chorus of rage and agony that was all too familiar. It was Thomas's voice, yet not as they knew it. It was twisted by something otherworldly, a sound that no human throat should produce.

George stood, his chair toppling, his face a mask of resolve carved from a lifetime of suffering the sins of his forebears. "We have to end this," he said, and there was a terrible certainty in his voice. "Before it ends us."

Marlene's eyes flickered to the windows where the darkness pressed against the glass like a living thing. "But how? How do you fight a curse that's in your blood?"

Eleanor, with a sorrow that seemed to age her further, if such a thing were possible, clasped the journal to her chest. "We break the cycle. We end the pact, no matter the cost."

The scream came again, this time joined by another, and another—different voices, the same torment. The Whitley family, bound by blood and darkness, moved as one toward the hellish choir.

Sarah reached for the carving knife, the blade catching the candlelight as she moved past the abandoned feast. "Then let's finish this," she said, her voice carrying the weight of an executioner's axe.

The ancestral evil had come to claim its due, but the Whitleys would no longer be its hapless prey. As they ascended the stairs to face the gathering darkness, they were not just a family, but a lineage awakening to the final act of their harrowing legacy. The last stand of the Whitley bloodline had begun.

Staircase steps groaned under the burden of the Whitley procession, a macabre march toward an uncertain redemption. The upper halls of the estate unfurled like the innards of some great beast, dark and twisting. Sarah led the way, her grip on the knife unyielding, her resolve steeled by the chorus of screams that drew them inexorably forward.

As they reached the landing, the house began to betray itself. Walls shuddered, the patter of hidden mechanisms echoing within, like the clicking of insect legs. Panels slid open with the rasp of old secrets, and the darkness oozed out from these newly revealed cavities of the Whitley home.

The first of the hidden rooms yawned wide, an abyssal maw that drew Sarah's gaze. The sight within seized her breath—a tableau of horror arrayed like some grotesque gallery. Corpses, long desiccated, were mounted on the walls, their clothing dating back decades, perhaps centuries. Each was positioned as though frozen in a final plea, their open mouths a silent testament to the Whitley's grim legacy.

"God..." Marlene gasped, her body trembling like a leaf in the storm of revelation. "All this time..."

George moved ahead, eyes hollow yet burning with a vengeful fire. "No more," he growled. "We put an end to this now."

But as they ventured deeper into the home's dark heart, Sarah felt a pull, a siren call from the journal still clutched in Eleanor's brittle hands. It beckoned her, promising answers and, perhaps, the means to end the cycle.

A sudden, bone-jarring crack split the air, and the house seemed to convulse around them. Eleanor stumbled, the journal slipping from her grasp and thumping to the floor, its pages fluttering open as if desperate to speak its truths.

Sarah snatched it up, the aged paper rough against her fingers. The words were a cipher of madness, detailing rites and rituals, sacrifices made in the name of protection, and the ghastly pact with a malevolent force that had birthed the Whitley curse.

The structure of the house continued to groan and mutate around them, walls peeling back to expose more hidden rooms, more secrets. It was as if the estate itself was coming apart, unfurling its history in a last, perverse display.

Amidst the chaos, Thomas's voice, now a distorted echo of his former self, bellowed from the depths of the house. "You can't hide from what's inside!"

Sarah's eyes, wide with the terror of realization, met her mother's. Marlene's face was drawn, ghostly pale, but within her eyes lay a sparking fury. "We must destroy the journal," Marlene said, voice barely above a whisper, yet carrying the weight of finality.

The sound of movement stopped them cold—a scuttling, as if something was moving within the walls themselves. Sarah's breath hitched. In the dim light, she could see the outline of something inhuman, a shadowy figure that seemed to stretch and twist with the architecture of the house.

Eleanor's voice cracked like a whip. "No! The journal—it's all that keeps it at bay!"

"Or what chains it to us!" Sarah countered, the knife in her hand gleaming with an almost otherworldly light. Her decision teetered on the precipice of destiny.

Another room unveiled itself before Sarah, beckoning her with a grim invitation. Inside, the remnants of what appeared to be a failed ritual circled an ancient, stained altar. The very air around it vibrated with an ominous energy.

Sarah approached, the journal's contents etched into her mind. She could destroy the book, attempt to sever the link between the entity and her family, risking unleashing the full wrath of the darkness. Or, she could embrace the knowledge within, bind the entity to her will, and assume the mantle of protector—becoming the very thing she feared.

The house seemed to pulse, an arrhythmic beat that mirrored the hammering of her heart. Dust fell from the ceiling in soft showers, a prelude to collapse, or perhaps a sign of the entity's growing impatience.

Outside, the wind howled, a mournful dirge that sang of endings. The Whitley estate, once a bastion of familial tradition, now stood as a crumbling edifice to terror and madness.

The screams had quieted, replaced by a sinister silence that pressed in on Sarah. Her family stood frozen, caught in the gaze of fateful decisions and revelations too ghastly to comprehend fully.

As the walls of the Whitley home continued their inexorable decay, Sarah clutched the journal against the fading candlelight, the shadows dancing across her determined face. The final choice loomed before her, and within the beating silence of her ancestral home, she made her decision.

The night was deep, and the house waited.

The ruins of the Whitley estate lay scattered like the bones of some colossal creature, picked clean by time and the voracious appetite of the elements. What once stood as a grand manor was now a gnarled skeleton, groaning in the biting November wind that swept through Harrowgate, carrying whispers of the past to those who would listen.

No soul had laid eyes on Sarah Whitley since that fateful Thanksgiving night. She had vanished as if swallowed by the earth itself, leaving behind the accursed journal—the harbinger of the family's downfall. The townspeople spoke of the Whitleys in hushed tones, a mingling of fear and morbid curiosity staining their words. They wondered, they gossiped, but none dared approach the shattered remnants of that once-imposing abode.

In the center of what had been the grand foyer, the journal lay open, its pages fluttering like the wings of a trapped bird in the throes of a dying gust. The text, once written in a meticulous hand, now seemed to squirm and wriggle, the ink bleeding into shapes and symbols that defied understanding.

As the sun began its descent, casting the world in the soft gold of twilight, a car approached, winding its way up the long-abandoned drive. A young couple, filled with dreams of restoration and a fresh start, stepped out, their eyes wide with the naive excitement of new homeownership.

"This place is going to be beautiful again, you'll see," the man said, his arm wrapped protectively around the woman's shoulders.

She nodded, her smile bright yet edged with a hesitant anxiety as she glanced at the decrepit structure. "It's just so... sad looking. But we'll fill it with love and light, right?"

They didn't see the pages of the journal turn, as if by an invisible hand, nor did they hear the soft, sibilant laughter that seemed to seep from the very ground on which they stood.

Inside the car, forgotten in the back seat, a toddler babbled happily to himself, his innocent eyes fixated on something that moved in the shadows of the car's interior. Something that wasn't supposed to be there.

Night was falling, and the house—its appetite whetted by the promise of new life—seemed to stir. The boundaries between past and present blurred, the sins of the forebears a thick essence in the air, potent and ready to ensnare the next lineage.

As darkness embraced the Whitley estate, so too did it welcome the newcomers. Whether as a new beginning or a continuation of an endless, haunted night, only time would tell. For the legacy of the house was not written solely in the blood that stained its floors, but also in the spirits that lingered, watching, waiting, ever hungry for the next chapter in the Whitley saga to unfold.

The end.

Threshing Floor

The horizon bled the last streaks of amber and mauve as the sun sank behind the sprawling Nebraska cornfields. Arthur Morrow stood at the edge of the threshing floor, his eyes tracing the serried ranks of cornstalks that swayed like weary sentinels in the evening breeze. The final preparations for the harvest had been laid out with meticulous care, as they had been for generations, but there was no celebration in his movements, no pride in his gaze. Only a grim satisfaction that spoke of duty and the dark anticipation of things to come.

Judith watched her husband from the shadowed porch, her eyes narrow slits against the dying light. "It's almost time," she murmured, more to herself than to Lena, who stood beside her, shivering despite the warmth of the autumn evening.

Lena's voice held a tremor that belied her usually fiery spirit. "The town's all abuzz about the Morrow harvest. They say it'll be a bounty like no other."

Judith's lips tightened, her response barely audible. "They always do."

The air was thick with the scent of overripe corn, and as the light faded, the whispers seemed to grow louder. It was an old town tale that the corn whispered secrets on the eve of the harvest. Tonight, the whispers felt like screams clawing at the back of Lena's mind.

Inside the house, the family dinner was a somber affair. Caleb sat at the head of the table, his knife slicing through the roast with precise, controlled movements. The sound of the carving was a staccato rhythm that seemed to echo the tension that hung in the air. "Tomorrow, we thresh at first light," he stated, his voice as flat and hard as the plains themselves.

Ethan, sitting across from him, speared a potato with a little too much force. "Can't wait to get it over with," he drawled with a smirk that didn't quite reach his eyes.

It was then, as the family engaged in the pretense of normalcy, that the evening's ominous peace was shattered. Arthur stood abruptly, his chair scraping back violently against the wooden floor. "Found something by the north field," he rasped, throwing a burlap sack onto the table with a dull thud.

Judith's hand flew to her mouth, while Lena, driven by a morbid curiosity, edged closer. The sack was stained dark, and when Arthur unfurled it, the sight within stole the warmth from the room.

It was a rabbit, or what was left of it. The creature's limbs were splayed at unnatural angles, its once soft fur matted with clotted blood. But it was the precision of the mutilation that was most disturbing—a series of intricate cuts, almost ritualistic in nature.

"Animals get into all sorts," Ethan said, his attempt at nonchalance falling flat in the heavy air.

"This wasn't any animal," Arthur countered, his eyes cold as he met Ethan's gaze. "This was a message."

Caleb leaned in, examining the carcass. "A warning," he agreed, his voice devoid of emotion. "It's starting again."

Lena's hand trembled as she reached out, then pulled back. "What does it mean?" she asked, her voice barely above a whisper.

Arthur's reply was as hard as the land he tended. "It means we've got more to do than just harvest corn this year."

As the Morrow family sat in silence, the mutilated rabbit on the table between them, the whispers of the corn grew louder. It was as if the land itself was alive with a malignant anticipation, eager for the rites to commence. Tomorrow, the threshing floor would be busy with the harvest, but tonight, it lay still, a mute testament to the sinister harvest that was yet to come.

In the darkness beyond the farmhouse, the cornfields rustled and hissed, not with the wind, but with the sibilant promises of an ancient malevolence that lay in wait, ready to claim what it was owed. And above, the moon—a silent witness—cast its pale light over the threshing floor, illuminating the stage for a Thanksgiving none would soon forget.

Morning broke with a chill that belied the season, casting a ghostly pallor over the Morrow lands. As the sun peeked timidly over the horizon, its rays fell upon something unnatural, a blemish on the rustic façade of the barn. Judith, with her morning cup of coffee steaming in her hands, froze at the sight of it. The barn door, usually a stoic guardian of their livelihood, bore strange symbols, slashed violently into the wood. They seemed to writhe under Judith's gaze, a stark contrast against the aging red paint.

She let out a breath she hadn't known she was holding, the steam mingling with the misty air, as she called over her shoulder, "Arthur!"

Arthur emerged from the shadows within the barn, his presence almost as foreboding as the markings that marred the door. His eyes followed Judith's outstretched arm, and the sight that met him caused his jaw to set firmly, his lips forming a thin, grim line.

"They're back," she whispered, the steam of her breath visible in the cold air.

Arthur's response was a gravelly growl. "It's been too long... we knew this was coming."

Behind them, the house remained silent, the rest of the family unaware of the grim portent lurking just outside. But the peace was not to last. Within the hour, the elder Morrows convened in the musty confines of the farmhouse cellar, the earthen walls lined with preserves and jars that bore witness to their clandestine meeting.

Arthur stood at the head of the room, his eyes shadowed, with Judith at his side. "The Harbinger's Mark," he declared, his voice reverberating off the walls. "It's been generations since it last appeared. The pact... it's resurging."

Judith's eyes, usually so composed, flickered with a fear that she had long buried. "We have done so much to keep it at bay," she murmured, "but it's never enough."

As the discussion turned to the ancient covenant that bound them to the soil and the darkness it harbored, footsteps echoed on the stairs leading down to the cellar. Caleb descended, his face set in hard lines, the muscles in his jaw working.

"I heard noises," he began, his voice betraying a tension that his calm exterior tried to mask. "I should have known you'd be whispering about family secrets."

Arthur met his son's accusatory gaze. "This is not just about family, Caleb. This is about survival."

Caleb slammed his fist against the wooden table, making the jars rattle. "Survival? What about living, Father? What about the truth?"

Judith reached out, her hand trembling as it brushed Caleb's. "You must understand—"

"Understand?" Caleb interjected, his voice rising. "I understand that we're bound to a legacy of shadows and whispers! Tell me, what price has this land not yet exacted from us?"

The silence that followed was suffocating, the air between them charged with the weight of unspoken histories.

Arthur's voice, when he finally spoke, was like the rumble of distant thunder. "The land gives, the land takes. You know this, son. We all play our part in the cycle. It's our duty, to the soil, to the town, to each other."

Caleb's eyes burned with a mixture of anger and desperation. "And what if I refuse to play my part? What then?"

Before the tense tableau could erupt, a sudden noise from upstairs pierced the moment—a thud, a shattering sound, and a sharp cry that couldn't be mistaken for anything but terror. It cut through the air, severing the thread of their standoff and drawing them back to the grim reality of their legacy.

The family rushed upstairs, fear fueling their steps. As they reached the kitchen, the source of the commotion became heart-stoppingly clear. The window lay in shards, and a rock, wrapped in paper etched with the same symbols as the barn door, sat ominously on the kitchen floor.

Lena stood against the far wall, her hands over her mouth and her eyes wide with fear. The vibrant red of her hair seemed to dim in the shadow of the ominous message before them.

Caleb moved first, striding to the rock and unfurling the paper with a fury that made the paper crackle under his touch. His eyes scanned the symbols, and his body tensed as if he were bracing against a blow.

"It's a warning," he said, his voice cold as the winter frost. "The Harbinger's Mark... it's just the beginning."

Outside, the wind began to howl, sending waves of unease through the stalks of corn that encased the Morrow farm. The whispers had begun to sound like chants, and in the air, there was the scent of a Thanksgiving none of them could predict, one that would be carved deep into the marrow of their bones. And the threshing floor waited, hungry for more than just the harvest it was promised.

Lena stood frozen, the chaos of the shattered window a stark contrast to the stillness of her form. Her lips, usually so quick to spill laughter or defiance, were clamped shut in a line of dread. The paper, with its cryptic symbols, seemed to mock her with a secret only it knew.

Arthur's gaze was locked on Lena, assessing, his thoughts obscured behind the weathered mask of his visage. "Lena," he started, his voice a baritone command, "you've been with us for nigh on two decades. You know the cost of the soil."

Her voice, when it finally came, trembled like a leaf in a storm. "I know what you've told me, what I've seen... but this," she gestured towards the stone and paper, "this is different, Arthur. It feels different."

"It's the same evil," Arthur replied, his tone final. "Just... bolder than before."

Caleb's fists clenched at his sides. "How much bolder will it get, Father? How much more will it demand from us?"

Judith's eyes flicked to her son, then back to the symbols. "The same as it always does. Everything."

The kitchen was silent except for the whisper of the wind sneaking through the jagged edges of the broken window. The family stood in a tableau of fear and frustration, the tension palpable.

Ethan's arrival was like a gust of air in a stifling room. He came bounding in, his humor a stark contrast to the dread that hung over the kitchen. "What's this? Some kind of Thanksgiving prank?" He picked up the stone and examined it, his laughter failing to mask the unease in his eyes.

"No prank," Caleb said, snatching the stone from his brother's grasp. "It's a message."

"A message?" Ethan chuckled, though the sound was hollow. "What, like 'Happy Thanksgiving from the local cult'?"

Judith turned a sharp gaze on him. "This is no time for jokes, Ethan."

"Seems like the perfect time to me," Ethan retorted, the levity slipping from his tone. "Laughter's better than just staring at each other, waiting for the sky to fall."

Caleb turned away, the strain on his face deepening. "Sometimes the sky does fall, little brother. And sometimes the ground opens up to swallow you whole."

Lena moved closer to Ethan, her eyes imploring him to understand. "It's not the sky we should worry about. It's what's beneath our feet. It's always been what's beneath our feet."

The exchange was cut short by a knock at the door, hesitant at first, then growing insistent. Judith's head whipped towards the sound, her thin lips pressing tighter together. "Who would be calling at this hour?"

Arthur moved towards the door, the lines of his face etched with resolve. "We're about to find out."

He swung the door open to reveal Mayor Donnelly, his face ashen, his hands trembling. "Arthur..." he started, then paused to glance over his shoulder at the fields that lay beyond. "There's something you need to see."

The family followed the mayor, their footsteps cautious, the crunch of the gravel underfoot seeming excessively loud in the tense silence. As they approached the edge of the Morrow land, where the corn stood tall and foreboding, the reason for the mayor's visit became horribly apparent.

Mysterious lights, like will-o'-the-wisps, danced above the fields, casting an otherworldly glow on the stalks that swayed not with the wind but with some unfathomable rhythm. Lena's breath caught at the sight, and even Ethan's quicksilver grin faded.

Caleb's voice broke the silence, his tone more of a command than a question. "What's happening in our fields?"

Mayor Donnelly shook his head, his usually jovial face now lined with concern. "It's been seen all over, Caleb. People are scared. They're saying it's a bad omen."

Arthur's jaw tightened. "They're not wrong."

Lena, standing a little behind, wrapped her arms around herself. The lights seemed to beckon, to call to something deep within her, something she didn't dare acknowledge.

Judith stepped forward, her voice barely above a whisper. "We've always known the harvest was veiled, that the soil's bounty was bartered with something... ancient. But this," she gestured at the luminous display, "this is different."

The family stood, the glow of the lights painting their faces in hues of dread. In the town below, doors were shut tight, and curtains drawn, as whispers of omens grew into a cacophony of fear.

The Morrow family knew the truth lay hidden beneath the land's fecund cloak. As the lights continued their spectral dance, the questions hung in the air, unspoken yet suffocating.

What was the cost of the Morrow harvest? What ancient pact held the family to this land? And as the veil thinned with the approach of Thanksgiving, what would come calling for its due?

Under the moon's watchful eye, the Morrow homestead stood as a bulwark against the creeping dread that settled over the fields. Inside, Arthur's words echoed, a grim drumbeat in the fraught silence. "This year's harvest demands a greater price."

Caleb's hands were rough, the skin cracked like the dry earth that bordered their property, as he ran them through his hair, pulling at the roots. "What price?" he rasped, the question directed at no one and everyone at the same time.

Arthur's eyes were stones, unyielding. "The price we've always paid, only... it wants more."

Judith's fingers twisted a dishtowel until the fabric strained. "It's the blood," she said, and her voice was the sound of autumn leaves being crushed underfoot. "It's always been the blood."

The words felt like a shroud descending upon the family, and for a moment, the only sound was the house settling, as if it too were bracing for what was to come.

Outside, the winds began to howl, a lamentation that foretold the calamity brewing on the horizon. Caleb moved towards the window, his gaze fixed on the distant fields where the lights had danced their macabre ballet. "I found another one this morning," he said, almost to himself. "A cow, drained and left in the north field. It's escalating."

Judith's eyes met her son's reflection in the glass. "It's feeding," she corrected, her voice a hushed terror.

Ethan, always the one to lean on humor, had no jests left. "Who's doing this? Who's capable of something like this?" His eyes sought his father's, begging for an explanation.

Arthur's voice was a distant rumble. "It's not a question of who, but of what." He turned to face his sons, his visage a testament to years of carrying a terrible knowledge. "The land gives, and it takes away. We've known that since your granddaddy's time. But this land," he paused, his eyes haunted, "it takes more than it gives."

The knock at the door wasn't a surprise this time, but it was no less unwelcome. Caleb moved to answer it, his movements heavy, like he was wading through waist-high water.

It was Sheriff Hollis, his hat held in his hands, his brow furrowed with worry lines that were deep and numerous. "Caleb, Arthur..." he began, shifting uncomfortably. "There've been incidents at the Jenkins and the Ellery farms. Accidents, they're calling them, but..." His voice trailed off as he looked at the Morrow men, the unspoken truth hanging between them like a guillotine's blade.

"What kind of accidents?" Caleb's voice was a taut wire.

"Fires," the sheriff replied. "Barn fires. Livestock lost, and the Jenkins boy..." He paused, swallowing hard. "He's in a bad way at the hospital. They don't think he'll..."

Ethan cut in, "That's not accidents. That's something else."

Sheriff Hollis nodded. "I know. And I think you know too."

Arthur stepped forward, the authority of his years commanding the space around him. "We need to gather the townsfolk. They need to know what we're up against."

The sheriff looked like he wanted to argue, then thought better of it. "I'll round them up. Meeting at the town hall in an hour."

After he left, the family didn't speak. There was a pact here, not just with the land, but with each other—a covenant of silence woven through the generations.

Lena's voice, when she spoke, was like the breaking of a dam. "How can we just stand here? People are getting hurt, Arthur. Caleb, we can't let this..." Her plea hung unfinished, the unspoken horrors too vast to voice.

Caleb moved to her, his hand reaching out then falling to his side. "We don't have a choice, Lena. We never did."

Judith's voice was a steel thread. "We do what we must to protect our own, to protect this town. It's the burden we bear."

As the family prepared to face the townspeople, the unease was a palpable thing, wrapping its fingers around their throats. They knew that the horror that had haunted their lineage was no longer content with cattle and whispered threats.

Arthur's final words before they departed were a benediction and a curse. "We thresh the wheat from the chaff," he said, looking each of them in the eye. "We pay the price for the harvest. And this year... we'll pay in blood."

The door closed with a sound like a tombstone settling into the earth, leaving the family to gather their resolve and their secrets like armor. The Morrow legacy was one of blood and earth, and as the night deepened, so too did the certainty that the coming days would see that legacy written anew in crimson across the harvest moon.

Lena's hands trembled as she pulled the chain to illuminate the attic. Dust motes danced in the beam of light like macabre little spirits frolicking before an impending storm. She didn't want to be here, in the musty dark of the Morrow homestead's past, but something drew her—some whisper of intuition, or perhaps it was just the need to understand the madness seeping into her family.

She moved hesitantly between old trunks and furniture shrouded in white sheets, each object a silent sentinel to Morrow secrets. Then, her eyes caught a glint of leather from an old chest. Lena reached out, her fingers brushing against the cold metal of the latch. The chest popped open with a protesting creak, revealing an ancient tome nestled among moth-eaten clothes.

The book was thick, its leather cover cracked and moldy with age. Lena coughed as she disturbed the years of accumulated dust. The tome felt wrong, its presence an aberration. She hesitated, then with a surge of resolve, opened it to a random page.

The words were scrawled in a tight, spidery script, almost illegible, and the language was archaic. But the illustrations that accompanied the text left no room for doubt. They depicted rituals, horrific and detailed, with figures that were too elongated to be human, standing around a pit that seemed to pulse with an unnatural life. The book fell from her hands, as if it had suddenly become red-hot.

"Lena? What are you doing up here?" It was Caleb's voice, soft and concerned, filtering up from the bottom of the attic stairs.

She composed herself enough to call down, "Just looking for some extra blankets."

Caleb didn't come up, and she was thankful for it. She wasn't ready to share the grim find, not yet. She returned the tome to its resting place, her mind reeling from the implications of the images she had seen. It was all connected, she knew. The mutilated livestock, the missing vagrants, the accidents—it was all bound to the Morrow land, to their blood.

Arthur stood outside under the gnarled branches of an ancient oak tree, a sentinel that had stood watch over the Morrow land for centuries. The night was eerily silent, as if the world was holding its breath. He felt it then, a slight chill in the air, a shift in the breeze. A voice whispered through the leaves, a rustling that was both familiar and chilling.

"You know the price of the covenant, Arthur Morrow."

The voice was not heard with the ears but with the heart, and it was the ancestral spirit of the Morrows, the harbinger of their pact.

Arthur's voice was barely a whisper, "I know."

"You hesitate. The seed of the covenant must be sown, or the land shall reclaim its bounty, and your lineage will wither with the crops," the spirit intoned, the leaves shivering with its power.

Arthur clenched his jaw, his hands balled into fists at his sides. "It's asking for too much, more than ever before."

The leaves rustled with what might have been impatience. "The entity cares not for your mortal tribulations. The pact must be honored. The harvest must be secured."

Arthur lifted his eyes to the moon, seeking solace in its unchanging face. "And if we refuse?"

"The soil is rich with the blood of your forebears, but it can always be enriched further," the spirit said, the threat clear and cold.

Arthur's heart was a heavy stone in his chest. There was no escaping the covenant. There never had been.

As he turned to walk back to the house, the spirit spoke once more, "Remember, Arthur Morrow, the harvest is nigh, and the threshing floor awaits its tribute."

The message hung heavy in the air as Arthur descended into the homestead, the weight of his ancestors' choices a mantle on his shoulders. The pact had sustained them, but at what cost?

Inside, the silence was oppressive. Judith stood by the hearth, her face ghostly in the flickering firelight. Caleb was silent, his expression stony, while Lena avoided his gaze, her own face pale. Ethan alone seemed to be wrestling with the desire to speak, to perhaps offer some plan of defiance.

Arthur looked at each of them, the family he had protected all these years, and knew that the time for secrets had passed. The truth, as grim and grotesque as it was, would have to be laid bare.

The Morrow family was at a precipice, and dawn would bring a reckoning that would shake the very roots of their existence. They would go forth and prepare the ground, for the seed of the covenant was calling, and its harvest was death.

The rising sun cast an auburn glow over the sprawling Morrow cornfields, its light touching the dew-kissed stalks with a false promise of serenity. The monstrous threshers stood at the field's edge like primordial beasts, steel limbs poised to rend the earth asunder. Their engines roared to life, a cacophony that shattered the morning's peace and set the crows to a frantic escape. The air vibrated with the energy of the machinery, an unnatural fervor that seemed to grip the workers as they set about their grim task.

Ethan, the younger Morrow, always felt the rush of the threshing. It was a dance with danger, a testament to man's will imposed upon nature. But today, the thrill was tainted, the excitement undercut by a gnawing anxiety that clawed at the edges of his consciousness. He shook it off and forced a laugh, slapping the back of a nearby worker with feigned cheer.

"Let's make this year's yield the envy of Nebraska, eh?" he called out, the falsity of his bravado unnoticed by the others.

As the day wore on, the sky turned a grim steel gray, heavy with unshed rain. Ethan maneuvered a thresher down a particularly overgrown row, the mechanical jaws devouring the golden stalks with unrelenting hunger. Then, the machine shuddered, a guttural cough echoing through the gears. Ethan cursed and killed the engine, the sudden silence an ominous counterpoint to the chaos that had reigned moments before.

Climbing down, he trudged over to the stalled thresher, the heavy soil of the Morrow fields clinging to his boots. He reached into the jam, his hands searching for the offending blockage. His fingers closed around something hard and decidedly not plant-like. With a mixture of effort and revulsion, Ethan cleared the debris.

At his feet lay a grim tableau – bones, unmistakably human, their edges gnawed and weathered. Amongst the remains were trinkets, crudely fashioned from twigs and twine, their shapes suggestive of symbols long forgotten by those who walked above the soil. Ethan's breath caught in his throat, his usual nonchalance crumbling before the macabre discovery.

He looked across the fields to where his father stood, a solitary figure against the darkening sky, watching. Ethan couldn't decipher the look in Arthur's eyes, but he knew that acknowledgment, a shared realization that the past never truly died in these lands; it merely slept.

Ethan covered the remains with a burlap sack and signaled for the other workers to continue, his voice devoid of its usual humor. He'd report this, of course, he had to. But not now, not while the harvest was at stake.

Back at the homestead, Judith Morrow's hands flitted from task to task with an absent-minded frenzy. The whisper of her prayers wove through the kitchen like smoke, silent pleas to a deity she wasn't sure was listening. Her eyes darted to the windows, to the shadows that seemed to crowd closer with the approach of dusk.

Her husband and sons were out there, amongst the corn and the secrets, and she was here, wrestling with the knowledge of what those secrets meant. The mutilations, the whispers of vanished souls – they were omens, and Judith felt the sharp edge of terror that they presaged.

She'd hear the creak of the old floorboards and turn sharply, half-expecting to see a ghost from her past, or worse, something new and terrible. But it was only Lena, her daughter-in-law, carrying a basket of linens.

"Can I help you with anything, Judith?" Lena's voice was gentle, an attempt to bridge the gap that had formed between them.

Judith shook her head, her words a mere murmur, "The day is full, and the night will be longer."

Lena watched her with concern but respected her silence, knowing that some fears were too deep for words.

As night fell and the workers retreated from the fields, the Morrow family gathered in their home, the heaviness in their hearts mirrored by the storm clouds that gathered above. They ate in silence, the only sounds the clink of cutlery and the wind that began to howl around the eaves of the house, a harbinger of the tempest to come.

Thanksgiving was upon them, but there was little to give thanks for. The threshing had begun, and with it, the awakening of something that the Morrow family had long feared. The past was resurfacing, demanding its due, and before the night was over, they would all have to face what they had sown in the blood-soaked soil of their inheritance.

After the meal, Lena found Caleb lingering by the hearth, his gaze lost to the flames that crackled and popped with a life of their own. The firelight danced across his features, carving shadows that seemed to whisper of the same darkness that had settled over the fields.

"Caleb," Lena began, her voice steadier than she felt, "we need to talk."

He didn't turn to look at her, his jaw set in a hard line. "Now's not the time, Lena."

"It's never the time, according to you," she snapped back, her frustration finding its vent. "But after what I saw in the attic..."

Caleb whirled around, his eyes sharp as flint. "You were in the attic?" There was a danger in his tone, an urgency that bordered on panic.

Lena's resolve wavered, but she held his gaze. "Yes. And I found the chest, Caleb. The one with your grandfather's journals, the..." Her voice trailed off as she struggled to voice the horrors scrawled in those dusty pages.

"You shouldn't have done that." Caleb's voice was low, a growl that seemed to rise from the very depths of his being. "Those are family matters."

"Family matters?" Lena's laugh was bitter, hollow. "Is that what we're calling it now? We're not a family, we're caretakers of a curse!"

Caleb's hand shot out, gripping her arm with a strength that made her wince. "Don't say things you don't understand."

Lena's voice was a whisper, but it carried the weight of her fear and resolve. "I understand more than you think. I know about the sacrifices, the... agreements made with whatever lies beneath these fields. And I know about the disappearances every harvest. The vagrant that's gone missing, it's starting again, isn't it?"

He released her, his face a mask of anguish and anger. "Lena, you have to trust me. It's for the good of the town, for our family."

"Trust you?" Lena's voice rose, a crescendo of desperation. "How can I trust a man who won't tell me the truth? Who keeps secrets soaked in blood and darkness?"

Caleb turned from her, staring back into the flames. "It's not about what you know, Lena. It's about survival. This land, this town, it needs... it demands a price."

"Then let's leave!" Lena's plea was fervent, her hands reaching for his, seeking an anchor in the storm that was their life. "We can get out. We don't have to be bound by this... this horror."

Caleb's hands enveloped hers, his touch gentle in contrast to the harshness of his words. "And go where? This is our life. The land provides for us, for everyone here. Without it, we're nothing."

Lena pulled away, her eyes shimmering with unshed tears. "I'd rather be nothing than a part of this... this unholy bounty."

Caleb looked at her then, really looked at her, and Lena saw the conflict warring in his eyes. He loved her; she knew that much was true. But the land and the legacy of the Morrow name held him in a grip as unyielding as the soil that nurtured their cursed crop.

They stood in silence, the crackle of the fire underscoring the void between them. Lena knew that her confrontation had set something irrevocable in motion. She could feel the threads of their lives fraying, the unraveling of a tapestry woven through generations with a dark and monstrous thread.

Outside, the storm broke, the first drops of rain pattering against the windows like the fingers of the dead, seeking entry to the warmth of the living. Lena turned from her husband and walked to the window, her heart a thrumming bird in a cage of ribs.

As she watched the heavens open and the rain wash over the fields, she whispered to the night, "What have we done?"

And though she spoke to the darkness, it was the land that answered—a low, mournful wail that rose with the wind, as if in reply.

Ethan had always been the foil to the Morrow family's stern legacy. His laughter had once filled the homestead's halls, a counterpoint to the perpetual whispers of the corn. Now, his voice was sharp, slicing through the tension in the air with a precision that left a silence in its wake.

"You think this is about the harvest?" Ethan's voice was laced with disbelief, a bitter edge to his usually light tone. "You're blind, Father. We're threshing souls, not just corn."

Arthur Morrow stood rigid, the lines in his face deepening like furrows in the field. "Your disrespect has grown intolerable," he growled.

"Disrespect?" Ethan scoffed, his eyes wild and accusing. "What do you call what we're doing to this town, to these people?"

"It is our burden to bear," Arthur replied, a touch of ancient sorrow in his voice.

Ethan's laughter was harsh, joyless. "A burden? No, a burden is a heavy load. What we carry... it's a plague."

Caleb entered the room, the scent of rain clinging to his clothes, the debate drawing him like a moth to flame. "Ethan, this is not your place. It's bigger than us."

"Bigger than us?" Ethan rounded on his brother, the brother he had once idolized. "When did you become as blind as he is?"

The elder Morrow's gaze could have stripped the paint from the walls. "You will not speak to your brother in that manner."

But Ethan was beyond caring for the sacred hierarchy that had imprisoned his family in servitude to the earth's dark appetites. "It's a sickness, Caleb. Can't you see it? The land's poisoned with it!"

Lena, listening from the doorway, felt her breath catch. Ethan's words were dangerous, the kind that once uttered, could never be taken back. Her eyes met Caleb's for a fleeting moment, a silent plea for peace, for sanity.

Arthur's next words were quiet but they carried the weight of a death sentence. "If you cannot bear our legacy, Ethan, then you have no place here."

"You're exiling me?" Ethan's face was a mask of mock incredulity, but beneath it, there was a glimmer of relief, of freedom.

Arthur's nod was final. "By morning, you'll leave. And if you ever return, you will be met not as a Morrow, but as a stranger."

Caleb moved as if to protest, but a look from his father quelled any dissension. Ethan's gaze lingered on his brother, a silent conversation that ended with a sorrowful nod. Then, without a word to his father, Ethan strode past Lena and out into the rain-drenched night.

Lena felt the air thicken with unsaid words, with the weight of an inevitable doom. As Arthur and Caleb spoke in hushed, grave tones, Lena slipped outside, the need to breathe free of the house's oppressive atmosphere overwhelming her.

The rain had eased into a drizzle, leaving the air fresh with the scent of wet earth. Lena made her way toward the barn, needing to put distance between herself and the stifling air of the homestead.

As she approached, the barn loomed large against the night sky, its walls etched with shadows. Lena's heart stumbled when she saw them—symbols, the same as those from the journals, now branded into the barn's wood.

Her mind reeled. Had it been Caleb? Or had the darkness they courted now marked them as its own?

She heard voices, low and fearful, and tucked herself against the barn's side, peering around the corner. Several townsfolk stood huddled together, their own livestock in tow, each animal marked with a symbol that matched the barn's.

"It's a warning," one man muttered.

"Or a claim," another replied, her voice tinged with dread.

Lena's stomach churned. This had gone beyond the Morrow's control, beyond the clandestine horrors of the harvest. It was spreading, like rot through ripe fruit.

She hurried back to the house, her mind racing with desperate plans. There had to be a way out, a way to save her children from this legacy of darkness.

Inside, she gathered her children from their restless sleep, whispering promises of safety, of a new beginning. She bundled them into the car, the engine turning over with a comforting purr.

But as Lena pressed the accelerator, the car shuddered, then stalled. She tried again, her pulse hammering in her ears. Nothing. A third attempt met with the same inexplicable failure.

Lena stepped out into the misty night, the rain a cold kiss upon her face. She rounded the vehicle, her eyes searching for an explanation, but found none.

Turning back to the house, a chilling realization settled upon her. The house, the land, the very air they breathed—it was as if an invisible barrier had risen around them, sealing them within its malevolent embrace.

Lena's breath came in ragged gasps as she understood the true nature of their entrapment. It wasn't just about keeping threats out. It was about keeping the Morrows in.

And as she looked up at the darkened windows of the house, the silhouette of Arthur Morrow watching from within, Lena knew the horror they faced was only just beginning.

The week leading up to Thanksgiving had always been busy in the town, but this year, the energy was different. It was tense, expectant, as if each person could sense the thrumming beneath their feet, the pulse of something ancient and angry, waiting to be sated.

In the schoolyard, children clung to their mothers, whispering of the nightmares that had disturbed their slumber. Shadows, they said, tall and shapeless, that whispered promises of plenty in exchange for silent, unnamed horrors.

At the heart of the community, the town hall stood stoic and unassuming, a sentinel over the townsfolk. But today, it was the epicenter of raw emotions and whispered fears as the town meeting commenced.

The wooden chairs arranged in neat rows were filled with residents, each carrying the burden of the unsettling events. Murmurs filled the room like the rustle of corn stalks in the wind, each whisper a thread in a tapestry of growing unease.

Caleb stood at the front of the hall, his presence commanding yet wrought with an inner turmoil that seemed to crackle around him like static. He cleared his throat, and the room gradually fell into a hushed silence.

"We're here to discuss the preparations for the harvest feast," he began, his voice steady. "We all know this year has been... challenging. But we must stand united as a community."

A man stood up from the back, his voice carrying clear and sharp. "United? With all that's been happening? The livestock... the symbols... What are we not being told, Caleb?"

Caleb's jaw tightened. "We are doing all we can to ensure the safety and prosperity of this town."

"But are we safe, Caleb? Are our children?" a mother asked, her voice laced with a fear that tugged at Lena's heart from where she stood, leaning against the back wall.

Caleb's gaze swept the room, lingering on the faces of his neighbors, his friends. "We have always been protected. This year will be no different."

"But the ground," another voice rose, "it trembles. I've felt it beneath my feet. What does it mean?"

Caleb's hand clenched at his side. "It means nothing. The earth shifts, it's natural."

"Natural?" It was Ethan, who shouldn't have been there, his voice a jagged edge cutting through the tension. He stepped into the light, his eyes alight with a defiance that bordered on desperation. "Is that what we're calling it now?"

Caleb's stance shifted imperceptibly, the air around him growing heavy, his patience fraying. "Ethan, you have no place—"

"No place?" Ethan's laugh was devoid of humor, echoing off the walls. "I have every right to be here, to speak the truth. We are tethered to something unspeakable, and it's demanding its due!"

The room erupted in an uneasy chatter, the seed of chaos sown.

Caleb's voice rose, raw and powerful. "Enough!" His fist slammed down on the podium with a force that left a crack in the wood, a small gasp escaping from the gathered crowd.

Ethan met his brother's blazing eyes with a steady gaze. "The shadows grow long, brother. Can you not see them?"

The townspeople looked around, a collective breath held, as if expecting the darkness to manifest before their eyes.

A subtle tremor passed through the floor then, a shiver of the earth that went unnoticed by many, but not by Lena. She felt it coil around her spine, a serpent biding its time.

Arthur Morrow rose from his seat, his voice the calm before the storm. "We are a community bound by the land. It gives us life. Respect it, honor it, and we will continue to thrive."

Ethan's scoff was a red flag to Caleb's bull. "Thrive? This is not living. It's surviving at the whim of—"

"Enough, Ethan!" Caleb roared, his composure shattered like glass. He advanced on his brother, the room holding its breath.

Ethan stood his ground, but his eyes... they held a sorrow, a resignation that he had played his final card in this deadly game.

Lena couldn't stand by any longer. She stepped forward, her voice cutting through the heavy silence. "This is getting us nowhere. Fear will only tear us apart."

Caleb and Ethan paused, the fury in Caleb's eyes dimming as he turned to face his wife. The room waited, the very air charged with expectation.

"Let us focus on what we can control," Lena continued, her voice a balm to the raw nerves of the townsfolk. "Our unity, our strength as a community. Let us trust in the Morrow's guidance as we always have."

A murmur of agreement rippled through the crowd, the tension dissipating as if her words were the antidote to the poison of fear.

The meeting ended not long after, with plans hastily drawn and tasks assigned. But as the townspeople filed out, the shadows seemed to linger, dancing at the edges of sight, a portent of the harvest to come.

The chill of the November air did little to cool the fevered whispers of the town as Lena walked home, her mind awhirl with the knowledge that this year, the harvest was more than a tradition—it was a reckoning.

The Morrow house stood silent, the wind whispering through the brittle corn like hushed incantations. Inside, the hearth's fire crackled—a beacon of warmth against the creeping cold that seeped through the walls. Arthur Morrow sat at the head of the ancient oak table, his lined face illuminated by the flickering light, eyes fixed on the empty chair across from him, the matriarch's chair. Judith had retreated to the sanctity of her room, her presence absent but her spirit heavy in the air.

Caleb entered, the sound of his boots echoing in the stillness. "It's time," he said, his voice devoid of emotion, a mere messenger of fate.

Arthur nodded, the weight of the years and the burden of legacy bowing his shoulders. "Gather the family. It must be done as it always has."

The somber ritual began, each member of the Morrow family wordlessly taking their place at the table, save for Ethan, whose seat remained ominously vacant. Lena's hands trembled ever so slightly, betraying her dread. She knew, as they all did, that this Thanksgiving eve was unlike any other.

Arthur's gaze fell upon her, and for a moment, Lena saw the fracture in the iron-clad man before her. "The land demands its due," he said, his voice a gravelly whisper, as if speaking the words louder would make them more real, more terrifying.

Lena's voice was steady, belying the fear in her heart. "And we have always paid it. But why must it be one of us?"

Arthur's eyes met hers, a flash of sorrow passing through them. "Because that is the covenant. The blood of the Morrow must feed the land that sustains the town."

Caleb's fist clenched, a surge of suppressed anger coursing through him. "Father, there has to be another way. We've never turned on our own before."

Arthur's stare was unwavering. "The signs have been ignored for too long. The whispers of dissent have angered the soil. It thirsts for a purer offering."

Silence enveloped the room, thick and oppressive, as Judith's shuffling footsteps approached from the hallway. She entered, her silhouette ghostly. "The ancestors whisper," she intoned, her voice barely above a whisper, "and their words are clear. We abide, or we all perish."

Lena's breath hitched, her eyes searching for her children, the youthful innocence that had no place in this archaic barbarism. "You can't mean—"

Arthur's face hardened, the patriarchal mask returning. "It is decided. The firstborn of the firstborn. Our traditions have kept us, sustained us. This is the way."

Outside, the wind rose to a howl, as if to underscore the gravity of his decree.

Caleb's voice broke the spell. "Ethan must be found. He cannot be absent. Not tonight."

Arthur's gaze flickered to the empty space where Ethan should have been, his disapproval a tangible thing. "Then find him. He must stand with us or against us."

The door creaked open, sparing them from further conversation. Ethan's frame filled the doorway, his face a storm of conflict. "Against," he said, his voice resonant with finality. "I've seen enough to know there's no prosperity in this path. No future."

Arthur stood, a towering figure of stoic resolve. "You would defy the very roots that feed you?"

Ethan's defiance was palpable. "I would defy any tradition that demands the blood of my kin."

Lena looked between the men of her family, her heart torn. The Morrows had always been the rock upon which the community was built, unyielding and enduring. But now, as the foundation crumbled, she wondered if the harvest was worth the horror it cloaked.

Arthur turned, facing the window where the last light of day fought against the encroaching night. "Then prepare, all of you," he commanded, his voice steady as the ground that shook beneath them. "The sacrifice will proceed at midnight. The Morrow bloodline will feed the land, or we will all suffer the consequences."

The room fell into a chilling silence, each Morrow locked in their own turmoil. Outside, the shadows lengthened, reaching towards the house as if in anticipation, ready to envelop them in the darkness of their own making.

Under the blood-red moon, the Morrows convened in the shadowy expanse of their cornfield, a hallowed ground that had seen the passing of countless seasons and the silent witnesses of the family's dark tradition. A cold November breeze danced through the stalks, rustling them into a dissonant chorus as if they murmured secrets long buried beneath the rich Nebraska soil.

Caleb stood apart, his tall form a solitary silhouette against the silvered husks, his heart pounding a relentless beat that echoed the turmoil within. He had been raised on the lore of the land, on the sacrosanct duty of his bloodline, but the price of the prosperity had never seemed so stark, so drenched in undeniable dread.

Lena's eyes were fixed on her husband, the fiery red of her hair muted under the moon's crimson glow, her thoughts swirling like the wind through the corn. She clutched her shawl tighter, as if it could shield her from the truth of the night, the truth of the man she loved and the history they shared.

"The children," she whispered, her voice barely audible. "How do we face them after tonight?"

Caleb's response was strained, as though each word was a piece of his soul, torn and offered to the indifferent wind. "We tell them we did it for their future, for the town's survival. We tell them we had no choice."

"But is that the truth, Caleb?" Lena's voice was now a blade, sharp and cutting to the marrow. "Or do we simply fear to break the chains our ancestors forged?"

Before Caleb could respond, Ethan's voice sliced through the tension. "Caleb, Lena, this is madness. Look around you. The earth will continue to turn, the seasons will change, harvests will come and go. But if we do this, if we spill Morrow blood by our own hands, we won't be able to wash it away. It'll stain us forever."

Judith's hand reached out, resting on Ethan's arm, her touch as frail as her voice. "The harvest moon won't wait. The hour draws near, and the land grows impatient."

Arthur's form emerged from the shadows, his aged face cast in sharp relief by the eerie light. "Enough talk," he stated, the finality in his voice brooking no argument. "We are here not to debate but to act. The prosperity of many depends on the sacrifices of few."

As the family's discord hung in the air, a chilling gust swept through the field, bending the corn in servile obedience. It was as if the land itself responded to Arthur's command, a silent assertion of the ancient pact that bound the Morrow family to this land.

Judith stepped forward, her movements echoing the ceremonial gravity that the moment demanded. "The altar is prepared," she announced, her eyes not meeting anyone else's, knowing that what lay before them was a chasm too vast to gaze into without losing a piece of oneself.

One by one, they approached the heart of the field, where a stone altar stood—ageless, cold, and stained with the passage of time and the deeds of generations. The implements of their forebears were arrayed with care, glinting dully under the light of the harvest moon.

Arthur took his place at the head of the altar, his presence a stark reminder of the lineage they all shared. "We do this for the greater good," he intoned, his voice carrying across the field. "For the Morrow blood has always been the linchpin of the covenant."

Ethan's hands clenched at his sides, the lines of his face etched with conflict. "Father, there is no good in this. It's an endless cycle. When does it stop?"

"When the land no longer requires it," Arthur replied, a hint of something unrecognizable flickering in his eyes—resignation, perhaps, or a sorrow too profound to name.

Caleb, caught between the father he revered and the brother he loved, the wife he cherished, and the children he would die for, felt the crushing weight of his lineage bearing down on him. In that moment, the whisper of the corn seemed to swell into a cacophony of voices, the ancestors calling, demanding, beseeching him to uphold the tradition that had cursed and blessed them in equal measure.

The hour was close, the choice laid bare in the moon's merciless light. And as the clock in the town square struck the eleventh hour, the Morrow family stood at the precipice, their next actions fated to ripple through the very essence of their being, through the town that lay in oblivious celebration, and into the annals of a history written in shadows and blood.

The silence of the night was a shroud, and under its cover, the Morrows prepared to enact a ritual that would seal their fate and that of the town tethered to the lifeblood of their fields. With the moon hanging heavy above, judgment itself seemed to await the outcome of the Morrow's harrowing choice.

The eleventh toll of the town clock faded, leaving a void that was swiftly filled by the susurrus of the cornfield. This was the hour when night creatures stilled, when even the breeze seemed to hold its breath. Caleb's hand was steady as he reached for the ceremonial blade passed down from generations whose faces were etched into the Morrow family tapestry, their eyes empty yet accusatory.

Lena's gaze never left her husband, her body taut with a fear that transcended the chill of the night. "Caleb," she uttered, her voice a mere wisp, "remember who you are."

Arthur's eyes were steadfast upon the stone altar. "We remember who we are by doing what must be done."

Judith's lips moved in silent prayer, or perhaps a plea for forgiveness from a deity she no longer understood.

The moment stretched, each second a lifetime, until the ground beneath them began to tremble. A low rumble cascaded through the soil, growing louder, a deafening roar that threatened to split the earth.

The Morrows steadied themselves, their eyes wide with a terror that was as much about anticipation as it was about the impending revelation.

And then it rose.

The entity was not a creature of flesh and bone, but a living, breathing manifestation of the earth itself. Dirt, cornstalks, and the decay of life long past swirled into a towering form that loomed over the Morrow family, its presence an oppression on the senses, a weight that promised a suffocation of the soul.

Arthur's voice, once commanding, now quivered with a veneration bordering on mania. "We give to you, who gives to us."

Judith swayed, her eyes affixed to the churning mass of earth and plant. "The cycle continues," she murmured, her voice lost to the din.

Caleb's arm froze mid-air, the blade catching the moonlight as he looked upon the horror before him. "What are you?" he demanded, his voice a mix of fear and defiance.

The entity did not speak in words, but its voice was clear—a resonance that filled their minds, a pressure that sought to crush their wills. I am the Threshing Floor, the reaper of what is sown, the guardian of the harvest. I am the hunger beneath, the price of the bounty above.

Ethan recoiled, his eyes aflame with horror and a burgeoning resolve. "This ends, it ends with us!" he cried, his voice barely carrying over the tumult.

Lena, tears streaking her pale cheeks, grasped Caleb's free hand. "We can choose," she insisted, her voice firm. "We can choose not to feed it."

The entity writhed, the ground beneath them buckling as it drew closer. Arthur stood his ground, but his certainty was a façade beginning to crumble. "It demands," he whispered, his voice carrying a truth they all knew but had never dared to acknowledge. "It always demands."

The Morrows, surrounded by the whispering stalks and the oppressive gaze of their ancestors, stood on the brink of damnation.

Caleb's grip on the knife faltered, his soul torn asunder between the loyalty to the land and the love for his family.

Judith's whisper cut through the tension, a knife-point of sanity in the maelstrom. "The truth," she said, her voice steadying, "we are its servants, but we have also been its jailers. We decide whether it starves or feasts."

A cacophony of howls erupted from the town as the entity turned its gaze towards the flickering lights beyond the field. Hunger was its creed, and its appetite was voracious.

The Morrows stood against the darkness, the blade glinting—a symbol of their power and their prison. With the entity awaiting its tribute, they were the fulcrum upon which the fate of all would tip. The façade of the Morrow legacy was shattering, and beneath it lay the raw and undeniable truth of their existence.

In the distance, a child's cry pierced the night, a reminder of innocence and the future. Caleb felt it slice through the fog of tradition and terror. It was a call that beckoned towards a different path, a plea for change that could not be ignored.

The entity towered, its form a grotesque monument to the cycle of sacrifice. And as it drew its power from the very land that the Morrows had tended, the question that hung in the air was clear: Would the cycle continue, or would they dare to defy the legacy etched into the very soil they called home?

The answer lay unspoken as the Morrows faced the monstrosity before them, their decision poised like the blade at Caleb's side—a harbinger of life or death.

The aftermath was a landscape of ruin. The town's quaint main street, once lined with the hopeful bustle of Thanksgiving preparations, now lay in a tangle of debris. Windows, like the vacant eyes of a corpse, stared blindly into the night, and the scent of smoke clung to the crisp autumn air like a malignant spirit. The earth still bore the scars where the entity, a horror born from the greed of generations, had clawed its way towards the heavens, a perverse mockery of ascension.

In the Morrow household, Lena's silhouette was etched against the dimming light, her once vibrant hair now a crown of disheveled shadows. Her skin, where it was not smeared with the earth of the entity's touch, was pale, almost translucent, a stark canvas to the frenetic pulse visible at her throat. The transformation—or was it possession?—that held her was not of the body but of the essence. Lena Morrow, the firebrand, the beacon of change, now stood as a conduit to something ancient and unyielding.

The surviving townspeople, those not claimed by the entity's wrath or driven mad by its revelations, wandered like lost souls through the wreckage. Eyes that had once greeted neighbors with warmth now slid away, heavy with the knowledge of what had transpired. Lips trembled with the effort of unspoken confessions, of the terror that whispered in the quiet moments, the realization that the foundation of their lives had been a lie—a bargain with an unspeakable darkness.

In the town square, where families had gathered year after year to give thanks, stood Ethan, his lean figure now appearing to bear the weight of the world. His laughter, once the melody that could ease the most furrowed of brows, was nowhere to be heard. In its stead was a brooding silence that spoke volumes of the torment within.

Caleb stood at the fringe of the desolation, his broad shoulders hunched as if he could bear the burden of their sins upon his back and away from the broken spirits around him. His hand, still stained with the remnants of the ritual, trembled, not with fear, but with a rage that simmered like the fires of hell itself.

Arthur, his figure stooped, his shadow merging with the failing light, watched the remnants of his legacy with an expression of profound grief. "The land was ours to tend, ours to protect," he muttered to no one, his gravelly voice a shattered echo of the authority it once held.

Judith's hand found his, her touch feather-light yet laden with a strength forged in the bowels of their shared nightmare. "The land is not to blame," she whispered, her words not for him alone but for the ears of all who remained. "We must look to the morrow, not with fear, but with the hope that from this ruin, we can forge a new path."

Their eyes, the aged and the young, the broken and the defiant, turned towards her. Judith Morrow, the silent matriarch, spoke again with a clarity that cut through the veil of despair. "We have reaped the whirlwind, but we are still here. We breathe, we bleed, we stand. We are more than the legacy of this entity."

A murmur rose among the survivors, a collective breath drawn in the wake of her words. Hope, that most fragile and indomitable of human conditions, began to flicker like the first light of dawn against the night's oppression.

As night deepened, the entity, a sentinel of malice and hunger, continued its silent vigil over the town. Its form had receded, but its presence remained—an ever-present threat, a reminder of the cost of their prosperity. The Morrow family, once the unspoken rulers, now stood amidst the ruins, their choices laid bare before the dawn that threatened to rise on their final day.

Caleb's gaze found Lena's, and in her eyes, he saw the reflection of what they had become. Her voice, when she spoke, was not her own, but it was filled with an urgency that he could not deny. "It is not over," she said, her words carrying the weight of the ages. "It waits, it watches. We must decide."

The Morrows, and all who remained, gathered in the shadow of the entity's silent watch. They were the wounded, the survivors, the bearers of truth—and their next steps would determine the fate of a town once bound to the cycle of the Threshing Floor. The harvest had ended, but the reaping was just beginning.

The dusk bled into a darkling night, carrying with it the heavy silence of the aftermath. The ruined fields lay fallow, stretching out like a shroud beneath the wan glow of a crescent moon. The land that had thrived under the Morrow's stewardship was now a barren expanse, tainted by the residue of an ancient malevolence.

Under this baleful moon, a lone car traversed the undulating road towards the remnants of the Morrow estate. Inside, a family of four—two hopeful parents and their children, innocence untouched by the grimness of their destination—spoke of new beginnings and the promise of fertile soil.

"Nebraska's got the best corn in the world, they say," the father remarked, a note of pride threading his voice as if the land's past victories were his own.

His wife, a woman whose eyes danced with dreams of space and sunsets over fields of gold, nodded, her voice lilting with a hope not yet tempered by the truth. "And the space for the kids, Jim. A place to grow, not just for the crops, but for them too."

In the backseat, a boy and a girl, twins with the sun-kissed hair of their mother and the robust build of their father, pressed their noses to the glass, eyes wide at the expanse of the night.

"Do you think we'll have a horse?" the girl asked, her voice a tremulous mix of excitement and the weariness of a long journey.

"Maybe two," her brother chimed, with the confidence only a child can possess.

But the land was not ignorant of their coming. It lay in wait, the memories of blood and sacrifice etched deep into its clods. The soil, which should have been resting, preparing to once again burgeon with life come spring, was instead an open wound, seeping with the echoes of the Morrrows' sins.

As the family approached what remained of the town, a shadow flickered at the periphery of their headlights—a fleeting whisper of movement that caused the father to slow the car.

"Deer, maybe?" his wife suggested, but her voice was uncertain, a thread of anxiety weaving through it.

"Just the night playing tricks," he assured her, though his hand tightened on the wheel.

Meanwhile, in the remains of the Morrow house, Lena, her essence stretched thin between worlds, felt the shift in the air. The entity within her stirred, a low and ominous vibration that resonated with the arrival of new lifeblood at the threshold of its domain.

"They come," she intoned, the words slipping from her lips like a secret too long kept.

Caleb, standing by a window with panes that reflected only the desolation within, turned towards her sharply. "Who?" he demanded, though he knew the answer before she could give it.

"Future... Fodder..." The words were fractured, as though the very act of speaking them was a puzzle her human form could barely contain.

Outside, the car rolled to a stop in front of the Morrow's driveway—a hesitation that came too late, a realization dawning as the headlights illuminated the husk of the house, skeletal against the night sky.

The family exchanged uneasy glances, the silent communication of those on the precipice of a decision that could not be undone.

Back within the shattered embrace of the homestead, Ethan, with eyes that had seen too much, whispered, "What have we done?"

Judith Morrow, now the cornerstone in the rubble, placed a hand over her heart, where the throb of the land's pain echoed. "What we always do," she said, her voice a fortress against the chaos. "We survive. But survival comes at a cost."

Arthur, his body a map of the land's sorrow, clenched his jaw, the creases in his face deepening with resolve or regret—it was hard to tell. "We cannot—" he began, but the rest was lost to the groaning of the house as the wind caught its broken frame, a dirge for the fallen.

In the car, the mother turned to her husband, her eyes a mirror to the fear that suddenly clawed at her heart. "Jim... maybe we should—"

Before she could finish, a sound, strange and discordant, carried to them on the wind. It was neither human nor animal, a symphony of the earth's unrest—a siren call to those who would heed it.

Inside the car, the children shivered, the romantic visage of a rural life eclipsed by the visceral fear of the unknown.

"Let's go," the father said abruptly, the words a command that brooked no argument.

As the car reversed, tires crunching over gravel as if in haste to escape, Lena's voice rose, an aria of grief and warning. "The cycle..." she sighed, "turns."

The car disappeared down the road, leaving behind the quiet dread that settled over the land like dew. In its wake, the Morrow family emerged, specters against the darkness of their once fertile dominion.

"Do they know?" Ethan murmured, his question more for the stars than those that lingered with him.

"They will," Judith responded, her gaze fixed on the horizon, where the last light of the car's taillights vanished into the night.

Arthur turned away from the sight, the lines of his face etched with a grim anticipation. "They always do."

The Morrow family, bound by blood to the earth beneath their feet, stood in silent vigil as the entity's pulse beneath the ground promised a rebirth of horror with the coming of the new season.

The fallow fields awaited the thaw, the seeds of tomorrow's nightmares nestled within, and the cycle prepared to begin again.

The end.

Pilgrim's Regress

The November sky hung low and sullen, as if it too lamented the shortening days. In the belly of Jason's beaten-up Chevy, the four friends chattered excitedly about their Thanksgiving road trip through the picturesque wilderness of Maine. It was a tradition, they'd agreed, a much-needed escape from the rigidity of college life.

Jason was at the wheel, his scruffy beard barely concealing the wry grin that played on his lips as he listened to the others. Emily, with her keen brown eyes scanning the roadmap spread across her lap, was insisting they were close to their first waypoint, a so-called 'must-see' landmark known to locals as the Whispering Pines.

"Come on, Em," Jason teased, his eyes briefly meeting hers in the rearview mirror. "The only 'whispering' I want to hear this weekend is the sound of turkey calling my name from the oven."

A hearty laugh erupted from the back seat, where Travis sat beside his girlfriend, Laura. "Man, you think about food more than a linebacker thinks about the next play."

Laura leaned forward, the concern in her voice cutting through the banter. "Guys, it's getting really foggy. Should we maybe stop and wait it out?"

But the playful mood in the car was infectious, and the fog was just another adventure, a spectral adversary to taunt on their way to a well-deserved break.

"You worry too much, babe," Travis said, wrapping his arm around Laura. "Besides, Jason here claims he can drive through anything."

Famous last words, they'd soon find out. As they wound deeper into the backwoods, an impenetrable fog descended like a shroud. Within minutes, the road vanished, the trees became phantoms, and the laughter died in their throats.

"Jason, seriously, pull over," Emily's voice was a mixture of worry and command. "We could hit a tree or..."

"Or what? The Boogeyman?" Jason joked, but the humor was forced now. His foot eased off the accelerator, the Chevy creeping forward as if it too feared what lay beyond the white veil.

That's when they saw it. A sign, so weathered it was nearly reclaimed by the encroaching wilderness, announced their unplanned arrival: "Welcome to New Plymouth - Established 1620."

"A whole town hidden out here?" Laura's tone was incredulous, a stark contrast to her usual calm.

"Maybe it's some kind of reenactment place?" Travis suggested, peering out as the vehicle edged forward.

Jason brought the car to a stop as the fog seemed to open up like curtains, revealing New Plymouth. They were indeed a spectacle, but nothing like any reenactment they'd seen or heard of. The village was a slice of the seventeenth century perfectly preserved, as if each building, each cobblestone street, had been sealed under glass, untouched by the passing centuries.

"Well, this is definitely not in the travel brochure," Emily murmured, her voice laced with fascination.

The air was still, the only sounds were the soft rustling of the trees and their own breathing. Even the fog seemed hesitant to enter the village proper.

"Maybe we should ask for directions," Laura said, "and maybe get out of this fog."

The four friends gathered their courage and stepped out into the crisp air. Their arrival hadn't gone unnoticed. Faces peered from behind curtains, and doors creaked open cautiously.

Then, as if on cue, the fog began to dissipate, revealing the true extent of New Plymouth's quaint charm. Villagers dressed in what appeared to be authentic pilgrim attire milled about, some pausing to observe the newcomers with a cautious curiosity that bordered on suspicion.

Elijah Goodwin emerged from a stately home that seemed to serve as the settlement's focal point. His striking blue eyes scanned the group before a smile broke his stern demeanor.

"Welcome, travelers," he greeted, his voice smooth like a sermon. "It's rare we get visitors on such an auspicious day. Come, join us in our preparations. Today is a day of giving thanks, after all."

Jason exchanged a look with his friends. They shared a nonverbal agreement that was part skepticism, part thrill for the unscripted detour their trip had taken.

"We didn't mean to intrude," Jason began, but Elijah raised a hand.

"No intrusion at all. Providence, I'd say. It's been a long time since New Plymouth has had fresh faces to share in our harvest feast."

As they walked through the village, the initial trepidation melted away, charmed by the rustic authenticity of New Plymouth. Little did they know, their names had just been etched into the roster of an ancient and unfathomable tradition, one that would demand more from them than mere thankfulness. The feast they'd been invited to would prove to be unlike any other—a celebration that hungered for something primal, something that the mist had concealed with merciful opacity. But for now, they were simply enchanted visitors, stepping into a page of history that refused to turn.

The houses of New Plymouth huddled together like pious congregants, their wooden facades aged to a soft gray, as if leached of color by the weight of centuries. The smell of roasting meat and woodsmoke filled the air, a rustic perfume that spoke of simple lives and hearty appetites. The square was alive with villagers, their movements practiced and sure, a dance of tradition played out beneath the gaze of leafless trees.

Elijah led them to the common house, a large structure that loomed at the heart of the settlement, its massive central chimney like the spine of some ancient leviathan. Its door swung open to reveal a hall festooned with autumn's bounty—dried corn husks, pumpkins, and bunches of herbs hung from the rafters.

Inside, a long table was set with a care that bordered on reverence. Pewter plates gleamed in the light of dozens of candles, and the faces of the villagers reflected the flames, their expressions an eerie mask of anticipation.

"Please, be seated," Elijah gestured with a sweeping hand. "You are our honored guests."

The group exchanged glances, unease threading through the warmth of their welcome. They took their seats, the benches worn smooth by countless sittings. Laura's hand found Travis's under the table, her grip tight.

"Y'all sure know how to make folks feel special," Travis said, his voice a bass rumble in the hushed room.

Elijah's eyes crinkled at the corners. "Here in New Plymouth, we believe that every soul God brings to our table is a cause for celebration."

A door at the far end of the hall opened, and Abigail stepped through, her presence like a silent peal of a bell. She carried a tureen of soup, the steam rising around her, framing her in an ethereal halo. Her solemn green eyes met Jason's, and something passed between them, a silent recognition that felt as old as the earth.

The feast began with a simple grace, Elijah's voice resonant. "We give thanks for the harvest, for the hands that nurtured it, and for the strangers that grace our table. May they find warmth in our company and peace in our midst."

The food was a testament to the labor of the land; venison stew, root vegetables, and breads so hearty they seemed hewn from the very soil they sprang from. Yet for all its richness, each mouthful seemed laced with the tang of the unknown.

Jason felt Abigail's gaze upon him throughout the meal, and when she spoke, her voice was a whisper against the din of conversation.

"You do not find our ways strange, Jason Clarke?" Her lips barely moved, the words meant only for him.

He shrugged, attempting nonchalance. "Every family has its own traditions."

"Traditions," she echoed softly. "Yes, the ties that bind blood to blood, and the living to the dead."

Emily's eyes were sharp, missing nothing, but the warmth of the room, the food, and the company had worked their subtle alchemy. Even she found herself caught up in the pageantry of it all, the shadowy corners of her mind whispering that not all was as it seemed.

Laura's laughter peeled out, a touch too loud, a veneer over the nervousness that danced in her eyes. "This is like stepping into a history book. It's kind of magical."

Elijah smiled at her words, the blue of his eyes deepening. "We aim to preserve not just the body of our heritage, but its soul."

The meal continued, course after course, a seemingly endless array of dishes, each more elaborate than the last. The conversations around the table grew more animated, the villagers sharing tales of harvests past and winters survived. Yet, beneath the conviviality, there lay a current, a thrumming energy that Jason felt in his bones.

It was Travis who finally put words to the unease. "So, what's the price of admission to this little slice of heaven?" he asked, half-joking, half-serious.

Elijah turned to him, his smile unwavering. "Only that you share in our gratitude, Travis Green. And perhaps," he continued, his gaze sweeping over them, "that you help us preserve it."

The firelight flickered, casting the room momentarily in shadow, and in that flicker, something primal and ancient seemed to leer back at them. The feast was not yet over, and as the laughter and storytelling swirled around them, the friends were unaware that they had become part of a narrative far older and darker than any of them could imagine.

The clatter of pewter and the hum of old hymns faded as the friends retreated to the guest quarters provided by their hosts. Emily lingered behind the others, her gaze catching on the edges of shadows that seemed to cling a bit too fondly to the corners of the rooms.

"Something on your mind, Em?" Jason asked, noting her furrowed brow.

She shook her head, forcing a smile that didn't quite reach her eyes. "Just... impressed by the authenticity of this place. It's like they've captured a moment in time and refuse to let it go."

Travis laughed, a hearty, dismissive sound. "Or maybe they just don't have the budget for renovations. This place could use some of that TV makeover magic."

Laura, linking her arm with Travis's, shot a reproachful look at Emily. "Come on, it's like an adventure. Like we're in one of those interactive museums."

Emily's response was cut short as a procession of children skipped past them, their voices weaving a haunting melody that lingered in the air long after they had gone. The tune was unfamiliar, a series of notes that seemed to descend with each step they took, burrowing into the listener's psyche.

Travis stopped one of the boys, his broad hand gentle on the child's shoulder. "Hey buddy, what's the song?"

The boy, no older than eight, peered up with unblinking eyes, his innocence undercut by the weight of his gaze. "It's the song of thanks. For the harvest. For the feast. For the gift."

Laura smiled, though the boy's words sent a chill through her. "What gift?"

But the boy only smiled, a cryptic twist of his lips, and scampered away to rejoin the procession.

They found their way to the guest quarters, a modest building with beds that bore the imprints of countless previous occupants. The group settled in, the weight of the feast sitting heavy on their stomachs and minds.

It was Laura who first noticed the carvings on the bedposts, her fingertips tracing the crude shapes. "Look at these," she murmured. "Are these... symbols?"

Travis leaned in, his brow knitting. "They look old. Maybe some sort of... I don't know, pilgrim thing?"

Jason, already engrossed in a tattered book he'd found on a shelf, glanced over. "Pilgrim thing?" he echoed absently.

The carvings were a series of interlocking shapes, neither fully geometric nor entirely organic. There was an intentionality to them, a language of lines and curves that seemed to whisper of hidden things.

"That one looks like a cornucopia," Emily observed, "and that—" She pointed to a series of concentric circles, "—reminds me of a labyrinth."

Laura's laugh was tinged with nerves. "A maze to get lost in?"

Travis's humor had faded, his eyes tracing the symbols. "Or something to trap..."

The room fell into a contemplative silence, each lost in thought, the language of the carvings as indecipherable as the unsettling sensation that crept over them.

Jason finally closed the book with a snap, breaking the spell. "This place is a living museum, guys. It's all about the ambiance. These symbols are probably just part of the show."

Emily didn't seem convinced. She drew her legs up onto the bed, wrapping her arms around them. "Ambiance doesn't explain the children's song, or the way the villagers look at us... like we're..."

"Special?" Laura offered, her voice hopeful.

"Or chosen," Emily replied, the word hanging in the air like a prophecy.

The group settled into an uneasy sleep, their dreams a tangle of autumn leaves and whispered chants, the lines between past and present blurred by the murmur of the settlement.

In the dead of night, Jason found himself wandering the empty halls of the main house, drawn by a thirst for knowledge that bordered on obsession. The old tomes he found were bound in leather that creaked with age, the pages within inscribed with a meticulous hand that spoke of a time when each word was precious.

He found a passage, his fingers tracing the words as he read aloud to the silent hall, "And so it was that the bounty of the earth was given, and in return, the earth demanded its due. A cycle unbroken, a pact sealed in blood and bone."

A floorboard creaked behind him, and Jason spun around, expecting to see one of his friends. Instead, Abigail stood in the doorway, her presence as haunting as the text he'd just read.

"You should not be here," she said, her voice soft but firm.

Jason's heart raced, but he held his ground. "Why? What are these books?"

"They are our history," Abigail replied, moving closer. "The story of New Plymouth. But some chapters are not meant for outsiders."

Jason's skepticism wrestled with the raw sincerity in her eyes. "What are you hiding?"

Abigail's gaze never wavered. "The question, Jason Clarke, is not what we hide, but what you are willing to see."

Outside, the wind picked up, howling through the settlement, carrying with it whispers of the past, or perhaps, omens of what was to come. The chill that seeped through the cracks was not just from the cold. It was a warning, a precursor to the bitter harvest that awaited them as the last leaf fell, signaling the end of the facade and the beginning of the truth.

The whispers didn't cease with the falling of night. They grew into an orchestra of unseen murmurs that clawed at the fringes of sleep, prying the friends from their uneasy dreams. Laura's breaths came in short gasps, her sleep fitful and pocked with flickers of shadow and light.

Beside her, Travis turned restlessly, his subconscious wrestling with a sense of impending dread. Something visceral tugged at him, a primal alarm that whispered of flight over fight.

Jason's mind, however, couldn't surrender to the spectral hands of sleep. The words from the ancient tome echoed in his skull, "a pact sealed in blood and bone." He knew that Abigail hadn't just happened upon him; she was a sentinel, guarding knowledge that Jason was now determined to unearth.

And then there was Emily, her back to the wall, eyes wide open and staring into the dark. She felt the vibrations of the house, a subtle shift in the air that suggested movement, purpose. Slipping from her bed, she approached the window, her gaze drawn to the flicker of torchlight beyond.

"Guys," she whispered urgently, a hand on Jason's shoulder, "there's something going on outside."

Jason followed her gaze to see the procession of settlers emerging from their homes, moving with an unsettling synchronicity toward the outskirts of the village. Their faces were obscured by hooded cloaks, the torches in their hands casting an otherworldly glow on their path.

Travis and Laura were now alert, their hearts syncing with the pace of the unexpected parade. Without words, the four friends dressed swiftly, quietly, a mutual curiosity fueling their movements as they moved to follow.

They kept to the shadows, trailing the procession at a safe distance, careful not to make a sound. The land beyond the village dipped into a shallow valley where the fields lay barren, waiting for next year's sowing.

In the center of this desolation stood an ancient oak, its branches clawing at the night sky, leaves long since fallen. It was here the settlers gathered, forming a circle around the tree, their torches creating a ring of fire that seemed to hold back the darkness with tenuous strength.

Jason felt a knot tighten in his gut as he watched the villagers begin their ceremony. The trance-like state of the participants was palpable, even from afar. Their chants rose in a language that wasn't quite English, syllables twisted into something older, something far more sinister.

Emily clutched her notepad to her chest, scribbling notes with a trembling hand. "It's like... like something out of a harvest rite," she murmured, "Something pagan, something..."

"Dark," Laura finished, her gaze locked on the scene before them.

There was a rhythm to the ceremony, an ebb and flow that spoke of ritual and ancient practices. The settlers moved as one, their bodies swaying, their voices joining in a crescendo that reached toward the heavens as if in supplication... or in command.

As the ceremony reached its peak, the settlers parted to allow a figure to move to the forefront. Elijah Goodwin stepped forward, his piercing blue eyes reflecting the firelight. In his hands, he held an effigy woven from straw and cloth, its form grotesquely humanoid.

"Hear us, O bountiful earth," he intoned, his voice carrying across the field, "Accept this effigy, this... vessel of our thanks, and grant us another year of your grace."

The effigy was lifted high, and the crowd's fervor intensified. Jason's throat constricted as he watched the effigy tossed into the branches of the oak, where it hung, a suspended offering to an unseen deity.

"This isn't just Thanksgiving," Emily breathed, her voice barely above a whisper, "This is a sacrifice."

Travis's face was set, his jaw clenched. "What the hell have we stumbled onto?"

As they watched, hidden in the shadows, the ceremony concluded with a final, thunderous chant. The settlers began to disperse, the trance dissipating as if it had never been. But the ground itself seemed to remember, the energy of the ritual seeping into the soil, feeding something that lay beneath.

Laura reached for Travis's hand, her grasp seeking solace in familiarity. "We should go back," she said, her voice unsteady, "before they see us."

But even as they turned to leave, the truth clawed at the edges of their awareness, the knowledge that they had witnessed something primeval, something that thrived on the ignorance of outsiders. Something that would not, could not, be sated by mere effigies for long.

And in the darkness, the eyes of New Plymouth watched, hungry and knowing.

The return to their temporary lodgings was silent, each step punctuated by the quickening of their pulses. They could feel the weight of unseen eyes pressing upon them, a testament to the chilling revelation they had all silently acknowledged.

Once inside, Jason turned to the others, his gray eyes stormy with the churn of his thoughts. "We need to understand what's going on here, what that... that ritual meant."

Emily nodded, her notes clutched like a talisman. "We're missing pieces. Too many pieces. That effigy, the chants—they're part of something bigger. Something deeply rooted in this place."

Travis's posture was rigid, the revelations of the night stoking a fire within. "An effigy is a symbol, a stand-in. But for what—or for whom?"

Laura's voice was a fragile thread in the tense atmosphere. "This is all wrong. We're just supposed to be here for Thanksgiving, not... not this."

Their discussions were abruptly cut short by a knock at the door. It was firm, demanding attention. The four friends exchanged wary glances, the earlier unease blossoming into dread. Jason approached the door, his hand steady despite the tremor that threatened his resolve.

Elijah Goodwin stood there, his presence looming even in the doorway, a smile playing on his lips as though he were unaware of the nocturnal expedition his guests had embarked upon.

"Good morning, my dear friends," Elijah's voice was as smooth as honey, yet it sent a chill down their spines. "I trust you slept well?"

His gaze lingered on each of them, a knowing look that suggested the opposite. Jason felt a coil tighten within him, but he managed a polite nod. "We did, thank you. To what do we owe the honor of your visit?"

Elijah's smile widened. "Today is a day of great joy for New Plymouth. You see, we have a tradition here—a special honor given to select guests. And we have chosen you four to be the guests of distinction at our Thanksgiving feast."

The words hung in the air, laced with an edge that scraped against Jason's nerves. Emily's grip on her notepad tightened, the whites of her knuckles betraying her calm exterior.

"That's... very generous of you," Travis said, his voice betraying none of the unease that lay beneath. "But what does this honor entail?"

Elijah's eyes sparkled with mirth. "Oh, all will be revealed in time. For now, rejoice! For you are blessed amongst visitors."

As he left, the door closing behind him seemed to seal their fate. The room felt smaller, the air thicker.

Jason turned to face the others. "We're not safe here. That wasn't an invitation—it was a proclamation. We're part of their plan now, whatever the hell that is."

"We have to leave," Laura said, her voice desperate. "Before the feast, we have to get out of here."

But their plans for escape were interrupted by another figure at the window. It was Abigail, her green eyes alight with urgency. Jason moved to meet her, and the others followed.

"I need to speak with you," she said to Jason, her voice barely above a whisper. "Alone."

The others hesitated, but Jason nodded, stepping outside with her. They walked in silence until they were out of earshot, beneath the boughs of trees that whispered secrets.

"What is it?" Jason asked. "What do you need to tell me?"

Abigail's gaze was solemn, her voice tinged with a sorrow that belied her years. "You and your friends... you're in danger. The honor—they speak of it with reverence, but it's a lie. The previous honorees... they didn't leave New Plymouth. Not as they arrived."

Jason's stomach dropped. "What happened to them?"

"The land requires a sacrifice. A true sacrifice," she said, her eyes welling with tears. "My father believes in the old ways, the ways of blood and harvest. The feast is a front, a mask for something older and far more sinister."

"And the effigy?" Jason's thoughts raced back to the twisted figure hanging from the oak.

"A vessel," Abigail confirmed. "But it's not enough. It's never enough."

Jason's mind worked feverishly, connecting the dots of this perverse puzzle. "The guests of honor..."

"They become the offering," she finished, her eyes searching his. "You must leave, Jason. Tonight. Before the feast."

The urgency in her voice was palpable, yet beneath it lay something else—a connection that sparked between them, dangerous and undeniable. Jason took her hand, the warmth there a small comfort against the chilling truth.

"We'll leave, Abigail. But you should come with us."

Her laugh was bitter, a sound that held little humor. "And where would I go? This is my home, my prison."

The words hung between them, a testament to the forbidden bond forming under the shadow of the ritual oak. They were two souls caught in the web of New Plymouth's dark legacy, each seeking a way out, yet bound by the very thing they sought to escape.

And as they stood there, the land watched, the ancient hunger stirring beneath the soil, waiting for the feast to begin.

The day had aged into a somber afternoon when Travis decided to stretch his legs, unable to shake the cabin fever that the group's grim predicament had intensified. He informed the others of his need for fresh air, his instincts as a former quarterback telling him to recon the playing field. "I'll be back before dusk," he reassured Laura, who watched him with eyes shadowed by her tormented dreams.

The woods around New Plymouth were dense, the trees ancient, their twisted limbs scratching at the sky. Travis' boots crunched on the carpet of dead leaves, his breath visible in the chilly air. He couldn't shake the feeling that he was being watched, but he pushed deeper into the forest, driven by a gnawing curiosity that felt like a splinter in his mind.

The further he wandered, the more the woods seemed to close in on him, as if they were alive, whispering secrets in a language only they understood. That's when he saw it—a fresh mound of earth at the base of a gnarled oak, like a grave with no marker. His heart hammered against his ribs as he approached, the soil looking disturbed, recently turned.

He knelt beside the mound, his hands hesitating before digging into the cold earth. What he uncovered would haunt him for the rest of his days. A hand, pallid and lifeless, emerged from the grave, its fingers curled as though clinging to life. The rest of the body followed, a previous 'guest of honor' no doubt, their face a frozen mask of terror.

Travis recoiled, horror-struck, the ground catching his breath. This was the grisly truth of New Plymouth's hospitality. He had to warn the others—they needed to leave, now.

Laura's sleep had been anything but restful. Visions had plagued her—a tableau of horror that unfolded each time she closed her eyes. She saw the settlers in their puritanical garb, their faces contorted in fervent ecstasy as they danced around an altar that throbbed with an otherworldly pulse. Atop it lay a figure, bound and screaming—a sacrifice to appease whatever ancient entity the land craved.

She awoke with a start, her breath ragged, her skin slick with sweat despite the autumnal chill that had settled in their room. The nightmares were getting worse, and the dark circles under her eyes were proof that sleep offered no sanctuary.

Emily had always believed in facing her problems head-on, and this time was no different. She sought out Elijah with a determined stride, her mind armed with questions that demanded answers. She found him in the settlement's modest chapel, a structure that seemed to groan with the weight of its own history.

"Elijah," she began, her tone as steely as her resolve, "What are these 'traditions' you uphold with such zeal? What do you mean by 'sacrifice'?"

Elijah turned, his smile never reaching his piercing blue eyes. "My dear Emily, your mind is clouded with the complexities of the outside world. Here, we are simple folk. Our traditions are merely expressions of our gratitude for the bounty we receive."

Emily wasn't swayed. "Gratitude... or something else? I've seen the fear in the people's eyes. I've heard the whispers in the night. This is more than just Thanksgiving."

His demeanor shifted then, the mask of geniality slipping. "You are an intelligent woman, Emily. But there are things beyond the ken of your understanding, rituals that stretch back to the very founding of New Plymouth. We are the keepers of a covenant, a promise made long before the first pilgrim set foot upon these shores."

Emily's blood ran cold as the implications of his words sank in. "And the price of breaking that covenant?"

Elijah's gaze was unflinching. "Devastation. Starvation. The land here is... hungry. It requires nourishment of a particular kind."

The depth of the town's fanaticism was laid bare, a chilling realization that sealed the fates of those caught in its grasp. Emily knew then that the stakes were far higher than any of them had imagined. They weren't just fighting for their freedom—they were fighting for their lives.

The air in the chapel felt thick, oppressive, as if it too was a captive of the grim secrets it housed. She left without another word, her thoughts racing, a plan beginning to form. They needed to act, and they needed to act fast.

The threads of the nightmare were weaving tighter around them, the dark tapestry of New Plymouth's legacy threatening to engulf them all. But there was still time, a narrow window to escape the closing snare—if only they could see it in time.

Evening draped its cloak over New Plymouth, and in the half-light, the stark severity of the settlement was softened, the edges blurred. A deceptive peace lay upon the land as Jason and his friends gathered in the house they'd been assigned, the mood somber.

"We need to leave," Travis declared, his voice a low rumble, as he recounted the horrific discovery in the woods. "Tonight."

Jason paced the floor, his gray eyes hard with resolve. "We need a plan. They'll be watching the roads, the woods. They've done this before, and they're prepared for runners."

Laura sat by the hearth, the firelight casting dancing shadows upon her face. "But we know the forest now, at least better than before. And we can't stay. My dreams... they're warnings."

Emily looked toward the window, her eyes reflecting a resolve as sharp as flint. "They expect us to be a part of their... harvest festival tomorrow. That gives us the cover of the feast to slip away."

Abigail entered the room quietly, her presence like a wraith, unnoticed until she spoke. "It won't work." Her voice was a melancholic melody, the tune of a heart divided.

All eyes turned to her, questions unspoken.

"You don't understand the forces you're dealing with," Abigail continued, moving closer to the hearth, seeking warmth but finding none. "The woods themselves will betray you. They serve the Old Gods as much as we do."

Jason's voice softened. "Abigail, tell us. What is it that you do here? What gods demand such... devotion?"

Her gaze met his, and for a moment, it was as if the shadows retreated. "They are ancient, as old as the earth itself. Our forefathers made a pact with them. Prosperity for sacrifice. Every harvest, we pay our dues. If we don't..."

"What?" Travis interjected, his patience frayed.

"The land dies. The curse is real. Our fields will wither, our children will starve. We are bound to this land, and in turn, it is bound to us."

Laura's voice trembled with fear. "And the sacrifice? It's not crops, is it? It's people."

Abigail nodded, a tear escaping down her cheek. "Once, it was animals, but as the years passed, the Old Gods grew... hungrier. And now they will not be sated with less than human souls."

Silence fell like a shroud.

Emily broke it, her tone urgent. "You care for Jason, don't you? Help us stop this."

Abigail's internal struggle played out across her features, a tempest of duty and affection. "Stopping it is impossible. But escaping... perhaps I can do something. There's a place, a weak spot in the enchantment that holds the woods. I can show you."

Jason stepped toward her. "Why would you help us?"

"Because," she whispered, a haunted look in her solemn eyes, "I have seen what the Old Gods do to those who are sacrificed. And because... I cannot bear to see that fate befall you."

It was settled. They would leave under the guise of nightfall, under the pretense of joining the celebration. But as the shadows grew long and the time neared, a palpable dread settled over the group. There was the sense that the earth itself was aware of their plan, that the settlement was listening through the walls, the ground, the very air they breathed.

They prepared in silence, each lost in their own thoughts of what awaited them in the darkness of the woods, and what horrors they were leaving behind. The feast would be their diversion, the final act in the grotesque play they had been unwilling cast in.

As the first call to gather sounded throughout New Plymouth, a sinister sunset painted the sky in blood and fire, an omen of the night to come. The friends took a collective breath, stepping out into the twilight, moving toward the gathering with feigned solemnity.

Their hearts beat to the rhythm of impending flight, but the path to freedom was shrouded, winding through the shadows cast by the Old Gods of New Plymouth.

The Thanksgiving sun rose reluctantly, as if it too dreaded the day's grim festivities. The town of New Plymouth awakened to the distant echo of chopping wood and the murmur of somber voices preparing for the evening's feast. A thick fog hugged the ground, and the autumn air was heavy with an expectancy that was almost electric.

Travis's instincts had him up at dawn, a restlessness that wouldn't allow him to stay indoors. He nudged Laura awake, his voice barely above a whisper. "Come with me. Let's take a walk before this place comes alive."

She followed without a word, her usual brightness dimmed by the weight of the previous night's revelations. They moved through the settlement, the eerie quiet of the early hour magnified by the thickening mist that seemed to swallow the sounds of their footsteps.

Travis led them away from the main path, toward the forest that bordered the settlement. He had noticed something during their previous, hurried excursions—a pattern in the trees, unnatural and deliberate. As they neared the treeline, the sight that greeted them was chilling: a series of ancient symbols carved into the bark, forming a boundary.

"What is this?" Laura's voice quivered, her fingers tracing the outlines.

"I think it's a warning... or a ward," Travis murmured, his eyes scanning the forest beyond. "Abigail mentioned the woods serving the Old Gods. This might be how they keep whatever's out there at bay."

Their exploration led them to a hollow, where the earth dipped into an obscured opening. Laura stumbled upon it first, a gasp escaping her as she nearly lost her footing. The ground beneath the leaves gave way to reveal a concealed entrance, stone steps descending into darkness.

"We shouldn't," she whispered, but curiosity and fear were a potent mix that fueled Travis's determination.

"I need to know," he said, his hand finding hers. "Stay close."

The steps were worn, slick with moisture and age. The chamber they descended into was vast, the air thick with the scent of decay. Along the walls, crude shelves were carved into the rock, laden with remains—bones arranged with purpose, artifacts that whispered of rituals and offerings.

Laura's breath hitched, her hand tightening around Travis's. "This is their altar, isn't it?"

"It looks like it," Travis confirmed, his gaze locked on the remains. "These people... They're serious about what they do here."

Among the relics, they found a journal, its pages yellowed with age. Travis flipped it open, the scrawling handwriting documenting years of feasts, each entry more macabre than the last. His voice, when he read aloud, was a mix of horror and disbelief. "They believe the sacrifices give them power, prosperity... It's a cycle. And this year, we're a part of it."

They didn't notice the shadow until it moved, detaching itself from the darkness. Elijah Goodwin stepped forward, his piercing blue eyes cold and unyielding.

"You should not have come here," he intoned, his voice resonating in the chamber.

Back at the house, Jason felt the first stirrings of unease as time stretched on without a sign of Travis and Laura. He exchanged a look with Emily, the unspoken concern sparking action.

"We have to find them," he said, grabbing his coat.

The settlement was coming to life now, the sounds of preparation a dissonant backdrop to their mounting fear. As Jason and Emily searched, they realized that they were being herded, subtly, by the movements of the townspeople, toward the center of the settlement, where the feast was to take place.

In the center stood a grand table, laden with harvest bounty, a sickening display when juxtaposed with the knowledge of the true cost of such abundance. Elijah Goodwin presided over the scene, his gaze sweeping over his flock with an air of possession.

Travis and Laura were there, pushed forward by unseen hands, their faces pale but resolute. Elijah's voice rose, the timbre both comforting and commanding as he spoke of gratitude and blessings, of sacrifices made for the greater good.

The friends were united now, the veneer of honored guests dissolving rapidly as the true nature of the feast became apparent. They were surrounded, the eyes of the settlement upon them, hungry and expectant.

As the sky darkened toward evening, the Thanksgiving feast took on a macabre tone, the flickering torchlight casting long shadows. A hush fell over the assembly as Elijah lifted his hands, signaling the beginning of the Binding Feast. The sense of dread was palpable, a living thing, as the friends braced themselves for what was to come.

Each moment stretched, taut as a bowstring, as the townspeople began a low chant, a sound that seemed to come from the earth itself. And from the shadows, figures began to emerge, their faces obscured by masks that were not just disguises, but something far more ancient and terrifying.

The friends stood close, their minds racing for any means of escape, but they were penned in by tradition and terror, the Thanksgiving of New Plymouth a trap from which there was no easy release.

Jason's hand clenched into a fist under the table, his nails digging crescents into his palm. The chant from the townsfolk swelled, a sinister melody that crept along his spine. He leaned in, whispering harshly to his friends. "We're not going to just sit here and be part of this sick pageant."

Emily's eyes, sharp and assessing, met his. "What's the plan, then?" Her voice was a thread of steel wrapped in velvet, calm but ready to snap into action.

Before Jason could reply, Elijah's voice cut through the din, smooth as the surface of a still pond, but with something lurking beneath. "Our honored guests," he began, his eyes locking on each of them in turn. "You have been brought here to share in our most sacred tradition. You have been chosen not just to witness, but to partake in the prosperity of our harvest."

Laura's face had drained of color, and she glanced around, her chest rising and falling with quick breaths. "I don't like this," she whispered, her eyes darting to Travis, seeking reassurance.

Travis, ever the anchor, put a hand on her shoulder—a small gesture, but it stilled her shaking. "Stay sharp," he murmured, the muscle in his jaw working.

As the feast commenced, the dishes presented were a grotesque mirror of a Thanksgiving meal. A stew that bubbled ominously, its contents indiscernible; bread that was dark as the soil; pies that seemed to move of their own accord, their filling a mystery that no one wanted to solve. The air was thick with the aroma of herbs and something else—something metallic and ancient.

Elijah stood at the head of the table, his eyes on Jason as he lifted a goblet. "To our guests, may you bring us the blessing of renewal, as we have done for generations."

The toast was a signal, and as the townsfolk drank, the atmosphere tightened, charged with expectation. It was now or never.

Jason pushed back from the table, his chair scraping loudly against the floorboards. "This isn't a feast—it's a farce!" His voice thundered above the crowd, breaking the spell for a moment.

Elijah's gaze narrowed, the warmth vanishing like smoke. "Do not mistake our hospitality for weakness," he replied, his tone a growling undertow.

With a swift glance that conveyed a world of strategy, Jason gestured to the others. They stood, knocking over their chairs, and bolted. The settlement erupted into chaos, the chanting turning into cries of anger as the villagers surged forward.

Jason and his friends were halfway to the edge of the settlement before they heard the pounding footsteps behind them. They were being chased, hunted through the twisted pathways between houses and around corners that seemed to shift and play tricks on the eyes in the growing dusk.

Elijah's voice echoed, rising above the clamor, "The Old Gods demand their due! You cannot outrun destiny!"

The chase was disorienting, the landscape of New Plymouth a labyrinth that ensnared. They darted through an archway of intertwined branches that led into the forest, the very woods that Travis and Laura had explored earlier.

Branches snagged at their clothes, roots threatened to trip them, but fear lent them speed. Jason's breath came in sharp gasps, his mind racing for a plan. Emily was at his side, her focus unwavering, while Travis and Laura followed, their unity unspoken but unbreakable.

A clearing loomed ahead, moonlight filtering through the dense canopy. It was a respite, a moment to catch their breath and plan their next move. But the respite was an illusion, for the circle of masked figures emerged from the shadows, surrounding them.

Jason's mind was awhirl with panic and adrenaline. They were in the heart of the settlement's darkness now, the true face of New Plymouth revealed in the moon's cold gaze. They were trapped, not by the settlers, but by the very history they had sought to escape.

There was no conclusion here, no neat ending to their ordeal. As the circle tightened, Jason knew they would have to fight, not just for survival, but for the truth buried beneath the twisted roots of New Plymouth. The table was set, and they were the main course, but they were not ready to be devoured by the darkness just yet.

Their backs against each other, the four of them stood defiant in the clearing, the moon above casting a surreal glow on the encroaching figures. Emily's voice was calm but carried the edge of a knife. "We won't go down without a fight," she stated, her eyes darting, assessing their situation with a strategic mind.

Laura's breathing was heavy, her normally soothing voice now tinged with desperation. "There has to be a way out," she pleaded, searching for an exit in the ring of masked beings.

Travis stood tall, his physical presence a comfort to Laura and the others. "We stand together," he growled, ready to use his strength to protect his friends.

Elijah's voice, once melodic and enticing, now thundered through the trees. "You cannot deny the Harvest God its prize. The ground has been parched, the bloodline thinned. We need you to complete the cycle, to water the earth with blood, to feed the roots of our prosperity."

It was then that the earth beneath them began to tremble, a low rumble that grew into a roar as if the very soil of New Plymouth rebelled against its occupants. A chill wind sliced through the clearing, carrying with it a foul stench of decay and ancient rot.

From the trembling ground, a figure began to rise, the soil parting as if giving birth to a horror from the bowels of the earth itself. What emerged was a thing of nightmares, a grotesque mockery of the human form, its body a mass of writhing tendrils and its face a shifting mass of shadows and light.

"The Harvest God," whispered Emily, her voice laced with horror.

Jason's eyes met the creature's, and what he saw was an endless abyss, a hunger that was ancient and insatiable. "We won't be your sacrifice!" he shouted, defiance igniting in his chest.

The creature let out a sound, a guttural cry that was both a howl of rage and a beckoning call to its worshippers. The townsfolk, as if entranced, moved closer, their eyes hollow, their movements puppet-like as they advanced.

But it was in this moment of terror that the unexpected happened. A fracture appeared within the circle of townspeople, and through it stepped Abigail, her solemn green eyes now alight with an inner fire.

She moved with purpose, her voice rising above the din, clear and strong. "No more," she declared, her soft-spoken demeanor now fierce and commanding. "This ends tonight."

Elijah turned to her, his voice dripping with betrayal. "Abigail, my child, you would defy your heritage, our very essence?"

Her reply was resolute. "I defy a heritage that demands the blood of the innocent. I choose them," she said, gesturing to Jason and his friends.

The Harvest God let out a bellow of rage as Abigail joined the circle of friends, her presence an act of rebellion that sparked confusion among the other settlers.

Jason, seizing the moment, spoke up, "If blood is what you want," he snarled at the creature, "then come and get it."

With those words, the group lunged into action. Travis led the charge, his fists swinging with the force of his entire being. Laura, her fear now sharpened into focus, followed suit, moving with a grace born of desperation.

Emily's analytical mind worked rapidly, her movements precise, targeting weaknesses with the precision of a surgeon. Jason stood with them, his leadership not in commands, but in the solidarity of his stance beside them.

And at the forefront, a surprising ally, was Abigail, her betrayal of New Plymouth a catalyst that began to sow doubt among the other villagers. Her eyes met Jason's, a silent promise that she would fight with them until the end.

The Harvest God advanced, the ground itself seeming to pulse and writhe with its every step, the tendrils that made up its form reaching out with a hunger that had known centuries.

The air was thick with the sounds of battle, the cries of the settlers, the inhuman howls of the Harvest God, and the determined shouts of Jason and his friends. The fight for survival had begun, and the heart of New Plymouth beat with a frenzied rhythm, as if sensing the possibility of its own demise.

In the chaos, Emily's mind raced. The legends, the whispers of the settlement's dark past that Elijah had proudly recounted, now played over in her head. She remembered the tales of the Harvest God, bound to the earth, its power linked to the soil from which it sprang. "The land," she muttered, an idea sparking to life. "The land is the key!"

Jason, hearing her, tried to make sense of her words while dodging a swing from one of the entranced townsfolk. "What about the land?" he yelled back.

"It's where the creature draws its strength! We need to disrupt it—break the link!" Emily's shout was barely audible over the cacophony of the skirmish.

Laura, who was back to back with Travis, fending off the settlers with a ferocity that belied her kind nature, caught on to Emily's plan. "How do we break it?" she called out, breathless.

Emily, her mind whirring, locked eyes with Jason. "The effigy!" she shouted, a light of realization in her eyes. "The one in the center of town, it represents the bond to the land. Destroy that, and we might have a chance!"

Understanding dawned on Jason's face, a mix of awe and terror. "You mean the wooden sculpture? The one they adorned with all those carvings and offerings?"

"Yes!" Emily's voice was now tinged with urgency. "It's not just symbolic. It's a totem, a focal point for the Harvest God's energy!"

Without another word, Jason turned to Travis and Laura. "Cover us!" he ordered.

Travis nodded, his jaw set. "Go!" He turned to Laura. "Stay close."

Laura nodded, understanding the gravity of their task. Together, they became a bulwark, a human shield as Jason and Emily darted through the melee towards the town center.

Abigail, still within the fray, moved with a grace that was almost otherworldly, her actions causing ripples of hesitance among the villagers. Her betrayal was more than an act; it was a breaking of chains that held the settlers in thrall.

The creature roared in fury, sensing the plan unfolding. It thrashed, sending villagers flying with the wild sweeps of its appendages.

Emily and Jason reached the town center, the effigy looming before them, an eerie sentinel in the moonlight. The totem was grotesque, adorned with carved symbols and dried blood, offerings hanging from its twisted limbs.

Jason looked around frantically. "We need fire," he gasped, searching for something to ignite the effigy.

"Here!" Emily had found a torch, discarded in the commotion, its flame still licking the air hungrily.

Taking the torch, Jason thrust it into the base of the wooden structure. The dry wood caught quickly, the flames eager to consume the tainted symbol.

As the effigy burned, a piercing scream rent the air, the sound coming from the Harvest God as it writhed in apparent agony, the link between it and the land weakening.

Back at the clearing, the settlers were faltering, their movements sluggish, their expressions confused, as if awakening from a deep trance. The strength of the Harvest God waned, its tendrils retracting as the effigy smoldered and cracked.

Travis and Laura, amidst the settlers, sensed the shift. They stood their ground, protecting the space, giving Jason and Emily the time they needed.

But the creature was not defeated yet. With a desperate surge, it lashed out at the closest target—Travis and Laura.

"Travis!" Laura's scream was one of both warning and terror as the tendrils coiled towards them.

Without a second thought, Travis pushed Laura out of the way, taking the full brunt of the attack. The tendrils wrapped around him, pulling him towards the writhing mass of the Harvest God.

"Laura!" Travis's voice was strained, but his eyes locked onto hers, a silent message of love and sacrifice.

Laura, scrambling to her feet, tears streaming down her face, looked for something, anything to help Travis. Her eyes landed on a piece of the burning effigy, a flaming branch that had fallen to the ground.

With a cry that mingled grief with rage, she seized the flaming wood and charged at the Harvest God, driving the fire into the heart of the tendrils holding Travis.

The creature let out an unholy shriek, its form convulsing as the fire from the effigy, now a weapon in Laura's hands, burned it.

The townsfolk, now mostly free from the creature's control, watched in horror and fascination as the battle unfolded, their once blind fervor dissolved in the face of the raw courage displayed by the outsiders.

The Harvest God, aflame and in agony, released Travis, its form beginning to crumble as the link to the land and its totem broke down.

Travis, released but weakened, collapsed, with Laura at his side, her defiance never wavering as she stood over him, a guardian even in her despair.

The night air filled with the sounds of crackling flames, the creature's death throes, and the heavy, ragged breaths of those fighting for their lives. The heart of New Plymouth was exposed, beating with a vulnerability that had not been seen for centuries.

As the creature's form diminished, the soil of the settlement seemed to sigh, a release of tension that had been held for far too long. And in that moment, the struggle was no longer just about survival, but about the shattering of a cycle of darkness that had held sway over the land.

The outcome of the battle hung in the balance, the fabric of New Plymouth's sinister legacy tearing at the seams. And as the friends stood together, their fate intertwined with the crumbling horror before them, the true reckoning of Pilgrim's Regress was only just beginning.

The smoldering remnants of the Harvest God cast an eerie glow over the charred ground of New Plymouth. The once-mighty entity, now reduced to ashes and dying embers, lay scattered by the very hands it sought to dominate. As the chilling wind swept through, it carried away the remnants of the terror that had gripped the land.

Jason stood still, his chest heaving, the adrenaline slowly ebbing from his veins. His eyes scanned the devastation around him, the horror of what had transpired sinking in. The villagers, those not lying motionless on the ground, stared back at him and his friends with a duality of fear and gratitude, unsure whether to approach their liberators or flee from the saviors who had slain their god.

Beside him, Emily clutched her side, blood seeping between her fingers. Her breaths were shallow, her face pale beneath the smudges of dirt and blood. But her eyes still burned with the fierce determination that had led them to this moment of tenuous victory.

"We need to get out of here," Jason murmured, his voice a hoarse whisper, his arm instinctively wrapping around Emily's waist to support her.

Emily nodded, the action setting off a grimace of pain. "I can't... I can't walk far, Jase."

He looked down at her, gray eyes meeting brown in silent conversation. "You won't have to. I'll carry you if I have to." The resolve in his voice left no room for argument.

From the shadows, Abigail watched them, her expression an enigma. The flames reflected in her solemn green eyes, hinting at the turmoil within. The legacy of her father, Elijah Goodwin, lay in ruins at her feet, yet the subtle tilt of her head and the ghost of a smile suggested that the tale of New Plymouth might not end with the fall of the Harvest God.

Laura, her face streaked with tears and soot, hovered over Travis, who was slowly regaining consciousness. His broad chest rose and fell with labored breaths, and when he opened his eyes, the pain in them was quickly masked by the relief of seeing Laura safe.

"Trav, can you stand?" Laura's voice trembled as she helped him to sit up.

"With you by my side?" Travis grunted, attempting to rise. "I can do anything."

They shared a smile, brief and fragile, before Travis winced, the movement reigniting the agony from his wounds.

Laura looked toward Jason and Emily. "We have to move. Can he walk?"

Jason assessed Travis with a critical eye before nodding slowly. "We don't have a choice. We need to find shelter, tend to our wounds. We're sitting ducks out here."

The night had fallen silent, a stark contrast to the cacophony of battle that had filled it just minutes before. Now, the only sound was the soft crackling of the final remnants of the Harvest God burning out.

"Where will we go?" Laura's question was barely above a whisper, her gaze sweeping the desolate surroundings.

"Anywhere but here," Jason said, his voice resolute. "We head into the woods, find a place to hold up until daybreak."

Travis managed to get to his feet with Laura's help, and together, the group made their way into the treeline, leaving behind the settlement that had almost become their grave.

As they trudged through the underbrush, the forest seemed to close in around them, the trees whispering secrets in a language only the wilds understood. Emily leaned heavily on Jason, each step an act of willpower. Laura kept a watchful eye on Travis, ready to catch him should he falter.

The deeper they went, the more the woods seemed to change, the shadows growing longer, the air colder. The normal sounds of the night were absent, as if the creatures that called the forest home had decided to witness in silence the exodus of the few who had stood against the darkness and survived.

The occasional look back revealed nothing but darkness, yet the sensation of being watched, perhaps followed, clawed at the edges of their weary minds.

They didn't speak; words were precious, and their breath even more so. They walked, each step taking them further from the nightmare, but the question remained—would they ever truly escape?

New Plymouth and its sinister secrets lay behind them, but the echoes of the Harvest God's cries, the villagers' chants, and the haunting possibility of Abigail's silent pursuit followed them through the darkness.

The remnants of the settlement were far behind them now, the twisted silhouettes of the cabins swallowed by the gaping maw of the forest. Yet, with each step, the weight of unseen eyes seemed to press closer against their backs, a psychological specter that would not be shed by mere distance.

It was Travis who first heard the rustling. A hushed, deliberate movement—a whisper against the forest floor. He halted, Laura bumping into him from behind, her whispered apology cutting off as she too noticed the change in the air.

Jason and Emily stopped, turning back with a synchrony born of shared dread. They listened, but heard only their collective breathing and the thudding of their own hearts.

"Do you think they're following us?" Laura's voice was a thin thread of sound.

"Could be animals," Travis offered, though his skeptical gaze searched the murky woods. "Or..."

He let the word hang between them, the unsaid possibilities more terrifying than any creature that might prowl the Maine wilderness.

Emily, pushing through the pain, straightened up as much as she could. "No. They're not animals. They're waiting."

"Waiting for what?" Jason's voice cracked like a whip in the quiet.

"For us to break. For us to stop and never start again," Emily's response was a bleak whisper. Her eyes were bright with a feverish intensity that belied her weakening body.

They moved on, the decision unspoken yet unanimous. To stop was to invite death—or worse, to become part of the dark legacy they sought to escape.

Time lost meaning as they pushed through the night. The moon, hidden behind the thick canopy, offered no guidance, no indication of the hours slipping by. Only when the first tendrils of dawn began to seep through the boughs did they allow themselves a moment of respite.

They found a clearing, a small reprieve from the oppressive closeness of the woods. In the gray light of early morning, they looked at each other, really looked, and saw the toll the night had taken.

Laura's face was gaunt, the vibrancy of her eyes dimmed by exhaustion. Travis' broad shoulders slumped, his strength sapped to the very marrow. Emily was a ghost of her former self, the vibrant will flickering behind a facade of pain and blood loss. And Jason, their pillar, bore the haunted look of a man who had peered into the abyss and knew it stared back at him.

"We can't keep going like this," Laura said, her voice breaking the hush that had settled over them. "We need help."

Jason nodded. "At first light, I'll go. Find a road, a ranger station, anything."

"I'm coming with you," Emily said, attempting to rise.

He placed a hand on her shoulder, gently but with an underlying firmness. "You need to stay. Rest."

A flare of the old Emily sparked in her eyes. "Don't you dare tell me what I need—"

But the fire died as quickly as it came, her energy spent. She nodded, acquiescing.

They settled into the clearing, their bodies crying out for rest, even as their minds warned them against it. The light grew stronger, the forest around them coming into stark relief. It was in this burgeoning daylight that they saw the figures approaching from the direction of the settlement.

Not the expected hostile procession of villagers, but a new group, their backpacks and cheerful voices clashing violently with the scene of escape before them.

Jason rose to his feet, the others following suit as the group came into the clearing. There were five of them, mirroring their own number—a cruel joke of fate. They were younger, buoyant with the thrill of discovery, unaware of the ruined settlement they were marching towards.

"Hey!" The leader of the newcomers, a young man with an eager face, called out to them. "Are you folks okay? You look like you've been through hell."

Jason exchanged a look with Emily, the unspoken conversation clearer than words. These kids had no idea.

"We're fine," he managed, his voice gravelly with strain. "But listen, you need to turn around. There's nothing for you back there. It's dangerous."

The newcomers exchanged glances, a mix of confusion and disbelief on their faces.

"Dangerous? We're just heading to New Plymouth, heard it was a hidden gem for Thanksgiving festivities," another of the newcomers, a bright-eyed girl, chimed in.

Emily's breath hitched, a sound of pure despair. The legacy of New Plymouth was reaching out, undeterred by the destruction they had wrought.

Laura stepped forward, her voice carrying a solemn warning. "There's no festivity worth what lies ahead. Please, just go back to wherever you came from."

But as the new group shrugged off their concerns, continuing on their path with the invincibility of ignorance, the four friends knew it was far from over. Something ancient had stirred in the ruins of New Plymouth, and the echoes of its power lingered in the land, calling to those who would listen.

As the newcomers dwindled into the distance, the four of them looked back toward the settlement, a sense of unfinished business creeping like a vine around their hearts. They could leave, yes, but the story of New Plymouth would not leave them.

In the silence of the forest, the embers of the Harvest God could still be felt, waiting to be rekindled. And in the depths of the woods, eyes watched, green as the forest and just as unforgiving. Abigail stood hidden, a sentinel to the legacy that would never die.

The legacy lived on, its roots deep in the soil of Maine, and as the new group approached the settlement, it seemed to breathe anew, waiting to claim the past, the present, and any future that dared to tread upon its cursed ground.

The end.

Stuffing the Void

The air in the attic of the old Langdon house was still, dust motes dancing in the slanting light that managed to pierce through the grimy window. It smelled of old fabric and the musk of time-forgotten. Michael Langdon's breaths were audible, heavy with the weight of a widower's grief as he sifted through the cardboard boxes labeled in his late wife's neat script.

His fingertips brushed against aged leather, and there was an immediate sense of the uncanny, as if his touch had disturbed a resting entity. He drew out the object, a cookbook by its shape and heft, but as peculiar as one of those arcane tomes whispered about in hushed tones and hurried superstitions.

The cover was a deep, worn brown, inscribed with faded gold lettering that spelled out no title but a cryptic symbol—a circle with intricate lines weaving an indecipherable pattern within it. Michael's gaze lingered on the symbol, feeling an odd pressure at the base of his skull, as if his very sight was being drawn into its convoluted design.

Opening the book felt like an intrusion, the creak of the spine like a groan from an awakened sleep. The pages were yellowed with age, edges frayed, each leaf appearing to be much more brittle than the last. It wasn't just the recipes, though they were strange enough with ingredients he could not recognize and directions that seemed to hint at something more than culinary technique. It was the notes, scribbled in the margins in a frenzied scrawl that spoke of caution and conquest.

Michael's breath hitched as he read a note that bordered a recipe for a dish named "Eternal Stuffing":

"Do not indulge too deeply. The void returns what you give tenfold."

His initial curiosity piqued with every turned page, each recipe becoming more outlandish, more fascinating and—dare he admit—more tempting. They called to a part of him that hungered for something beyond the taste of food, something that might fill the gnawing emptiness left by his wife's sudden passing.

He almost did not hear the creak of the attic steps or the soft call of his name. It was Sarah, her voice laced with concern.

"Dad? You've been up here for hours. Are you going to come down?"

Michael hastily shut the book, its whisper seeming to cling to the air around him.

"Yeah, I'll be down in a minute," he called back, his voice more hoarse than he intended.

As he descended the stairs, the weight of the cookbook in his hands felt as heavy as the burden of his own sorrow. The recipes within, he convinced himself, were nothing more than the fanciful creations of a mind more imaginative than his own. Yet as he moved away from the isolation of the attic, Michael could not shake the feeling that he was bringing down more than just a collection of forgotten dishes. He was bringing down an invitation, an invocation to a Thanksgiving where the void was not just stuffed, but where it would consume them all.

Sarah watched her father as he became increasingly tethered to the ancient cookbook. She noticed the slight tremble in his hands whenever he flipped through its pages, the way his eyes glazed over the scrawled notes in the margins. Her father, the pragmatic Michael Langdon, was always a man of routine and rationality. Yet here he stood, simmering with a fixation that she couldn't fathom.

"Dad, you gonna tell me what's got you all wrapped up in that book?" she asked, trying to keep the conversation light, though her voice betrayed a sliver of concern.

Michael looked up from the cookbook, his gaze momentarily foggy before clearing. "It's nothing, just some interesting recipes I thought I might try," he replied, forcing a thin smile that didn't quite reach his eyes.

"Recipes? Since when do you cook anything more complicated than spaghetti?" Sarah's tone was teasing but observant, picking up on the undercurrent of something unspoken.

"I guess... since now," he said and turned back to the book, his fingers caressing the aged pages as if to appease them.

That night, Sarah heard the clatter of pots and pans emanating from the kitchen far later than usual. Descending the creaky staircase, she found her father engrossed in cooking, his movements mechanical and precise. A pot simmered on the stove, and there was an aroma in the air that was at once mouthwatering and yet, inexplicably, made her stomach churn with a dull dread.

She approached silently, observing as Michael followed the recipe with an intensity that turned his knuckles white as he gripped the countertop. The recipe was for something called "Whispering Gravy," and it required an assortment of herbs that Sarah had never heard of, ones her father had somehow procured from the depths of the pantry.

"Dad, it's almost midnight. What are you making?" Sarah's voice cut through the bubbling sound of the gravy.

Without looking up, Michael replied in a monotone, "Just trying something new. It's important to... to experiment, you know?"

She nodded, though he couldn't see her. "But why now? Why this?" she pressed.

Michael paused, the spoon in his hand stopping mid-stir. For a moment, Sarah thought she saw a flicker of the father she knew, lost and searching for an answer. Then the spell seemed to snap, and he was stirring again, his response coming as if from far away. "I need to do this, Sarah. It's... it's part of moving on."

The gravy simmered, the steam rising in tendrils, and as Sarah breathed in, the scent carried a note that was almost metallic, like blood. She watched her father, his gaze now distant, locked in a trance-like state, following the recipe as if each step were a vital incantation.

As the gravy reached the prescribed thickness, Michael poured it over a slice of homemade bread, the liquid soaking in, turning the white to a deep, dark brown. He raised it to his lips, his eyes closed as if in prayer, and took a bite.

Sarah watched, breath caught in her throat. Michael chewed slowly, then stopped, his face contorting in confusion and then understanding, a myriad of emotions flickering across his features—fear, sadness, and something else, something that seemed like satisfaction mixed with horror.

"It's..." He struggled to find the words, his voice a whisper. "It's like tasting memories... ones that aren't mine."

"What do you mean, Dad?" Sarah's voice was barely above a whisper, her own fear mirroring the look in her father's eyes.

He didn't answer, his gaze turning inward as he took another bite, the gravy-stained bread shaking in his hand. Sarah reached out, touching his shoulder, and Michael flinched as if her touch had pulled him from a deep sea of dark thoughts.

"I'm fine, Sarah. It's just... it's very rich. Very potent."

Sarah didn't buy it, the unease in her gut told her there was something profoundly wrong with the scene before her. Her father was not a man given to flights of fancy or gustatory adventures. Yet here he was, consuming a recipe that seemed to hold him under a spell, his senses ensnared by whatever secrets the Whispering Gravy held.

As Michael took another bite, Sarah felt an overwhelming urge to snatch the bread from his hands, to toss that damned cookbook into the fire. But she didn't move. Instead, she watched, a silent sentinel as her father delved deeper into the culinary abyss, his craving for the dishes within the ancient book growing with every taste, every whispering bite that seemed to call forth shadows to dance in the dim kitchen light.

And the night grew heavier, the shadows longer, as if Harper's Cove itself held its breath, waiting for the void to be stuffed not with bread, but with the souls of those who dared to partake in the feast that was to come.

The chill of late November in Harper's Cove was more than a match for the warmth of any kitchen, but the chill that had settled in the Langdon house was one of a different kind. Michael had taken to the kitchen like a specter to a graveyard, his presence there constant, almost vigilant. The old cookbook lay open on the counter, its spine cracked with age, pages whispering each time the draft caught them just right.

Sarah had retreated to her room after witnessing her father's unsettling communion with the Whispering Gravy. But the quiet of the house was deceptive, for within its walls, a subtle malevolence was stirring, seeping into the fabric of the Langdon lineage.

She tried to sleep, but the images of her father's transfixed face haunted her, and the whispered words he spoke, tasting memories that were not his own. Her thoughts were a whirlwind, each more disturbing than the last. It was a relief when the sun rose, chasing away the shadows, if not the foreboding they left behind.

Over coffee the next morning, Sarah raised the topic again. "Dad, about last night—"

Michael cut her off, his voice more animated than it had been for weeks, "It was an experience, Sarah. The book, it speaks in ways I can't quite explain."

Sarah watched him closely. There was color in his cheeks, a vitality in his movement that had been absent since her mother's death. Yet his eyes, when they met hers, were like dark pools, unfathomable and remote.

Later that day, she found herself at the local bar, where she met Robert Evans, her father's lifelong friend. Robert's usual jovial demeanor faltered when Sarah broached the subject of her father's behavior.

"Mike's cooking? That's a switch." Robert's attempt at humor was half-hearted. "Must be some book to light a fire under that man."

"It's more than that, Robert. He's different. It's like... he's obsessed. And last night, he said the food made him taste memories. Memories that weren't his." Her voice dropped to a hush, her gaze steady.

Robert's easy smile waned, replaced by a frown as he rubbed his chin, "Memories that ain't his? That's a new one... Mike ever talk to you about the book's history?"

"No," Sarah admitted, "But there's something about it. It's changing him, and I'm worried."

They agreed to keep a closer eye on Michael, neither one admitting the depth of their concern.

The transformation in Michael wasn't just spiritual or mental; it was physical too. With each new recipe he mastered from the arcane book, the pallor of his skin seemed to gain warmth, the slouch of his shoulders straightened. But those eyes, they spoke of long, sleepless nights and whispers in the dark, the kind that would drive a weaker man to madness.

Days passed, and the voices that once were muffled murmurs grew more insistent, guiding Michael's hands to more elaborate concoctions. He was no longer the man who burnt toast; now, his kitchen was an alchemist's lab, his ingredients not merely spices and meats, but elements of something far more primordial.

It was on a day heavy with the threat of snow that Karen Stevenson visited. Her soft knock on the door was almost lost amidst the cacophony of simmering pots and the frantic rustle of turning pages.

"Michael?" Karen called out as she stepped into the kitchen. The sight that greeted her was a man far removed from the one she knew. Michael was robust, his hair darker than she remembered, but his eyes—those were the eyes of a man staring into the abyss.

"Karen," Michael greeted her, his voice deep, resonant, "you came at the perfect time. I've just finished something special."

She watched him plate the dish, an elaborate concoction that seemed to pulse with its own life. Karen, versed in the town's lore and given to superstition, felt a shiver course through her. "Michael, where did you learn to cook like this?"

"The book teaches me," Michael replied, gesturing towards the leather-bound tome. "It's more than just a cookbook. It's a gateway."

As he spoke, the kitchen lights flickered, a draft stirred, and for a moment Karen thought she heard a chorus of whispers, so many voices overlapping that it was impossible to pick out words. Her heart raced, "A gateway to what, Michael?"

He only smiled, a knowing, secretive smile that chilled her to the bone.

Karen declined to try the dish, claiming a fictitious ailment. As she left, she could feel Michael's eyes on her back, and she wondered if the warmth of his gaze was not, in fact, the heat of a hidden fire, one that threatened to consume everything she had ever known about her friend.

Michael returned to his cooking, to the whispers that now felt like old friends. And as he moved through the kitchen, there was a grace to his steps that seemed out of place in the quaint old house, a house that no longer felt like home but rather a temple to some forgotten and hungry god.

With each recipe completed, the voice grew clearer, guiding him, nurturing him into something else, something not entirely Michael Langdon anymore. And the void within him, the one left by his wife's passing, began to fill with the murmuring voices of the cookbook, the voices of those long past, and the promise of power and satiation beyond any mortal feast.

The cookbook was his companion now, its pages fluttering with a life of their own, as if in anticipation for the feast that was to come, a Thanksgiving where the harvest to be reaped was darker than any storm cloud on Maine's horizon. And within the walls of the Langdon home, the whispers grew into a cacophony, promising a celebration of a most macabre nature, one that Michael Langdon, whether he knew it or not, was orchestrating with the fervor of the damned.

The town of Harper's Cove seemed to hold its breath as Thanksgiving drew near, a palpable tension hanging over the cobblestone streets and quaint storefronts. It was as though the very air vibrated with the silent hum of something ancient awakening. The townsfolk moved with a wary step, their greetings to one another carrying a new edge of uncertainty.

Michael Langdon, however, was a flurry of activity. The once-quiet house on Willow Street now buzzed with preparations for the upcoming feast. He had extended invitations to a select few, his hands carefully crafting each card from heavy, cream-colored stock. The words, "A meal to remember," were inscribed in a flowing script that seemed to dance with an inner light.

He had spent the last few days in a state of perpetual motion, each task executed with precision and care. Today, he was engaged in a dance with death itself, the kitchen his partner, the ancient cookbook his guide.

Karen Stevenson had spent the days following her visit to Michael's kitchen buried in the archives of the town library. The dusty tomes and ancient newspapers whispered of past Thanksgivings, but none so sinister as what she feared was to come. Her fingers traced the lines of text that spoke of tragedies long past, her eyes widening as she pieced together a pattern. Each previous owner of the cookbook had met an untimely demise, their last days shrouded in talk of madness and darkness.

Robert Evans, in the meantime, had taken to stopping by Michael's house more frequently, if only to assuage the unease that had settled in his gut. He had laughed it off at first, but the humor had long since drained away, leaving behind a hollow pit of dread.

"Michael, you're sure goin' all out, ain't ya?" Robert's voice was strained as he watched his friend meticulously arrange an array of exotic herbs and spices. The once-familiar kitchen now seemed alien, transformed by the esoteric array of ingredients that filled the countertops.

Michael did not look up from his task. "It has to be perfect, Robert. They all have to taste it—the essence of the feast. It's not just food; it's a communion."

"A communion, huh?" Robert frowned, uneasy. "That's one way to put it."

As they spoke, the sound of a door slamming echoed from upstairs. Sarah, her face pale and drawn, descended the staircase. Her nights had been plagued with visions ever since the cookbook had opened its maw to her father. Her dreams were a twisted reflection of the reality her father was creating, filled with haunting specters and pleading whispers.

"Dad, we need to talk about this feast," Sarah said, her voice tinged with desperation. "I'm worried about what it's doing to you, to all of us."

Michael's eyes finally met hers, and in them, she saw a flicker of the father she once knew. For a moment, the fervor waned, and his brow creased with concern. "Sarah, this is something I have to do. It's not just for me, it's for her—your mother. It's a way to honor her memory."

A chill ran through Sarah. She opened her mouth to respond, but the sound of the doorbell cut her off.

Robert moved to answer it, finding the local pastor and several concerned neighbors on the threshold, their faces drawn and worried.

"Robert, have you seen the news?" the pastor asked, his voice urgent. "There's been another disappearance. Young Billy Thompson didn't come home last night."

Robert's heart sank. Billy was the third this month. The town was unraveling at the seams.

Michael, overhearing the conversation, paused. The voices from the book grew silent as if listening, waiting. The town's misfortunes seemed to orbit around the ancient tome's presence, each event a strand in a web with the cookbook at its center.

He approached the group at the door, his expression unreadable. "Perhaps what this town needs is a gathering—a celebration to bring us all together," Michael offered, the smoothness of his tone at odds with the tension in the air.

The pastor nodded slowly, his eyes reflecting the conflict within. "Perhaps you're right, Michael. We could use something to lift the spirits."

As the group dispersed, Sarah caught the gaze of the pastor, who gave her a look that said without words, "Be careful."

The air was filled with the whispers of Harper's Cove, the rumors of the missing, and the unease about Michael Langdon's Thanksgiving feast. But Michael had his own whispering to contend with, the voices of the book spurring him on, whispering of a meal that would be remembered for generations to come—as either a beginning or an end.

Michael returned to his preparations, each slice of the knife, each stir of the pot, an invocation. And outside, as dusk fell over Harper's Cove, the world seemed to hold its breath, waiting for the dawn of Thanksgiving Day.

The door to the Langdon home swung open, and a gust of wind snaked through the hallway, trailing the last whispers of autumn. The guests filed in, shrouded in their heavy coats and woolen scarves, each bearing the marks of life's toils. There was Judy, with her nervous smile, hiding the tremors that had begun to haunt her hands ever since her husband's passing. Craig, a local carpenter, carried a jovial facade, yet his eyes were sunken, clouded with the fatigue of sleepless nights. They, like the others, came seeking respite, a night of warmth and merriment to cast away the creeping dread that had settled over Harper's Cove.

Michael greeted them with a gravitas that seemed to stretch the fabric of the room. "Welcome, friends," he said, his voice a velvety balm to their frayed nerves. "Tonight, we partake in a feast unlike any other."

The dining room was a spectacle of shadows and flickering candlelight, the table a stretch of mahogany set with gleaming silver and crystal. It was there the dishes awaited, a parade of the exotic and the bizarre that drew gasps and murmurs from the gathering guests.

The first course was a soup, a concoction that shimmered with a pearlescent sheen, flecked with herbs that none could name. They sipped tentatively, and a chorus of sighs filled the room as the warmth spread through their bodies. But the comfort was fleeting, for as the warmth seeped into their bones, so too did a foreign sense of weightlessness, as if their very souls were untethering from their flesh.

Karen Stevenson, her fingers trembling, set her spoon down with a clatter. "Michael, this is... it's remarkable," she managed to say, her voice betraying her struggle to remain grounded in the here and now.

As the main dish was served, a turkey that was impossibly plump and golden, the air grew thick, syrupy. The scent was intoxicating, yet beneath it lingered a note of something ancient and rotting. Michael carved the bird with ceremonial precision, and the guests watched, entranced, as the slices fell away, revealing a stuffing that was a tapestry of textures and hues, moving and undulating as if alive.

Robert Evans stabbed a morsel with his fork, his usual bravado now a swallowed lump in his throat. "Mikey, this is... Christ, I can't even begin to describe it."

"Thank you, Robert," Michael replied, his gaze not leaving the carving knife. "It's a recipe that demands respect."

With each bite, time began to fold upon itself. The clinking of silverware was at once a distant echo and a deafening clatter. The guests' conversations were a babel of voices, some speaking in tongues long dead, others in laments that curled around the soul.

Sarah, sitting as far from the table as she could, watched her father, her eyes wide with a dawning horror. The guests around him, her father's friends, were changing. Their faces blurred and sharpened, revealing flashes of others—people who had no place in this time, this feast. She saw a woman in a bonnet, her eyes hollow with famine, and a man in a powdered wig, choking on his own bloodied laughter.

The laughter rose, a crescendo that drowned out the guests' growing unease, and the room expanded, the walls stretching into infinity. The ceiling was no longer there, replaced by a sky that boiled with storm clouds, lit by lightning that cast all in stark, ghastly relief.

Michael stood, his shadow vast and monstrous upon the stretched walls, the cookbook open before him. The pages fluttered as if caught in a gale that touched no other thing in the room. He read from it, his voice a cacophony of whispers, each word a thread weaving through the minds of his guests, stitching them into the tapestry of the cookbook's dark history.

As the final course, a pie of deepest black, was presented, the guests were no longer merely diners. They were pilgrims standing at the precipice of understanding, gazing into the abyss that Michael had spread before them on fine china.

The first forkful was hesitation made flesh. The second, a surrender to the inevitable. With each bite, they sunk deeper into the mire of the book's memories, caught in the throes of lives not their own, of deaths too gruesome to contemplate.

The pie was not fruit; it was darker, richer, and filled with a sweetness that clawed at the back of the throat. It was a flavor that spoke of endings, and as it settled in their stomachs, a collective dread settled over the room.

Sarah, unnoticed, slipped from her chair, her mind a whirlwind of fear and determination. She had to act, had to break the spell before the final, unspoken course was served—the course that would seal their fates.

And in the eye of the storm that was her father's legacy, Harper's Cove held its breath, the veil between this world and the next worn thin, fraying at the edges like the pages of the accursed book that lay open, whispering its terrible secrets to any who would listen.

Sarah's voice, once melodious and sure, now quivered like a plucked string as she implored the guests, "Please, we need to leave. All of us."

But her plea was met with vacant stares, their bodies anchored to the chairs as if by unseen shackles. Even Robert, who would have normally cracked a dismissive joke, was silent, his eyes glassy as he stared into the remnants of his plate, now slick with a sheen of black residue.

Across the room, Michael hunched over the open cookbook, its pages fluttering though no breeze came to disturb the stagnant air of the dining hall. Karen approached him, her steps hesitant but determined. She reached out a hand, not to Michael, but to the book before him. Before her fingers could graze the leather cover, Michael snapped it shut, his eyes snapping to hers.

"It speaks to me," he whispered, a tremor in his voice that matched the shake in his hands. "It whispers, Karen. At first, I thought it was grief... the silence after Martha's passing, but it's not. It's this... this damned book."

Karen swallowed, her instincts as a librarian who revered books warring with the primal fear that clawed at her insides. "Michael, we need to get rid of it," she said, her voice barely above a whisper. "It's not just a book. It's—"

"—a curse," Michael finished for her, nodding slowly. His face was pale, the lines of sorrow etched deeper by the candlelight. "I know. I've seen what it does. What it shows."

A collective gasp pulled their attention back to the guests. Judy, with her nervous smile now a rictus of horror, was clawing at her face, her fingers coming away with strands of gray hair. "I saw him," she cried out, her voice ragged. "My Tom... but not... not as I remembered. Twisted. Wrong."

One by one, the guests began to share their visions, each tale a tapestry of personal hells woven from the very fabric of their fears. Craig spoke of wooden figures, carved with his own hands, coming to life, their tiny mouths filled with accusations and truths he had never dared to voice.

The room twisted upon itself, the corners stretching into obscurity as the house itself seemed to digest the scenes unfolding within. Sarah, standing unnoticed in the archway, felt the walls pulse, as if the house was alive with the same malevolence that emanated from the book.

The air was now thick with the scent of ozone, the aftertaste of the pie mingling with a coppery tang of blood. It was as if the room was a mouth, and they, the courses yet to be fully consumed.

Michael's voice broke through the chorus of terror. "It's showing us... it's feeding us their deaths. The past owners of the book... their last moments."

The guests, bound by the unseen force, could only watch as the room filled with specters of the past, the ghosts of those who had once claimed ownership of the book. A colonial woman wept blood as she rocked the cradle of a child that would never cry again. A Victorian gentleman laughed maniacally, his body covered in festering boils, each bursting to release a swarm of flies.

Sarah's voice rose above the maelstrom, "Dad, stop it! You have to stop it!"

Michael turned to her, his eyes hollow. "I don't know if I can," he confessed, his voice a hoarse whisper. "I don't know if I want to."

The visions tightened their grip, the room now a gallery of grotesques, each more terrifying than the last. The dinner guests were not just witnessing these horrors; they were feeling them, the pain, the fear, the despair of every soul ensnared by the cookbook's dark recipes.

Sarah's mind raced, her father's admission igniting a spark of resolve within her. The book, the cause of all this madness, lay closed on the table, its cover innocuous yet ominous. She knew then that the key to their salvation lay within its cursed pages.

As she moved toward it, the room seemed to sense her intent, the air growing colder, denser, as if trying to smother her resolve. But Sarah Langdon was her father's daughter, headstrong and fierce, and she would not be deterred. The fight for their souls was just beginning, and the night was far from over.

The room had become a vortex of shadows, each one stretching like tendrils toward the book that now seemed like the heart of this darkness. Sarah's determination was a stark contrast to the oppressive despair filling the room, her footsteps steady as she made her way to the book.

But the house, animate with the vile energy of the cookbook, was not passive. The walls began to bleed, a slow ooze of black ichor that painted grotesque patterns, like ancient runes forgotten by time. The guests, their eyes wide with dread, watched the liquid darkness as it crept along the floorboards, pooling around their feet, and then began to rise.

Karen, caught between her desire to flee and her impulse to help, fixed her gaze on Sarah, willing her forward. "Michael," she cried out, reaching for him again, her voice now infused with an urgency that cut through the din of terror. "You have to let her try!"

Michael, trapped between the realm of the living and the tormented echoes of the past, looked as though he was struggling against the weight of an unseen force. His hands, once steady and sure as a surgeon's, now trembled violently.

Sarah was nearly upon the book when a howl erupted from the shadows. It was not the sound of any one guest, but a chorus of the damned, a cacophony of the many souls who had succumbed to the cookbook's allure. The sound pierced through the room, and Sarah stumbled, clutching her ears.

In the brief moment of her falter, the book seemed to come alive, its cover writhing like the skin of a serpent. The whispers that Michael spoke of earlier were now a guttural chant that filled the room, growing louder with each of Sarah's labored breaths.

She looked back at her father, her eyes searching for some sign of the man who had raised her, who had taught her that courage was not the absence of fear, but the triumph over it. But the man who met her gaze was a shell, his essence hollowed out by the parasitic tome before him.

Judy's cries had subsided into whimpers, and Craig sat silent, his face gaunt, as if the wooden figures of his visions had carved pieces from his very soul. Robert, the ever-jovial salesman, had no quips, no laughter to mask the dread; his spirit seemed crushed under the weight of his own private horrors.

"Michael!" Sarah's voice was a command now, echoing with more authority than her years should allow. "Fight it! Help me!"

And in that moment, there was a flicker of recognition in Michael's eyes, a spark of the man who had once been the cornerstone of his daughter's world. With a visible effort, he stood, the book falling open before him, its pages a blur of script that twisted and writhed as if alive.

Sarah reached for the book, her fingers brushing the ancient leather, and the house shuddered. A scream filled the air, not from any of the guests, but from the cookbook itself, a wail of fury and defiance.

Michael and Sarah, united in their defiance, held their ground as the images swirled faster around them, now a maelstrom of the macabre. It was as if the book was unleashing its entire morbid history upon them, desperate to protect its malevolent heart.

The scent of decay and the cloying sweetness of overripe fruit mingled as the air thickened. The guests, now seeming part of the furniture, were statues of terror, their faces masks of the dread that the book inflicted upon them.

As the visions threatened to overwhelm her, Sarah could see through the veil of the past. Scenes of the cookbook's origins played before her like a twisted play: pagan rituals in moonlit groves, blood offerings upon altars of stone, and chants that promised power at the most terrible of costs.

A colonial man, garbed in the tattered remnants of his finery, appeared before Michael, his eyes sockets empty, mouth moving in silent agony. He pointed a accusing finger at Michael, whispering a truth that froze his blood.

"It was always yours to bear, the legacy," the apparition hissed, voice like the scraping of bone on stone. "The lineage of blood and sacrifice. Your wife... she was just the beginning."

Michael reeled, his face a ghostly pallor as the implication of the spirit's words sank in. The lineage, the bloodline—he was a descendant of the original architects of the book's horrors.

The realization was a catalyst, breaking the spell of paralysis that held the others. They turned to look upon Michael, and in their eyes, he saw the reflections of their own nightmares, the shared horror that bound them all to the fate of the cookbook.

But before more could be revealed, before the lineage could be fully understood, the house itself convulsed, a deep rumble that seemed to come from the very bowels of the earth. The dinner table split, the fine china shattering, the remains of the Thanksgiving feast spilling onto the floor like the innards of a gutted beast.

And as the walls of Harper's Cove's oldest home continued to groan and bleed, and the guests stood transfixed by terror, Sarah's fingers finally closed on the pages of the cursed cookbook, her will set to tear away the veil of shadows that clung to its words.

Her actions, however brave, were not without consequence, for the house seemed to scream in protest, and the darkness clung tighter, more desperate.

The chapter would not end here, not with the void so close to being filled with the truths that should never be known. The history of horror was still being written, and its scribe was the cookbook that lay open, its pages a testament to terror.

Amidst the chaos, a chill wind swept through the ruptured home, carrying with it a whisper of rot and the unseen touch of those who had crossed into the void. Michael's eyes, wide and frantic, followed the spectral breeze as it weaved between the guests, who were now rooted to their seats by an invisible force.

Sarah's grip on the book tightened, her knuckles whitening. As she turned the pages, she could feel the resistive energy pulsing from the heart of the tome, as if the recipes were imbued with the breath of something inhuman, something that had been waiting, biding its time within the confines of ink and leather.

Robert staggered to his feet, his usual bravado a crumpled vestige of the past. "Mike, what is this?" His voice was a ragged thread of fear. "What have you done?"

Michael turned to his friend, the shadows of his own terror etched upon his face. "I—I didn't know," he stammered, the words catching in his throat. "I just wanted..."

His voice trailed off, swallowed by the growing din of the malevolent whispers that now seemed to emanate from every corner of the room.

Karen moved closer to Michael, her resolve steeled by the unfolding nightmare. "It's not just the book, is it?" she demanded, her voice rising above the whispers. "It's this house, it's you, Michael!"

He could not respond; the truth was a jagged pill, lodging itself in his throat, choking the very breath from him.

The guests watched in silent horror as the air began to shimmer with a sickly light, the barrier between worlds thinning until the room was teeming with the uninvited. Ethereal figures, clothed in the garb of countless eras, flickered in and out of existence around the table, their hollow eyes fixed upon the living. Their whispers merged with the chanting from the book, a symphony of the damned that resonated with the very frequency of dread.

Sarah, caught in the eye of this supernatural storm, felt the weight of her lineage, the heavy mantle of a heritage soaked in darkness and despair. "Dad, please," she pleaded, reaching out to him. "We need to break the cycle."

Michael, his consciousness a battlefield of wills, felt the pull of the cookbook, its demands for a final ingredient—a demand for a sacrifice that would satiate its hunger and seal the fate of all who had partaken in the accursed feast.

"Sarah, I—" Michael's voice broke, the strain of his internal struggle apparent in the tremor of his words.

But the entities crowding the room were growing impatient, their forms solidifying, as if the act of reading the cookbook had lent them substance. A spectral child, its eyes hollow and empty, reached for a carving knife, its small hand passing through the silver blade as it whispered, "More..."

The unspoken word hung in the air, a command that echoed in the minds of the guests, binding them to the will of the cookbook.

Craig's eyes snapped to Michael, understanding dawning like the first light of a terrible dawn. "You have to destroy it," he hissed, nodding towards the book. "It's the only way."

But the cookbook, as if sensing its impending doom, unleashed a torrent of images into Michael's mind—visions of his late wife, her laughter, her love, all intertwined with the dark knowledge that had led to her untimely end. It was a cruel juxtaposition, love interwoven with horror, and it anchored him to the spot, a statue of flesh and bone, his will ensnared by the book's malignant whispers.

Sarah's voice cut through the maelstrom, a beacon in the darkness. "Dad, look at me! You're stronger than this. You're stronger than it."

Her words seemed to reach something within him, a flicker of the old Michael, the one who laughed and loved, who was not a prisoner of grief. His eyes locked with hers, a silent plea for forgiveness—for help.

Outside, the winds of Harper's Cove howled, and the house, once a sanctuary of family and warmth, now groaned under the weight of its own haunted legacy. The entities, the uninvited guests of a feast beyond comprehension, closed in, their forms gaining clarity with every beat of Michael's racing heart.

And as Sarah held the cookbook, her father's battle with the darkness visible upon his contorted face, the entities moved closer, drawn to the nexus of their summoning, their intentions as obscure as the void from which they came.

The table, now split and shattered, bore the remnants of the feast, the remnants of sanity. And in the middle of it all, the cookbook remained open, its pages fluttering as though it were breathing, anticipating the next verse of its terrible history.

Karen's hands were steady as she flipped through the pages of an old grimoire she had brought from the library's restricted section, a collection of forgotten lore and protective incantations. Her voice, when she spoke, was a lifeline cast into the tempestuous sea of Michael's despair. "Michael, the book! It may fear fire, or there may be a rite, something we can use."

With each suggestion, the shadows in the room deepened, as if reacting to the threat of their demise.

Sarah, still clutching the cookbook, sought the support in Karen's words. "A rite," she echoed. "We can do this, Dad. We can end it."

Michael's focus wavered as he battled the seductive pull of the book. He nodded, a jerky, almost mechanical motion. "Fire, then," he managed to gasp. "We burn it, we burn them out!"

Robert, pale as death, scrambled to the kitchen, returning with a canister of lighter fluid and a box of matches. His hands trembled, but his resolve was clear. "If we're doing this, we do it now," he declared, his words a bare whisper.

They gathered around the open cookbook as if it were a serpent, coiled and ready to strike. Robert drenched the ancient pages in lighter fluid, the chemical smell overpowering the stench of decay that had begun to infiltrate the room.

Sarah hesitated, her gaze on the entity that had once been a child, now a grotesque parody of innocence. "Do it," she urged, her voice laced with desperation.

With a strike of a match, a small flame danced to life, its glow feeble against the encroaching darkness. Robert's hand shook as he brought the fire closer to the drenched pages.

A collective gasp filled the room, the entities recoiling, their forms wailing and contorting as the flame touched paper. The cookbook resisted, its pages seeming to scream in silent agony as they blackened and curled.

Michael's scream melded with the inhuman cries as the cookbook ignited, the images of his wife's smiling face twisting into expressions of pain and betrayal within his mind. The room spun, the entities' whispers turning to shrieks, the veil between worlds tearing further with each flicker of the rising flames.

But as the fire consumed the book, the house itself began to react. The walls bled shadows, and the floorboards writhed and buckled as if the building's very soul was being torn asunder. The visions that the guests had been suffering—their own personal hells—began to materialize, giving form to fear and madness.

Karen, clinging to the grimoire, began chanting, her voice steady as she recited a rite of banishment, each word a note in an ancient melody designed to soothe the fabric of a reality torn by the cookbook's evil.

The entities howled, their forms dissipating in the smoke, but not without a final, spiteful act. The child-like specter turned its gaze upon Sarah, and with a chilling smile, it lunged, its form dissolving into a mist that sought her mouth, her eyes, her very essence.

"No!" Michael's voice was a thunderous roar, his paternal instinct a sudden, fierce shield. He lunged forward, breaking the invisible bonds that had held him, intercepting the mist with his own body.

The darkness swirled around him, and he could feel it, cold and unyielding, as it entered his lungs, his heart, his soul. A freezing burn, like icy needles pricking from within.

Sarah watched in horror, her scream a silent accompaniment to the cacophony, her hands outstretched toward her father, the fire reflecting in her tear-filled eyes.

And then there was silence—a terrible, stretching silence that filled the room as the flames died down, leaving only embers where the cookbook had once been. The entities were gone, vanished with the smoke, but at what cost?

The house settled, the nightmare seeming to recede into the walls, into the very ground beneath them. But Michael lay still, his eyes closed, his chest barely moving.

Karen knelt beside him, her grimoire forgotten, her hand on his forehead. "Michael?" she whispered, fear a tangible thing in her voice.

Robert stood back, the spent matches in his hand, his face ashen, as if he couldn't believe the nightmare had been real.

But it wasn't over, they knew it wasn't. The silence was too heavy, the calm too pronounced. And as Sarah held her father's hand, feeling the weak pulse of his heart, she knew that the cycle wasn't broken, not yet.

Because in the ashes of the cookbook, amongst the charred remnants of its binding, a single page fluttered, untouched by the fire, its ink glistening in the dim light, waiting for the next reader to continue its legacy.

The silence was shattered as the single unburned page from the cookbook began to levitate, its corners curling as though gripped by an invisible hand. The ink on the page swirled and shifted, forming words that whispered into the minds of those present.

Sarah's voice was a thread of sound, "Dad, don't leave me."

Michael's eyes flickered open, the irises swallowed by an inky blackness that seemed to pulse with the same rhythm as the fluttering page. "I'm here," he rasped, but the voice that left his lips was not entirely his own. It was laced with something ancient, something that had tasted centuries of desperation.

Karen recoiled, the grimoire slipping from her fingers, her voice now a prayer, "Not him, please, not him."

Robert, a statue of disbelief moments ago, moved with sudden purpose. He snatched the grimoire from the floor, his eyes scanning the arcane symbols, looking for something, anything that could help. "We need to finish this," he said, his usual levity gone, replaced by a grim determination.

Sarah held her father's hand tighter, trying to anchor him to the world, to her, but the shadows within him writhed and fought, a tempest seeking to escape its mortal confines. "Fight it, Dad. Please, fight it."

Michael's other hand reached out, not to his daughter, but to the page. It stopped its flight at his touch, and the room was filled with the scent of ozone and brimstone. "It wants... to be whole," he uttered in the voice that was not his own.

Karen, finding her voice, a vessel of the grimoire's ancient wisdom, directed Robert. "The rite of sealing! On page 43, hurry!"

Robert's finger traced the lines of the text as Karen began to chant once more, her voice a commanding force that demanded obedience from the elements around her.

The page in Michael's grip screamed in silence, the ink bleeding off as if trying to escape its paper prison. Michael's body began to convulse, a battle of wills raging within him as he repeated a single word, a word that seemed to hold power, "Bind."

Sarah, tears streaming down her face, understood. She took up the chant with Karen, her voice a clarion call that pierced the supernatural storm. "Bind!"

The house itself seemed to take up the call, the walls groaning "Bind!", the very air pulsing with the word.

Robert, now reciting with the others, felt the power coursing through him, the grimoire hot in his hands, an ember that ignited courage within his soul.

The page, unable to withstand the assault of collective wills, ignited not in flame but in darkness. It was a void that sought to consume, but as it touched the skin of Michael's outstretched hand, it recoiled. There was something within him, within them all, that it could not devour—hope.

Michael, his voice clearer now but still heavy with the remnants of otherworldly intrusion, spoke with authority, "By the bond of blood and spirit, we bind thee!"

With a cacophony like the crack of thunder silencing an orchestra of discord, the void imploded, and the page disintegrated into a fine dust that settled like snow upon the embers of the cookbook.

But the room did not settle. The visions, freed from the paper prison, became corporeal nightmares that stalked the edges of the room. The last course was upon them, the final stand between the living and the spectral remnants of the cookbook's previous victims.

Robert's eyes, wide with horror, took in the scene—figures of men, women, children, all with the same hollow gaze, the same hunger that had driven the cookbook.

Karen, understanding too well the power of history and the weight of souls long tormented, shouted above the din, "We must give them peace!"

Michael, still clutching Sarah's hand, rose to his feet, the blackness in his eyes receding. "Let me be the vessel," he offered, his voice now wholly his own, but edged with resignation. "Let me take them where they need to go."

Sarah, understanding her father's intent, released his hand, her own voice a whisper lost in the chaos, "I love you, Dad."

As the entities converged, a maelstrom of lost souls, Michael began to speak words that were not from the grimoire, not from the cookbook, but from a place deep within, a place where love and sacrifice reside. The room brightened with an ethereal light, and the house shook to its foundations, a lighthouse standing firm against the storm of the void's final rage.

Dawn broke with a tenderness that felt out of place in Harper's Cove. Sunlight crept through the broken windows, casting a warm glow that contradicted the chill of the night's horrors. The house, once a symbol of familial warmth, now stood gutted, a carcass of memories strewn about in a macabre display.

Sarah, her once vibrant eyes dim with the residue of terror, sat on the porch steps, wrapped in a blanket that did little to ward off the coldness that had settled in her bones. The silence of the morning was oppressive, a stark contrast to the cacophony that had echoed through the walls just hours ago.

Beside her, the remnants of her father's last stand were evident in the scorched earth of the garden where the cookbook had been buried deep, its ashes a black smear against the frost-tipped grass. Her father,

Michael, was gone, having sacrificed himself to the void to grant peace to the spirits bound within the cookbook's cursed pages.

Robert, his usual jovial demeanor lost to the night's shadows, joined her, his movements heavy, as though he carried the weight of their shared experience on his broad shoulders. He sat down, leaving a respectful space between them, his gaze fixed on the horizon, avoiding the emptiness of the home they both knew was forever changed.

"We did it, Sarah," he said finally, his voice hoarse, the salesman's charm now just a faded facade. "Your dad, he... he saved us."

Sarah nodded, the motion automatic, her mind still grappling with the surreal truth of her father's transformation and sacrifice. "He was the bravest man I knew," she murmured, her voice barely carrying.

Karen Stevenson approached, her kind face marred by the night's trials, her eyes watchful as ever, but now rimmed with red. She brought with her a tray bearing a small pot of coffee and three cups, a gesture of normalcy in a world that felt anything but normal.

"Drink," she urged gently, her voice maintaining that gentle authority, even now. "We'll need our strength."

They accepted the coffee, the steam rising like spirits into the crisp morning air, the aroma a faint reminder of a time before the cookbook had consumed their lives.

"What happens now?" Sarah asked after a moment, her gaze on the blackened spot in the garden. "What if it's not really over?"

Karen set her cup down, her fingers laced tightly around it as though drawing comfort from its warmth. "We have to believe it is. We did everything we could. Your father's last act was one of incredible courage and love. The book's hold on this world has been severed."

"But what if severing isn't enough?" Sarah pressed, a shiver running down her spine that had nothing to do with the cold. "What if it can... come back?"

"It won't," Robert interjected with more confidence than he felt. "We made sure of it."

Yet, even as he spoke, an inexplicable chill settled over the trio, a silent acknowledgment of the unease that gnawed at them. The cookbook had been more than a collection of recipes; it had been a vessel of nightmares, and such evil was not easily forgotten or dismissed.

They drank their coffee in a silence punctuated only by the creak of the house settling and the distant call of a mourning dove. Each lost in their thoughts, they were unaware of the slight tremor beneath the ground where the cookbook had been buried, a tremor that was not from the earth, but something else, something that waited with the patience of eons.

As the morning wore on, the guests from the previous night's feast began to depart, their faces etched with lines of an experience no words could capture. They exchanged no goodbyes, only nods and glances that spoke volumes of shared suffering and resilience.

Sarah watched them leave, her heart aching with a mixture of loss and relief. Relief that they had survived, and a piercing loss for the man who had been her rock, her protector, her father.

The house behind them creaked again, a moan of age or perhaps something else, something akin to a sigh of relief or a sly chuckle. It was hard to tell, for Harper's Cove had always been a place where the line between the mundane and the supernatural was as thin as a wisp of fog upon the ocean.

They would leave soon, Sarah knew. The house would be closed up, left to heal from the wounds of the night's terrors. But even as they rose to go back inside, to gather what remained of their lives, a single thought lingered unspoken between them:

Evil, like the roots of an ancient tree, runs deep, and even the strongest flame may not burn it all away.

In the year that followed, Harper's Cove carried on with the quiet tenacity characteristic of small New England towns. The Langdon house remained empty, the locals superstitious of its past, whispering tales that mixed truth with lore. It stood as a spectral monument to that fateful Thanksgiving, the shadows within undisturbed by laughter or light.

As autumn once again bared the trees and chilled the air, a new family moved into the area, unknowing of the house's tragic tale. They were charmed by the town's quaintness, the leaves' fiery dance, and the welcoming smiles that were perhaps a touch too eager to dispel the gloom that hung over the old Langdon place.

One crisp morning, the town's annual book sale commenced. It was an event met with much anticipation, the chance to rummage through history and tales as told by the many volumes that passed through the residents' hands.

Among the stacks of worn paperbacks and musty-smelling hardcovers, there it was—a cookbook. Its leather-bound cover was too pristine amidst the others, the pages unmarked by time or use. It didn't belong there, yet it drew in eyes with an almost magnetic pull. There was no author's name, just an ornate title etched into the cover: "Culinary Rites."

A woman, the new librarian who had taken over after Karen Stevenson's abrupt resignation, picked it up. Her fingers traced the cover, a shiver running down her spine that she attributed to the breeze. "Interesting find," she commented to no one in particular.

"Yeah, it's been here since last year. Surprised no one's snagged it yet," the volunteer replied, an old man with spectacles perched precariously on the bridge of his nose.

"Well, I think it'll be perfect for my Thanksgiving dinner," the librarian smiled, the corners of her mouth lifting but not reaching her eyes. There was a strange gravity to her words, as if she spoke more than a casual truth.

The volunteer nodded, his own smile a rehearsed curl of the lips. "Sure thing, just be careful with those old recipes. They say some of them have a bit of... history."

The librarian chuckled, a sound that didn't quite dispel the chill in the air. "Oh, I love a bit of history with my cooking."

As she walked away, the cookbook under her arm, the volunteer watched her go with a glint of something unfathomable in his gaze. Harper's Cove had a way of keeping its stories alive, and he had lived long enough to sense when a story wasn't quite finished.

The leaves rustled as the librarian walked down the lane, the crunch underfoot punctuating each step towards the home she was still making her own. She mused on the recipes, the dinner she would prepare, and the warmth it would bring to her family's table.

Yet, as she turned the key in her door, a cool draft slipped past her, an uninvited guest eager to be part of the Thanksgiving festivities. It wound its way through the halls, the kitchen, up the staircase to where family photographs were yet to be hung.

In the air lingered the faintest scent of sage and something else, something not quite identifiable—a hint of decay, perhaps, or a whiff of desolation. It was gone as quickly as it had come, leaving only the anticipation of the holiday season in its wake.

That night, as the librarian sat by the fire thumbing through her new acquisition, the wind outside whispered through the trees, carrying with it a chorus of voices that had once dined at a table now long gone. They spoke of memories best forgotten, of a Thanksgiving where gratitude had been overshadowed by something far more ravenous.

And on the page where the recipe for stuffing lay, a small note was scribbled in the margin, the ink faded but the message clear:

"Feed the void, but never think it filled."

The librarian's eyes lingered on the words, her breath catching in her throat. There was a feeling in her gut, a gnawing sense of unease that she couldn't quite shake.

The clock ticked on, marking time in a home that had yet to learn its new inhabitants, in a town that held its breath as it watched, and in the fabric of a tale that was far from over. Harper's Cove knew all about cycles, about the ebb and flow of tides, and about books that, like the fabled phoenix, could rise from ash and memory to live again.

The librarian closed the cookbook, her heart beating an erratic rhythm. She would prepare the feast, of course. It was Thanksgiving, after all, and there was so much to be thankful for. But in the back of her mind, a thought took root—a worry that this Thanksgiving might just be more memorable than most.

As the fire crackled and the house settled into the silence of the coming night, a shadow flickered across the wall, formless and fleeting. It was as if the house itself was agreeing, in its own way, to the unspoken sentiment that filled the room:

A recipe remains, and with it, the taste of the past, eager to be savored once again.

The end.

The Gravy Boatman

The November fog was a living thing, creeping through the streets of Driftwood Bluffs with insidious intent. It clung to the windows of the Clark family home, a two-story relic from a bygone era that had seen better days, much like the town itself. Inside, Ethan Clark sifted through a box of his late father's possessions. His hands, once steady as a marksman's, now trembled with a cocktail of cold and memory.

He unearthed a collection of faded photographs, old medals of commendation, a pocket watch that had long since ticked its last tock, and at the very bottom, beneath a stack of weathered journals, a peculiar envelope. It was made of a thick, yellowing paper, sealed with a drop of crimson wax stamped with an emblem he couldn't quite place—a ship's wheel entwined with a serpent.

Ethan turned the envelope over in his hands. There was no postmark, no return address, only his name scrawled across the front in a handwriting that seemed to squirm and shift the longer he stared at it. He slit the seal with a knife, the wax cracking like a whispered secret.

Inside, a single card bore the invitation:

"You are cordially invited to join the Gravy Boat's Thanksgiving voyage. Redemption or oblivion? The choice shall be yours. Embarkation at midnight, Stygian River Dock. The Boatman awaits."

Ethan's breath hitched, a shard of cold stabbing into his chest. He dropped the card as if it burned him. The invitation fluttered to the floor, landing amidst the detritus of his father's life—and Ethan's own shattered past.

His mind catapulted him back to that night, three years ago, the night that had painted his badge with a stain no amount of polishing could remove. His partner's voice crackled over the radio, "Shots fired, officer down!" The scene had unfolded in a macabre dance of flashing lights and screaming sirens.

There had been a kid, no older than nineteen, a panicked look in his eyes, a gun in his trembling hands. Ethan had shouted for him to drop the weapon, his own firearm a heavy promise in his hands. But the kid had bolted, a rabbit in the jaws of fear, and Ethan's bullet had followed, a faithful hound unleashed.

Guilt had been his shadow ever since, a constant companion whispering of what should have been, what could have been.

Now, as he picked the invitation off the floor, his mind a maelstrom of past and present, he wondered if this was some kind of sick joke. Or perhaps a summons to confront the ghosts he had tried so hard to bury.

Outside, the town of Driftwood Bluffs prepared for its annual Thanksgiving celebrations. Strings of lights hung like beacons in the fog, illuminating windows filled with displays of harvest abundance. But beneath the festive veneer, a current of dread ran as deep and dark as the Stygian River itself.

The river's name was no mere affectation. Like the mythical river Styx, it seemed to exist between the worlds of the living and the dead, a boundary of mist and water where reality grew thin. And on Thanksgiving night, as legend had it, the Gravy Boatman would traverse these liminal waters, offering passage to those brave—or desperate—enough to accept.

Ethan's resolve hardened. He would meet this Boatman, come hell or high water. It was time to face the specters of his past, to see if redemption lay on the other side of the Stygian River.

Or if, like the river's namesake, all that awaited him was the chill embrace of the void.

The chime of the old grandfather clock in the hallway reverberated through the house, marking the arrival of another unwelcome hour. Ethan's gaze was pulled from the ghostly invitation as the doorbell echoed the clock's grim toll, a dissonant duet that seemed too orchestrated to be chance.

He opened the door, and there she stood: Diana, her silhouette almost spectral in the foggy halo of the porch light. Her sharp features were set in a familiar, defensive sneer, a look that had kept the world at arm's length since they were kids.

"Don't just stand there gawking, Ethan," she said, voice edged with the biting chill of the November air. "Are you going to let me in, or do I need to hold court on the doorstep?"

Her sarcasm sliced through the years of silence, and Ethan stepped aside, ushering her into the dimly lit foyer. She didn't move at first, eyeing the invitation in his hand with a lawyer's scrutiny. Her coat, as black as the waters of the Stygian River, brushed against the door as she finally stepped inside, shedding the fog like a second skin.

"So, you got one too," she said, her voice softer now, almost vulnerable, as she pulled a twin envelope from her purse. "The Gravy Boatman's little soirée."

Ethan grunted, a noncommittal sound that had become second nature, his default when words felt too heavy to wield. "Seems like it."

They moved to the living room, the heart of the house where their family had once gathered, now just another chamber in a mausoleum of memories. He gestured toward the invitation she held.

"You planning on going?"

Diana arched an eyebrow, her lips curving into a wry smile that didn't quite reach her eyes. "You think I'd pass up an opportunity to meet the spook of Driftwood Bluffs? Besides," she flicked a glance at his invitation, "we're in this together, aren't we? Like old times."

"Old times," Ethan echoed, the words leaving a bitter taste. The air between them was thick with unspoken accusations and regrets, a familial fog even denser than the one outside.

They sat, two estranged figures on opposite ends of the worn couch, the space between them cluttered with the debris of their shared history.

"So," Diana broke the silence, her voice sharp enough to cut through the tension, "what's the former hero of Driftwood Bluffs doing these days, apart from playing ghost hunter?"

Ethan's jaw tightened. He didn't need to look at Diana to feel her gaze dissecting him, analyzing his every move with the same calculated detachment she brought to her court cases.

"I keep to myself," he replied, meeting her gaze with a steely one of his own.

"Clearly." She leaned back, arms crossed. "And here I thought you'd have fled town after..."

She trailed off, but the air vibrated with the echo of her implication. Ethan felt the old wound in his psyche split open, the scar tissue of his guilt pulled apart by her probing words.

"I didn't run because I'm not a coward," he shot back, his control fraying.

"Could've fooled me." Diana's voice was a whisper, but it struck with the force of a shout.

Silence descended, a thick, oppressive blanket that smothered conversation. Ethan's mind raced with all the things he wanted to say, the apologies, the anger, the pleas for understanding—but the words calcified in his throat.

He stood abruptly, the invitation crinkling in his clenched fist. "We should get some rest. The boat leaves at midnight."

Diana nodded, standing as well, her movements deliberate, almost robotic. "Right. Because nothing says 'Happy Thanksgiving' like a trip down a river with Death's own ferryman."

Her attempt at humor fell flat, and she didn't wait for his response. She headed to the guest room, her footsteps a hollow echo in the silent house.

Ethan remained in the living room, the weight of the impending voyage bearing down on him. The Gravy Boatman had called, and whether siren or specter, his song was irresistible. But it wasn't redemption Ethan sought on the murky waters of the Stygian River. It was absolution.

The clock in the hall struck another hour, a somber reminder that time, much like the river, waits for no one.

Victor Daniels stood on the fog-laden pier of Driftwood Bluffs, his silhouette a monolith against the pale morning light. His coat was tailored to disguise the stoop of his shoulders, a garment sewn with the same care he'd stitched his public persona together. In his hand, he clutched the invitation, its edges frayed from where his fingers had worried it incessantly.

"Ferryman's got a taste for drama, don't he?" he muttered to the void before him, his voice booming across the water, unsettling a nearby flock of crows. "Dramatic bastard."

As Victor contemplated the eerily calm waters, a delicate rustling drew his attention. Down the bank, a slender figure knelt beside a whimpering form. It was Grace Harper, her face a mask of concentration as she tended to a small, injured fox. Her hands moved with gentle efficiency, wrapping a makeshift bandage around its paw.

"There you go, little one," she cooed softly, a sweet melody amidst the dank, oppressive air of the riverbank.

The fox darted a glance up at her, eyes reflecting a deep, almost human intelligence before it scampered away, disappearing into the mist.

Grace stood up, brushing the dirt from her knees, and turned to find Victor observing her.

"You got a kind touch, Miss Harper," he said gruffly, his tone an odd mix of derision and respect.

She met his gaze, her eyes a clear, resolute blue. "Every creature deserves a bit of compassion, Mr. Daniels. Even on Thanksgiving."

Victor snorted, shuffling his feet. "If you say so. Not much for holidays myself. Just another day, ain't it?"

Grace didn't respond, her attention shifting as the sound of ethereal oars cutting through the thick water reached their ears. Through the swirling mist, the Gravy Boat emerged, a spectral vessel manned by an even more spectral figure. The Boatman's eyes, like voids, fell upon each passenger, his stare as penetrating as a knife's edge.

As the boat drew closer, Ethan and Diana emerged from the treeline, their strides syncing despite the chasm of their estrangement. They halted at the sight of Victor and Grace, a silent acknowledgment passing between them all. The Gravy Boatman had drawn them together, each bearing the invisible scars of their past.

"Welcome," the Boatman intoned, his voice the rasp of leaves against gravestones. "I trust you all received your... invitations?"

They nodded, a collective action borne of unease rather than agreement.

"Good." The Boatman reached into the folds of his coat, producing four ladles, each with a name intricately etched upon the handle. "Your ticket to ride."

One by one, they took the proffered ladles, the metal cold and oddly heavy in their grasp. Ethan's hand was steady, Diana's defiant, Grace's trembling, and Victor's surprisingly hesitant.

"You will drink of the gravy when the time comes," the Boatman continued, his gaze lingering on each of them. "And you will face what lies within."

Victor, masking his sudden anxiety with a blusterous laugh, was the first to step onto the boat, the wood creaking under the weight of his life's choices. Grace followed, her movements tentative, while Ethan, with a protective glance at Diana, boarded with a grim set to his jaw. Diana hesitated, her eyes locked onto the Boatman's with a challenge before she too stepped aboard, the gap between the pier and the boat like the chasm between her and Ethan.

The fog seemed to caress the boat as it began to drift away from the pier, the shore receding into a distant memory. They sat in a silent circle, each lost in the labyrinth of their own thoughts, each sip of the Boatman's sinister concoction looming in their immediate future.

The river carried secrets, just like them, and as the Stygian waters whispered of dark things best left submerged, they all felt the unspoken truth; they were not just passengers on a boat but captives of their own haunted reflections.

The Gravy Boat slipped through the veils of mist as if it were a blade through silk, the only sound the lapping of the river against its ancient hull. The Boatman stood at the helm, his hands as still and sure as the dead. Mist curled around his feet like the fingers of ghosts, drawing a shroud over the world they left behind. The passengers sat, each with their own ladle held like a talisman, a silent vow that before this journey's end, they would drink.

Ethan's eyes, shaded a steely grey, scanned the riverbanks as they morphed into indistinct shapes, the reality of Driftwood Bluffs a fading whisper behind them. His mind, trained to dissect the facts, sought reason where there was none. "Why accept the invitation?" Diana's voice broke the silence, her tone sharp as the bite of winter.

Ethan glanced at her, his sister, the woman who had become a stranger to him. "Why do you think?" His reply was short, a clipped sound that seemed too loud in the encompassing fog.

Victor chuckled, the sound hollow. "Why indeed. Opportunity knocks but once, they say." He turned his gaze towards the Boatman. "What's your endgame, Ferryman? Riches beyond measure at the end of this Stygian cruise?"

The Boatman's lips twitched into what might have been a smile or a grimace. "All will be revealed in time, Mr. Daniels. Patience is the currency here."

Grace, her hands clasped tightly in her lap, spoke next. Her voice barely rose above a murmur, yet it carried the undeniable strength of her conviction. "I came for closure. To heal wounds, both seen and unseen." Her eyes met Ethan's for a moment, a silent plea for understanding.

The mist thickened, congealing into opaque walls around the Gravy Boat, the shore now nothing more than a memory. They had entered the realm of the Boatman fully, the world of the living slipping away with each stroke of the oars.

The conversation waned, the passengers retreating into their own minds, each grappling with the decisions that had led them to this moment. The ladles gleamed dully in the half-light, a morbid anticipation building in the air.

Suddenly, the boat shifted, a gentle sway that belied the change in the waters beneath. The river was deeper here, the current stronger, the sound of water churning against unseen obstacles below. The mist parted before them, revealing glimpses of something more—shapes that were not quite shapes, whispers that were not quite sound.

"The Stygian River has many faces," the Boatman rasped, breaking the silence as if sensing their collective disquiet. "It shows you what it wills."

Victor's face was etched with skepticism, but beneath it lay a tinge of fear. "And what is it willing us to see?" he demanded, his voice betraying the commanding boom it once had on the business floor.

"That, Mr. Daniels, is for the river to know and for you to discover," the Boatman replied, the rumble of his voice a dark undercurrent to the boat's steady progress.

Diana wrapped her arms around herself, as if feeling the chill of the mist. "What lies at the end of this journey?" she asked, her voice a blade slicing through the fog.

The Boatman's gaze met hers, a flash of ancient knowledge in his eyes. "The end is different for each soul aboard," he said cryptically. "For some, a new beginning. For others, an ending long overdue."

A shiver ran through the passengers, unbidden and sharp as a splinter. The boat continued its inexorable glide into the mist, the river's whispers now a cacophony of voices from the depths, each tale entwined with the murky waters of the Stygian River.

And as the Gravy Boat made its departure into mist, each passenger felt the inescapable pull of the journey they had embarked upon—a journey not just of distance, but of the soul.

As the river's current grew more insistent, the Boatman finally turned from the helm, his motion deliberate, the tattered edges of his coat drifting around him like smoke. He retrieved a large, tarnished ladle from the depths of his cloak, its surface stained with the patina of countless Thanksgiving eves.

"Time for the first course," he announced, his voice gravelly, a sound that seemed dredged from the riverbed itself. He dipped the ladle into a pot that none had noticed before, filled with a substance darker than the surrounding mists, thick and shifting with an inner turbulence.

One by one, he filled their ladles, the gravy sloshing against the sides with a life of its own. It exuded a rich, overpowering scent, a mingling of sage, thyme, and something indefinable—a scent that was less an aroma and more a presence, as if each breath inhaled the essence of countless bygone Thanksgivings.

The passengers hesitated, exchanging wary glances. But the unspoken code of the Gravy Boat was clear: refusal was not an option.

Ethan's ladle was the first to meet his lips, and the effect was immediate. His eyes rolled back as the taste triggered something primal, something long-buried. The mist around him seemed to coalesce, to darken, and then he was no longer on the boat but standing on a rain-slick street in Driftwood Bluffs, the night that had unmade him.

A younger Ethan, in uniform, with his service weapon drawn, face-to-face with a shadowed figure. A robbery gone wrong, or so the report would later read. But Ethan knew the truth—the hesitation, the split-second decision, the fallibility that cost a life. And now, that moment replayed, the gunshot echoing across years, the weight of the badge a leaden reminder of the cost of failure.

The gravy, it seemed, was not a mere conduit of memory but a summoner of specters.

Beside him, Diana gasped, her own ladle trembling in her grasp. Her vision was of a courtroom, a place where truth was her weapon. But the gravy cut through pretense, showing her a lost case, a client who suffered because she was too proud, too confident. The judge's gavel was a thunderclap of guilt, and the client's eyes, full of betrayal, now stared at her from across the Gravy Boat's deck.

Victor's laughter had turned to coughs, the sound of a man choking on his own history. He saw himself younger, more vigorous, at a boardroom table, signing papers that would dismantle families, lives, livelihoods—all in the name of profit. His empire was built on the ruins of others, and the ghosts of those lives now drifted around him, their accusatory whispers the only thing cutting through the fog.

Grace's flashback was a quiet agony. The hospital room was sterile, the beeping of the heart monitor a countdown. A mistake with the medication—a patient lost. Her hands, once her instruments of healing, now felt like instruments of harm. She shivered, the memory so vivid it was as if she could reach out and touch the cold skin of the patient once again.

The Boatman observed them, his expression unreadable. The manifestations of their guilt, brought to life by the gravy, now accompanied them on the boat, as tangible as the seats they occupied.

"You see," the Boatman intoned, his voice rising above the ripples of the past, "the gravy does more than nourish. It reveals. It punishes. It absolves—if you are willing."

Ethan blinked, the scene of the shooting dissolving back into the fog, his breaths shallow and ragged. He looked at his companions, each trapped in their own tormented tableau. The realization that they were all bound in this shared nightmare was as chilling as the mist that surrounded them.

The Boatman's eyes, dark as the river, watched them with an inscrutable gaze. "This is but the first course," he said, a statement that held the weight of a verdict. "There are more to come before we reach our final port."

And with that, the boat continued its relentless journey, the passengers holding their ladles like lifelines, bracing against the tide of their resurrected demons. The first course had been served, and the feast of souls was only just beginning.

The river whispered. Each ripple against the hull was a word, every splash a sentence from the past. The mists seemed to thicken, and the spectral voices of the wronged swelled in the heavy air, a chorus of accusations and laments.

Ethan, his face now a mask of stoic anguish, felt the relentless assault of the river's murmurs, as if the water itself had dredged up the echos of that terrible night. He fought to focus on the here and now, but the Stygian River seemed to flow through time as much as space.

Beside him, Diana clutched her ladle with white-knuckled intensity, the courtroom phantasm still playing in her mind's eye. Her usual sharp retort was a dull blade against the edge of her own guilt. "It's not real," she muttered, more to herself than to the others, her voice a thread of sound in the oppressive fog.

But the fog, a living thing, breathed her failings back to her. The faces of the jurors twisted into a jury of her own conscience. And from the fog, an apparition coalesced—a younger version of herself, full of bravado, oblivious to the iceberg of defeat that would sink her case and change her life forever.

"Do you hear them?" Grace's voice broke through the thick air, soft yet suffused with a tremor of fear. "The voices?"

Ethan nodded, his throat tight as if the mist itself coiled around it. Victor, whose usual bravado had been supplanted by a haunted look, grunted in affirmation, his usual flamboyance drowned in the echoes of his greed.

They all heard it—the murmurs of the past, a babble of voices speaking of lost hopes and dreams, of trust betrayed and lives unmade.

The Boatman, his form more shadow than man, steered them through the wails of the river, his silence a stark contrast to the cacophony of souls that swirled around them. "The river knows your sins," he murmured, the rumble of his voice somehow carrying over the din.

As the shared vulnerabilities began to bond them, the barriers they had built—of cynicism, arrogance, detachment, and denial—began to crumble like the banks of the river itself.

Diana, the sharp edge of her façade now blunted, turned to Ethan, her eyes searching for the brother she had known before the distance grew between them. "Ethan," she whispered, her voice cracked with the strain of impending tears, "I—"

But Ethan was staring into the fog, his jaw clenched, his gaze distant. "We can't undo what's done," he said, the words scraping out of him. "We can only face it."

Victor, his eyes now hollow, spoke in a voice that was no longer booming but brittle. "In the end, we are our choices," he said, as if speaking to the echoes that accused him. "Our legacy, nothing more than the memories we leave in our wake."

And Grace, who had always held herself apart, always the healer, never the patient, reached out. Her hand found Diana's, their grip a lifeline against the torrent of regret. "Maybe," she offered, her voice a melody of hope in a dirge of despair, "maybe we can still choose who we become."

The boat sailed onward, the river's whispers a cruel mimicry of their internal turmoil. And as the fog rolled in thicker, it seemed to pull the truth from their souls, laying it bare for the Boatman—and for each other—to see. The voyage was no longer just a passage across a river; it was a journey into the depths of their beings, and the river of echoes spared no one.

The Gravy Boatman loomed like a wraith over a steaming pot, the aroma of the thick, rich gravy mingling with the mustiness of the river. The boat had come to a languid halt in a wider basin of the Stygian, the water here a glassy black, mirroring the fog in an endless canopy above and below.

"Take," he commanded, his voice the grind of gravel on a tombstone. His ladle broke the surface of the gravy with a slow, deliberate motion, and as it poured into each bowl, it seemed to Ethan that the gravy was not merely a substance, but a living part of the river's essence.

Victor Daniels, his once imperious composure now shattered like brittle glass, watched the steam rise from his bowl with dread. With each billowing cloud, faces began to form—faces of men and women, young and old, each a visage of accusation.

He blinked, and they were there. In the vapor, he saw the youthful hope of an intern he'd callously dismissed. In the swirl, the despairing eyes of a partner he'd betrayed for a lucrative deal. And there, in the trembling surface of the gravy, the broken spirit of his own son, whose life had unraveled in the shadow of a father's towering greed.

Victor's breath hitched, a sound like the last gasp of a dying man. "No," he whispered, his voice a threadbare plea. "Not him..."

Grace watched him, her own bowl untouched. Her role had always been to heal, to bring comfort where there was pain. But the sight of the businessman, once so grandiose, now crumpled before the specters of his past, sparked a chilling realization within her. They were all bound to the ghosts of their actions, and here on this river, there was no escape, no salve she could apply, no wound she could mend.

As the gravy's aroma enveloped her, Grace's eyes flickered shut, and a face appeared behind her eyelids—one she had fought to forget. A patient, her patient, young and vibrant, with a life full of potential, gone too soon. The monitors' beeping had been a countdown, and the silence that followed was a void she had never filled.

She saw the moment of departure, felt the grip of the young hand in hers weaken, the light in those eyes dim to an extinguishable flicker. She had been the last person he saw, her words the last he heard, but it had not been enough. She had not been enough.

With the illusion so potent, so visceral, Grace could feel the coldness of death seeping into her bones, a chill she couldn't shake, a weight that threatened to drag her under the dark waters of despair.

"Why?" Grace murmured into the oppressive silence that followed Victor's sobs. "Why this torment?" Her question was not directed at anyone, perhaps not even the Boatman, but it hung in the air like an invocation.

"The price," the Boatman rasped, the word scratching the air, "is always paid in full, whether in flesh or spirit." His eyes, dark hollows beneath the brim of his tattered hat, seemed to absorb the light, the hope, the very essence of the souls before him.

Ethan reached for his own bowl, his hands steady despite the turmoil that clawed at his insides. The weight of the ladle in his hand felt like the heft of a gun, the decision to sip from it as consequential as the pull of a trigger. He hesitated, knowing that whatever he would see in the broth would be more harrowing than anything the river had whispered.

Diana, her eyes red-rimmed from unshed tears, turned to him. "Ethan, don't," she pleaded, her voice a wisp of the confidence it once carried.

But Ethan's gaze was unyielding, locked on the Boatman. "What's the endgame here?" he demanded, his tone sharp with the edge of a man on the brink. "What do you get out of this?"

The Boatman's lips, cracked and pale, twisted into a semblance of a smile. "Understanding," he croaked. "You will understand by the journey's end. All debts settled, all accounts closed."

As the passengers each wrestled with their specters, the boat began to move again, the current taking it gently forward. But forward to where, none could say. With the second course served, the feast of souls continued, the Gravy Boatman ferrying them not just across the Stygian River, but through the very shadows of their lives. And as the boat drifted into the denser fog, the line between the world of the living and the echoes of the past blurred into obscurity, with no promise of a return.

The river's whispers turned to murmurs, murmurs to roars, as the waters of the Stygian began their ominous rise. The thick fog churned as if the night itself was boiling. The Gravy Boat rocked gently at first, then with more urgency as the current swelled beneath it.

Ethan stood, bracing himself against the wooden table that once bore the Boatman's feast. He squinted into the impenetrable mist, searching for the cause of the disturbance, for the logic in the madness. Beside him, Diana clutched the edge of her seat, her knuckles white, her sarcasm washed away by the rising tide of fear.

"It's like the river's alive," Diana muttered, more to herself than to Ethan. "Angry."

Ethan nodded, his eyes never leaving the shifting fog. "It knows," he said, his voice barely carrying over the burgeoning tumult of the river. "It's feeding on something."

The water lapped hungrily at the sides of the Gravy Boat, greedily clawing its way up as if it meant to claim the vessel and all who sailed within. Victor's face had gone from ashen to ghostly, reflecting the terror that had settled in his bones. Grace's lips moved in silent prayer or curse—none could tell which.

Then, as the boat pitched and the first fingers of water crept over the side, the passengers saw them—apparitions in the water, figures suspended in the murky depths, reaching upwards with silent, pleading gestures.

Ethan's breath caught in his throat as one of the faces became clear, illuminated by a flickering light that seemed to come from nowhere. A boy, no older than ten, his eyes wide with the same terror that had gripped Ethan himself in a time long past. Next to the boy, a girl, her features mirroring the boy's, her expression one of desperate hope.

"Our past," Diana whispered, her voice breaking. "Oh God, Ethan. It's us."

Ethan's hands clenched into fists. "It's not real," he ground out, fighting the rising panic. "Just another of his damned tricks."

"But it feels real," Diana countered, her gaze locked on the younger versions of themselves. "Maybe that's all that matters here."

The apparitions of young Ethan and Diana beckoned to them, their mouths moving silently, as if trapped behind an invisible barrier that muffled their cries. As the real Ethan watched, water began to swirl around the children, threatening to drag them into the abyss.

Without thinking, Ethan reached forward, his hand plunging into the cold Stygian waters. It was like reaching into his own history, touching the raw, unhealed wounds of memory. The water around his hand boiled with the energy of his past, the guilt, the pain, the moments he had tried to forget.

Diana's hand found his shoulder, her grip firm. "We have to save them," she said, the steel in her voice belying the terror in her eyes. "We have to save us."

Together, they leaned over the edge of the boat, hands stretching towards their doppelgängers, the past so close they could almost grasp it. The boat groaned beneath them, timbers creaking in protest, as if aware of the sacrilege they were about to commit.

Grace reached out to steady them, her nurse's instinct to save life kicking in, despite the surrealism of the situation. "Be careful," she urged, her voice barely above the din.

Victor, forgotten for the moment, watched them with a mixture of awe and horror. In his bowl, the last of the gravy shifted, forming images he could not bear to see. He pushed it away, his chest tight with the knowledge that for all his wealth and power, he could not purchase escape from this nightmare.

Ethan's fingers grazed the boy's hand, the sensation electrifying, sending jolts of long-suppressed emotions coursing through him. Diana gasped as she too made contact, her breath coming in sharp, staccato bursts.

The children's lips moved more frantically now, a silent plea that Ethan and Diana understood all too well. It was the cry for help they had never been able to give voice to, the cry that had been drowned in a sea of adult indifference and their own helpless silence.

And as the boat pitched again, the apparitions began to fade, the murky waters claiming them inch by inch. Ethan's jaw set. They had come this far, faced the specters of their pasts head-on, and he'd be damned if he let them slip away now.

"We're not letting go," he declared, his voice a commandment against the chaos of the river. "Not this time."

The waters continued to rise, the past clawing at their hearts, demanding to be remembered, to be reconciled. And as the boundaries of time and reality dissolved around them, Ethan and Diana held fast to the visions of their younger selves, fighting to keep their heads above the water, both literally and figuratively.

The Gravy Boatman watched them, his expression unreadable. His feast had taken an unexpected turn, his passengers showing a resilience that intrigued him. What would they sacrifice to save themselves? Would they embrace their past, or would they drown in it?

The river surged, the boat rocked, and the past pulled at them with the inexorable tide of destiny, demanding an answer.

The chaos of the river had turned the Gravy Boat into a crucible of past and present, a twilight zone where the only certainty was the ever-present fog and the relentless, hungry current beneath. But amid the cacophony, a silence fell as the Gravy Boatman stood. The table before him, which had been clear moments ago, was now set with an ornate spread that seemed to manifest from the mist itself—a feast fit for the damned.

Ethan, still reaching into the water, felt a pull at his very soul. It was as though the river not only wanted the visages of their past but was intent on drawing out the essence of their very being. Diana's hand tightened on his shoulder, her resolve a lifeline in the maelstrom.

The Boatman's gravelly voice cut through the tumult, "The feast is served, but it's no mere food that awaits you on this table. It is absolution, it is condemnation, and for some, it may even be salvation." His eyes, dark as the river, settled on each passenger in turn. "But be warned, every choice has its price."

Ethan turned away from the river, from the fading memories, to face the Boatman. "What game are you playing with us?" he demanded, his voice rough with the strain of unshed emotion and the effort of holding onto the spectral children.

"No game, Ethan Clark," the Boatman replied, the corner of his mouth twitching in what could have been a smirk. "Simply the offering of a choice. Your past has weight, and that weight can drag you down or set you free. But first, you must confront it. You must decide."

On the table lay dishes covered with silver domes, the scent of a Thanksgiving meal rich and inviting, yet beneath it lay the cloying, metallic tang of fear. Victor Daniels, drawn to the display of opulence like a moth to a flame, approached the table. "And what if we partake?" he inquired, his voice betraying a hint of his usual bluster.

"To partake is to accept the journey's end," the Boatman intoned. "To feed on this feast is to consume your own soul's narrative, for better or worse. Your fate, like the gravy in your bowl, is yours to stir."

Diana's eyes, sharp and calculating, flitted from the Boatman to the table and back. "And if we refuse?"

The Boatman's gaze seemed to pierce through the fog, through flesh and bone, into the very marrow of their fears. "Then you shall remain adrift, lost between the worlds, a ghost amongst ghosts, forever hungry, forever seeking, never to find peace."

Grace Harper moved closer to the table, her gaze lingering on the covered dishes. "But if there's a chance for redemption..." Her voice trailed off, not a question so much as a hope whispered into the void.

"Aye, there is always a chance," the Boatman agreed, his voice softer now, almost compassionate. "But redemption is not granted; it is earned. And the price is steep."

Ethan felt the cold grip of the river release his hand, the apparitions of their younger selves dissolving like mist in the morning sun. With a heavy heart, he faced the feast. "And what if our past is too heavy to lift? What if the things we've done, the things we've seen, are too much?"

The Boatman's hat seemed to cast a shadow that engulfed his pale face, leaving only the gleam of his eyes visible. "Then you drink deep from the gravy, Ethan Clark, and you let the river decide. Will it be the weight that sinks you, or the baptism that purifies?"

As the reality of the Boatman's words sank in, the passengers regarded each other, the meal, and the murky river that had brought them to this precipice of the soul. The gravy, dark and thick, swirled in their bowls, a mirror to the abyss.

Ethan looked at Diana, a silent conversation passing between them. There was no trust in the Boatman, but there was an understanding that whatever lay ahead, they faced it together. The specters of their past may have faded, but the choices of their future loomed as large and as real as the Stygian River itself.

Grace reached for Victor's hand, offering a silent solidarity, but the old man seemed lost in his own reckoning, his gaze shifting from his own reflection in the gravy to the Boatman and back again.

The Gravy Boatman lifted a ladle, the contents dripping like liquid fate. "Now, who will feast? And who will fade?" His voice was the river, the fog, the night—inescapable, inexorable. The feast's truth awaited their answer, but the chapter of their destiny remained unwritten, the pen held in trembling hands.

The silence that had draped over the Gravy Boat was thick, suffocating, like the fog that hung in the air, dense and unyielding. Ethan's heart hammered against his chest, each beat a drum of war, calling him to a battle he was not certain he could win. His eyes met Diana's, and in that gaze, there was a silent accord that bespoke of the fear and determination that twined like thorny vines around their hearts.

Victor Daniels stood at the precipice of decision, the sheen of sweat on his brow betraying the cool demeanor he attempted to project. "If I drink," he began, his voice no longer the trumpet of his own triumph but a tremulous note of trepidation, "if I partake in this...this farce, will the ghosts of my own making finally give chase?"

The Boatman's chuckle was a low, ghastly sound that seemed to emanate from the river itself. "Victor Daniels," he intoned, his voice the finality of a tombstone's inscription, "the phantoms of your avarice will always pursue you. The question is, can you outpace the shadows, or will you be consumed by them?"

Grace's hand tightened on Victor's, her knuckles white as the mist. "It's not about outrunning the past," she whispered, her voice a lifeline through the despair. "It's about facing it, making amends...isn't it?"

The Boatman's nod was slow, deliberate. "To drink is to acknowledge, to partake is to dare the soul to rise above the black depths of its sins."

Ethan's breath was ragged as he stepped forward, the first to reach for the ladle. The silver tool seemed to pulse with a light that was not reflected from any earthly source. He looked into the bowl, and in the swirling darkness of the gravy, he saw the flash of a gun, the spatter of blood, the faces of those he couldn't save.

Diana's voice was sharp, a blade cutting through the haze of his hesitation. "Ethan, you can't let it take you. We decide, not him, not this...boatman."

With a nod that felt like the first step toward redemption or damnation, Ethan scooped the gravy, lifting it to his lips. The taste was rich, salty with the tears of his regrets, bitter with the tang of misdeeds, and underneath it all, the sweetness of hope. As the concoction seared his throat, his vision blurred, and he was back there, in the alley where his life had taken its darkest turn.

Next to him, Diana's breath hitched, her own ladle held suspended in time. Her eyes, once a clear, penetrating blue, were now clouded with doubt. "Ethan, what do you see?"

He could not answer, trapped as he was in the throes of his past.

Grace, the eternal healer, reached out to Diana, her hand shaking. "We all have our demons, our debts. Maybe it's time to pay them."

Victor's voice, now a mere shadow of his former self, murmured, "Perhaps it's time to settle accounts."

And then, the old man drank. In the silence, they heard the gulp, a sound so lonely and final, it was as if he were swallowing his last breath. His eyes closed, and for a moment, there was peace upon his face, a tranquility that had eluded him in life.

Grace watched, her own ladle cradled in her hands like the fragile body of a bird. With a nod to no one in particular, she drank, her face a serene pool that belied the roiling turmoil within.

The Gravy Boatman watched them, his eyes alight with the reflection of their torment, his face impassive as stone yet as expressive as the river that bore their fates.

"And now, Diana Clark," he said, his voice a siren call to the lost. "What of your story? Will you sup with your brother in the light, or will you sink in the darkness of your convictions?"

The air was a tapestry of suspense, every breath a stitch in the fabric of the moment. Diana, her heart a drumbeat in her chest, looked at the ladle, at Ethan, at the Boatman. The last ladle weighed heavy in her hand, not with gravy, but with the weight of souls.

The boat kissed the shore with the gentleness of a final breath, a soft sigh against the sands of the Stygian River's farthest reach. The mist seemed to part in reverence as Ethan and Diana, shoulders squared against the weight of their trials, stepped onto the bank. The ground beneath their feet felt unnaturally solid, as if welcoming them to a reality that had been denied to them for what seemed like eons.

Ethan's hand found Diana's, their fingers entwining with the familiarity of shared childhoods and the newfound intimacy of shared horrors. They turned, almost in unison, to cast a last look upon the Gravy Boat. It sat, an enigma of wood and whispers, the enigmatic Boatman a shadowed figure at the helm, his silhouette dissolving into the fog as if he were no more substantial than the secrets he ferried.

"The Gravy Boat," Diana said, her voice a mix of wonder and wariness, "it's like it was never really here."

Ethan, whose face had aged a decade in the span of a single, harrowing night, nodded. The stubble on his jaw was a testament to the time they had spent adrift on the murky waters, battling the specters of their past. "Maybe it wasn't," he murmured, his eyes still locked on the space where the vessel had vanished. "Maybe it was just... a vessel for our conscience."

Diana pondered this, her analytical mind grappling with the supernatural elements that defied her legal pragmatism. "And what of the others? Victor, Grace...?" Her voice trailed off, unable to finish the thought – the fear that they might not have survived their encounter with the Boatman's brew.

Ethan squeezed her hand. "They found their own shores, Di. Whatever that means for each of them."

The mist curled around their ankles as they turned from the river, facing the treeline that marked the beginning of a terrain that was familiar yet seemed alien after what they had experienced. The air was cold, biting, but beneath it there was a scent of earth, of pine, a reminder of life that continued unabated, regardless of the nightmares endured by those who walked its soil.

Ethan felt the pull of the ladle's last taste in his gut, a warmth that spread through his limbs, chasing away the chill of the fog and the dread that had clung to him like a second skin. "We should go," he said, his voice carrying a new timbre, one of resolve and the faintest touch of hope.

They walked, their steps cautious but determined, away from the river and toward the promise of a new beginning. The woods welcomed them, the trees standing like sentinels to guard their passage. The sounds of the forest were a symphony to their battered senses, the rustle of leaves and the distant call of a bird a soothing balm to their frayed nerves.

As they walked, the first rays of dawn began to pierce the fog, golden fingers that painted the world in hues of possibility. Ethan felt Diana's grip on his hand tighten, and he glanced at her, seeing not the hardened lawyer she had been, but the sister he had once known, her eyes bright with unshed tears and the dawning of understanding.

"We made it," she whispered, a statement that was both a question and an affirmation.

Ethan stopped, pulling her into an embrace that was both a greeting and a farewell to what they had been. "Yeah, Di," he said, his voice rough with emotion. "We made it. But I think..."

He paused, his gaze lifting to the horizon where the sun promised a new day, a new chapter. Diana followed his gaze, and together they stood in silence, watching the world awaken.

Behind them, the fog whispered secrets, the river flowed on, indifferent, and the Gravy Boatman, if he truly existed, had set sail for the murkier waters of other souls. Ahead, life beckoned with the clarity of daylight, a path forged by their own wills.

"We have a lot of walking to do," Diana finally said, a smile ghosting her lips.

Ethan returned the smile, the first genuine one in far too long. "Yeah, let's get going."

And with that, they stepped forward, into the light, into the uncertainty, into the rest of their lives.

The end.

Feast of the Wicker Man

The tires of Thomas Wakefield's old Chevrolet creaked and groaned as he navigated the crunching gravel driveway leading up to the Wakefield estate. The house, an imposing structure of grey stone and dark, ivy-draped timbers, stood sentinel over the undulating fields of Harvest Cove. November's breath had stripped the trees bare, and a frost had settled over the landscape like a shroud.

Thomas cut the engine and sat for a moment, gazing up at the family home. It was just as he remembered: timeless, yet filled with a silence that seemed to echo with whispers of the past. He could almost hear the rustle of the autumn leaves from his childhood, a dissonant chorus accompanying the town's peculiar fervor for its secretive traditions.

Opening the car door, the chilly air rushed in, biting at his skin and stirring the edges of his coat. He stepped out and was immediately met with the scent of burning wood that loomed in the air, a precursor to the coming feast.

Sarah, a figure of defiance, leaned against the porch railing, her green eyes fixed on the horizon. She watched her father with a cool, almost detached curiosity that one might afford a stranger.

"Nice of you to finally show up," she remarked, her voice carrying a hint of irony.

Thomas walked up the steps, his gaze briefly meeting hers. "The roads haven't changed much, still as unforgiving as the town's appetite for secrets," he replied, his skepticism a mask over his own disquiet.

Sarah turned her attention back to the distant fields. "They're building it again," she said, nodding toward the smoke that rose beyond the northern ridge. "The Wicker Man."

He followed her gaze. "Still holding on to old wives' tales to celebrate the harvest, I see." Thomas couldn't hide the dismissive edge in his voice, despite the unease that knitted his brow.

"They believe it's more than just tales, Dad. They believe it brings something... real."

Inside the house, the legacy of the Wakefields hung heavy in the air. Family portraits adorned the walls, stern faces from bygone eras staring down at them, silent witnesses to the cyclical march of the town's history.

As Thomas unpacked a few essentials, the quiet was broken by the distant sound of hammering and chanting. It was a rhythmic, almost hypnotic sound that seemed to resonate with the very heartbeat of Harvest Cove.

"You're not curious? About the Wicker Man, I mean." Sarah's voice, a mix of teenage indifference and genuine intrigue, pulled Thomas from his thoughts.

"I'm more concerned with what we'll find in the estate's affairs. There's a lot your grandfather never told us. The Wicker Man is just a spectacle, Sarah. Superstition." He brushed the conversation aside, but his eyes betrayed a flicker of uncertainty.

Sarah pushed off the railing and walked past him, her boots echoing on the wooden floor. "Superstition keeps this town alive, according to them. And they all look at us like we're the heretics for doubting."

Thomas followed her into the study, where ancient books lined the shelves, their spines creased with age. He ran his fingers along the titles, feeling the weight of his heritage. The Wakefield lineage was interwoven with Harvest Cove's lore, and the Feast of the Wicker Man was the thread that bound them.

"What if it's not all just belief? What if there's something to it?" Sarah's question hung in the air, her words heavy with an unspoken fear.

"Then we'll deal with it," Thomas said with a conviction he didn't feel, "as we always have."

Outside, the sun dipped below the horizon, casting long shadows over Harvest Cove. The chanting grew louder, more fervent, as if the town itself were calling out for something to stir beneath the frost-hardened soil.

The Feast of the Wicker Man was drawing near, and with it, the ancient entity that lay in wait. As darkness fell over the Wakefield estate, Thomas couldn't shake the feeling that this year, the harvest would yield more than just crops.

In Harvest Cove, the past was never truly buried, and traditions ran as deep as the roots of the old, gnarled trees that framed the skyline. The Feast was coming, and with it, the unraveling of the Wakefield family's precarious skepticism.

Sarah retreated to the dim comfort of her grandfather's study, the wood panels absorbing the last of the day's light, surrendering to the encroaching night. She wandered through the cluttered room, each artifact a testament to a history deeply rooted in the arcane. The old man had been a collector of oddities, a silent guardian of Harvest Cove's secret legacies.

She skimmed her fingers over the spines of leather-bound books, stopping at a volume whose title was obscured by time. Pulling it out, she blew off a layer of dust, revealing the faint words: "Rites and Remnants of Pagan New England." A cold shiver cascaded down her spine, as if the very act of acknowledging the book had invited a chill to dance upon her bones.

Opening to a page marked by a dried, crimson leaf, she found herself staring at a series of old pagan symbols, each accompanied by a cryptic description in her grandfather's tight, meticulous handwriting. Her gaze lingered on one symbol in particular, a spiral that seemed to draw her in, whispering of a cycle unbroken, demanding continuation.

"It's not just superstition, is it, Granddad?" she murmured to the emptiness, half-expecting the musty air to carry a reply.

Lost in the tome, Sarah didn't hear the soft footsteps behind her.

"What did you find?" Thomas's voice, skeptical yet curious, broke the silence.

Sarah jumped, nearly dropping the book. "Jesus, Dad! Don't sneak up on me like that!"

"Sorry," he replied, but his eyes were fixed on the open page. "What is that?"

"Some old book about Thanksgiving rituals," Sarah responded, masking her growing apprehension with nonchalance. "Look at this." She pointed to the spiral symbol. "They used to carve this into the trees around the harvest fields. It's supposed to represent life... or death. Rebirth, maybe. Granddad was obsessed with this stuff."

Thomas's interest piqued despite himself. "That symbol looks familiar. I've seen it around town."

"Exactly," she affirmed, "it's all over the place if you know where to look. It's like the town's hiding in plain sight, part of something... ancient."

Thomas nodded slowly, absorbing the weight of his daughter's words. "I remember your grandfather spending nights in this study, poring over these books. I always thought it was just his hobby."

Sarah closed the book and moved to the desk, where a pile of papers lay scattered. A leather-bound diary peeked out, its cover worn and corners bent from use. Pulling it from the pile, she felt a magnetic pull to its contents. She flipped through the pages, her eyes catching on a recent entry in her grandfather's shaky scrawl:

"The Feast approaches, and the signs are clear. The Man of Wicker must rise, but the soil thirsts for more than the dew of the morning's embrace. The old gods are restless, their whispers louder than the howling winds. We must appease them, lest the ground rejects our toil and the cycle falters. This year, the offering must be... substantial."

A knot tightened in Sarah's stomach, her heart beating an erratic drumbeat against her ribs. "Dad, listen to this," she urged, her voice barely above a whisper.

Thomas leaned over, his skepticism faltering as the words settled in the air, a harbinger of something neither could fully grasp.

"We should show this to Sheriff Collins," he said after a pause, a hint of urgency in his voice.

"No," Sarah objected, her rebellious spirit flaring. "Not yet. We need to know more, or she'll think we're just spinning tales like the rest of them."

"Fine," Thomas conceded, a plan formulating behind his stern gaze. "But we need to be careful. If what your grandfather wrote is true, there's no telling what this town is capable of."

They stood together in the fading light, the Wakefields, bound by blood to a town enshrouded in mystery, the Feast of the Wicker Man looming over them like a specter of a past long thought to be dead. As the shadows crept through the study, whispering of ancient rites and forgotten pacts, the line between legend and reality blurred, and Harvest Cove waited with bated breath for the coming sacrifice.

The sharp scent of fresh timber filled the air, clinging to the walls of Peter Granger's workshop like a stubborn fog. Sawdust carpeted the floor, a byproduct of the man's relentless labor as he stood, a solitary figure amidst the chaos of wood and tool. The workshop was an extension of the man himself—cluttered, raw, and intensely private.

Peter's hands, rough and calloused, worked with a precision that betrayed his otherwise wild appearance. Each stroke of the chisel, each cut of the saw, was deliberate, forming the sinews and skeleton of what would be the Wicker Man. It was not simply an effigy; to him, it was the embodiment of the town's prosperity, the centerpiece of the feast that defined their way of life.

He paused, stepping back to inspect the towering structure that had begun to take shape. The Wicker Man's outline loomed over him, a skeletal giant poised to touch the rafters. Peter's eyes, fierce and fervent, traced the contours of its form, seeking any imperfection. It wasn't just the framework that needed his touch; it was the soul of the thing. Without it, the sacrifice would be for naught.

A knock on the large wooden door broke his concentration. Peter frowned, not used to interruptions, especially now when the veil between his craft and his beliefs was at its thinnest.

"Mornin', Peter," greeted John Haskins, one of the townsfolk, as he entered, his eyes darting around the shadow-filled workshop. "I see the Man's comin' along."

"Every year you all act surprised," Peter replied, his tone gruff yet not unkind. "It'll be ready for the feast, always is."

John nodded, though an unease had settled over him, one that seemed to be shared by many in Harvest Cove these days. "Folks are talkin', Peter. They're sayin' this year's different. There's a... tension, like static before a storm."

Peter scoffed, a smirk playing upon his lips. "Superstition breeds in idle minds, John. Harvest Cove's no different now than it was a hundred years ago."

"But the omens, the signs. Old Whitlock's been ravin' about the patterns, the whispers in the grain. They say the land's hungrier this year." John's voice was barely above a whisper, as if the very air might carry his concerns to unwelcome ears.

Peter turned his back, focusing on a particularly stubborn piece of wicker. "The land's appetite doesn't change. It takes what it's given and gives what it takes. That's the way of it."

John moved closer, lowering his voice. "And what about what it's takin'? More accidents this year, more... disappearances. And the Whitlocks, they're stirrin' the pot, sayin' we need to be prepared for a greater sacrifice."

A hammering pulse throbbed at Peter's temple, his grip on the chisel tightening. "The Whitlocks have always been the shepherds of this town's soul, John. If they're preparin' us for somethin', then we best be ready to listen."

"But what if they're wrong? What if what we're doin'—"

"Enough!" Peter's voice boomed, echoing off the wood-paneled walls. "This talk borders on blasphemy. The Feast will proceed as it has always done. The Wicker Man will burn, and the land will be sated. That's our way, John. You know this."

John, visibly shaken, nodded slowly. "I... I know. It's just... my boy, Timmy, he's been hearin' things at night, whisperin' from the fields. He's scared, Peter. We all are."

Peter's eyes softened, a flicker of empathy breaking through. "Fear's a part of it, always has been. The harvest demands respect, and respect often comes from fear."

John seemed to contemplate this for a moment before giving a resigned sigh. "I s'pose you're right. We'll trust in the tradition, in the land. And in you, Peter. To guide us through this Feast."

"As I always have," Peter affirmed, turning back to his work as John departed. Alone once more with his creation, Peter whispered to the wooden figure, a twisted prayer for a silent god he both revered and feared.

"We'll feed you," he murmured, his hands resuming their work with renewed fervor. "We'll feed you, and you'll give us another year."

And with each curl of wood that fell to the floor, Harvest Cove inched closer to the Feast of the Wicker Man, to a night of fire and fear, from which the truth would emerge, raw and terrible, like the heart of the effigy Peter so lovingly crafted.

The Whitlock estate stood like an ancient sentinel over Harvest Cove, its stark, grey stone walls weathered by centuries of New England storms. Thomas Wakefield approached with an academic's curiosity, his daughter Sarah trailing with less enthusiasm, her gaze lost to the forlorn landscape.

Eleanor Whitlock awaited them in the foyer, her stature rigid, her steel-grey hair braided like a crown. The air was thick with the scent of old wood and lavender, the latter more suffocating than soothing.

She wore tradition like armor, her gaze fixed upon the Wakefields as if weighing their very souls.

"Thomas, Sarah," her voice was both a welcome and a warning, "how kind of you to accept my invitation."

Thomas extended a hand, his smile strained. "Mrs. Whitlock, it's been too long."

"Indeed, it has," Eleanor replied, her hand cold and firm within his. "Your father was a good man, kept the traditions of Harvest Cove close to his heart. I trust you'll do the same."

Sarah exchanged a glance with her father, her eyes rolling with the impudence of youth.

Eleanor turned her hawkish attention to Sarah, "And you must be Sarah. The last time I saw you, you were but a child."

Sarah offered a tight-lipped smile. "It seems a lot hasn't changed since then."

The matriarch's gaze sharpened. "Change is often silent, my dear, much like the roots of an old tree."

The grand clock in the hallway struck an ominous tone, the sound heavy with the history of the house. Eleanor gestured towards the parlor with a hand that commanded obedience without question.

"Please, sit," she said, leading them into a room that seemed more like a shrine to the past than a place for the living. The walls were adorned with portraits of the Whitlock lineage, eyes that followed too closely, whispers embedded in oil paint.

Eleanor sat across from them, her posture never yielding. "I must discuss the preparations for the feast," she began, her voice dipping with each word. "The Wicker Man must burn, and with it, our bonds to the land must be renewed."

Thomas, ever the skeptic, leaned forward. "And what exactly does that entail, Mrs. Whitlock? I'm more inclined to trust in modern agriculture than in... bonfires."

A shadow passed over Eleanor's face, her lips a thin line. "You may put your faith in science, Thomas, but here, we trust in the old ways. They have never failed us."

"The old ways," Sarah echoed, a subtle challenge in her tone. "And what about the disappearances? The accidents?"

Eleanor's eyes flicked to Sarah, a flash of irritation before she composed herself. "A tragic cost, but necessary. The land is fertile, the town thrives—does that not speak for itself?"

Thomas interjected, "At the expense of lives? I find that hard to accept."

Eleanor leaned in, her voice lowering to a grave timbre. "There are things in this world, Thomas, ancient and hungry, that do not bend to the will of man nor his conscience. We feed them, or they feed on us."

The silence that followed was thick with unspoken truths, the air charged as if before a thunderstorm.

Eleanor stood abruptly, her chair scraping against the wood floor. "I trust you will both respect our traditions during your stay. The Feast of the Wicker Man is not merely a celebration—it's a tether that binds us, one we dare not undo."

As she escorted them out, her final words hung between them, a dire prophecy. "This year, the feast must go on, lest the hunger beneath our feet turns to the flesh of our kin."

The door closed with a definitive thud, leaving Thomas and Sarah alone in the chill of the impending dusk. The whispers of the grain that John had spoken of seemed louder now, a cacophony only the earth could hear, and as the Wakefields walked away from the Whitlock estate, the notion of tradition was a shroud that threatened to suffocate.

Sarah glanced at her father, her voice barely above a whisper, "Do you believe her, Dad? About the... hunger?"

Thomas didn't answer, his skeptical mind warring with the primal fear that Eleanor's words had stirred. In the silence of his hesitation, the fields around Harvest Cove seemed to lean in, listening, as if eager for the reply.

Sheriff Ava Collins stood at the edge of the Wainwright's farm, her gaze fixed on the ghastly sight before her. The remains of livestock were strewn across the frost-hardened soil, their bodies eviscerated with surgical precision that no wild animal could accomplish. The cold morning air did little to dissipate the stench of death that clung like mist to the ground.

She crouched beside the nearest carcass, her leather gloves shielding her hands from the gore as she inspected the incisions. The cuts were clean, deliberate, and most unsettling of all, ritualistic. It wasn't the first time Harvest Cove had seen animal mutilations, but the frequency had spiked since the start of November.

Her deputy, a young man named Kyle who still held a youthful optimism about policing, was securing the perimeter. "What do you make of it, Sheriff?" he called out, the unease in his voice betraying his composed facade.

Ava stood up, her eyes sweeping the area. "Someone's sending a message," she murmured, though deep down she wondered if it was something—or someone—far more sinister.

As daylight stretched over the horizon, she noticed something peculiar near the woods: a pattern of footprints leading away from the massacre, spaced too evenly to be from a panicked flight. Ava followed the trail, her hand resting on the service pistol at her hip.

The footprints led to an expanse of open field, and there, scrawled into the earth with what appeared to be a stick or a bone, was a symbol—a circle entwined with what looked like roots or vines, but it was unlike any insignia the town or she knew of.

A shiver ran down her spine. Harvest Cove was a town that thrived on tradition, but this was something alien, a mark that had no place in the annual Thanksgiving lore. She took out her camera, snapping pictures for evidence.

"Kyle, have you ever seen anything like this?" she called over her shoulder.

"No, Sheriff. It looks old... pagan almost," Kyle responded, stepping beside her, his eyes wide with a mix of curiosity and fear.

Ava nodded, her thoughts racing. Pagan symbols, animal sacrifices—it painted a grim picture, one that didn't bode well for the coming festivities.

She made her way back to the sheriff's office, her mind a tempest of conjecture and dread. The office was a small building that had once been a general store, its walls lined with the history of law enforcement in Harvest Cove.

Sitting at her desk, Ava pulled out the town records, the pages yellowed with age. She began to search through them, looking for any reference to the symbol she had seen or similar events in the past. It was a forbidden area of the town's history, one that many, including herself, had avoided.

Hours passed, the only sound in the office the turning of pages and the tick of the old clock on the wall. Ava's eyes caught on an old entry, a barely legible scribble about a ritual, one predating even the earliest Thanksgiving celebrations in Harvest Cove. It spoke of an offering to the "ancient ones," a feast to stave off their wrath. There was no accompanying symbol, but the description of the ritual set a chill in her bones.

The door to the office swung open, breaking her concentration. It was Peter Granger, the carpenter, his intense eyes wilder than she remembered.

"Sheriff," he said, his voice urgent, "you need to stop poking around. Some things are best left buried."

Ava met his gaze, her resolve steeling. "That's not your decision to make, Peter. What are you afraid we'll find?"

Peter's lips twisted, a snarl contained with effort. "It's not fear, it's respect—something you've forgotten."

He turned and left as abruptly as he'd entered, leaving Ava with a sinking feeling in her gut. She picked up the phone, her fingers dialing Thomas Wakefield's number before she could second-guess herself.

"Professor Wakefield," she said when he answered, "it's Sheriff Collins. We need to talk—about the town's history, about what's really buried beneath the fields of Harvest Cove."

As she waited for his response, the sheriff's badge on her chest felt heavier than ever, a reminder that the truth, however horrific, was her burden to bear. And as the line crackled with Thomas's hesitant acknowledgment, the shadows of doubt began to stretch across the walls of her office, whispering of the darkness that lay ahead.

As the sun dipped below the horizon, Harvest Cove was swaddled in a chill that seemed to seep into the very marrow of its residents. Sarah Wakefield stood on the porch of her father's inherited farmhouse, feeling the biting wind whip around her, carrying with it the scent of impending snow and something else—something far less tangible. It was as if the wind itself was a harbinger, whispering warnings in a language she felt in her bones but couldn't understand.

Inside, Thomas was entrenched in his late father's study, surrounded by musty tomes and parchment-thin documents, his face lit by the glow of a single desk lamp. His brows were furrowed as he traced lines of text with a skeptic's scrutiny. Each knock of the weathered wind chime outside seemed to punctuate the unsettling history he was piecing together—a history that the townsfolk had kept shrouded in festivity and folklore.

A sudden draft swept through the house, causing Sarah to shiver. She pulled her jacket tighter, watching the fields that stretched out beyond their property. There, amidst the barren stalks of last summer's corn, she saw something flicker—an ephemeral light that danced and swayed like a flame, yet was too distant to be a torch or lantern.

"Dad!" she called out, not taking her eyes off the spectacle.

Thomas emerged, drawn by the urgency in his daughter's voice. "What is it, Sarah?"

She pointed towards the fields. "Look. Lights."

He squinted into the darkness. "Could be someone from town with a flashlight."

"That's not a flashlight," Sarah replied, her voice laced with a certainty that made Thomas pause. "It's like... like they're alive."

They stood side by side, watching the undulating glow. Then, as if on cue, the lights extinguished, plunging the field back into darkness.

"Did you hear that, too?" Sarah whispered, her green eyes searching his. "The whispers?"

Thomas shook his head, frustration and concern warring within him. "Whispers are just wind, Sarah."

But he had heard them—a chorus of indistinct murmurs that rose and fell with the wind. His logical mind clawed for a rational explanation while a primal part of him recoiled in alarm.

Inside, the phone rang, slicing through the eerie quiet. Thomas answered, his voice steady despite the disquiet that Sarah's observation had instilled in him.

"Professor Wakefield, it's Eleanor Whitlock," came the unshakable tone of the town matriarch. "I trust you're settling in well. I wonder if you and your charming daughter would join me for tea tomorrow morning. There are... preparations to discuss."

The cordiality of the invitation did little to mask its obligatory nature. "We'll be there," Thomas replied, hanging up without another word.

After the call, the house felt smaller, the shadows deeper. Father and daughter were silent, each lost in their own apprehensions about what Harvest Eve would bring.

Later that evening, as the town's children engaged in their own innocent pre-feast traditions, laughter drifting through the streets, Thomas and Sarah found themselves at the Harvest Cove Library. The building was old, the wood creaking with stories and secrets, much like the tomes it housed.

Sarah browsed through the stacks, her finger tracing the spines of books until she came across a series of old newspapers, bound in leather. The dates went back centuries, the pages yellowed and fragile under her touch. An article caught her eye—a story about a Harvest Eve from the 1800s where the celebration was canceled due to an "unforeseen tragedy," the details of which were curiously omitted.

She scanned the pages, searching for more, when a shadow loomed over her—a figure obscured by the dim lighting.

"Interesting reading?" came the voice, deep and unsettlingly calm.

Sarah jumped, turning to face Peter Granger, the carpenter. His presence in the library was like a wolf in a den of resting deer, jarring and unbidden.

"Just trying to understand the town's history," she said with a courage she didn't feel.

Peter leaned closer, his eyes intense. "Some histories are meant to die with the past, Sarah. Your father would do well to remember that."

Before she could muster a reply, he was gone, melding into the shadows between the bookshelves.

Sarah found her father, her hands trembling as she relayed her encounter. Thomas listened, his features hardening with resolve.

"We're not going to be intimidated by local superstitions or the people who peddle them," he said, his voice low but firm.

Yet, as they left the library, with the whispers of the wind caressing their ears and the specter of the unexplained lights lingering in their minds, the word 'superstitions' felt like a flimsy shield against the palpable dread that Harvest Eve had cloaked around Harvest Cove.

Thanksgiving Day dawned with a hush over Harvest Cove, the usual bustle of morning activity strangely muted, as if the town itself was holding its breath. A grey veil of clouds hung low, and the autumn leaves whispered secrets that seemed to unsettle even the oldest trees. The air held a chill that spoke of more than just the changing season.

Thomas Wakefield stood on the porch, watching as the townspeople began to converge on the central square. They moved with a sense of purpose that bordered on the ceremonial. Among them, Peter Granger walked with the weight of tradition on his shoulders, his gait slow, almost reverent, as he headed towards the open field where the Wicker Man would be built.

"Let's get this over with," Thomas muttered, more to himself than to Sarah. He felt the gnaw of a deep-rooted anxiety, an unspoken dread of what was to come.

Sarah, standing beside him, nodded, the memory of last night's lights and whispers still fresh in her mind. Her eyes, so like her mother's, held a tumult of fear and fascination. "I have a bad feeling about this, Dad."

As they approached the square, the scent of the old world filled their nostrils; a blend of earth, sweat, and something darker, a smoldering that wasn't yet fire. The crowd was a tapestry of anticipation, their faces a mix of fervor and solemnity as they watched Peter and his chosen few begin the construction of the effigy.

Eleanor Whitlock stood by, her sharp eyes scanning the assembly as if looking for something out of place, her lips a tight line. "Professor Wakefield," she called out, "your timing is impeccable."

Thomas approached her, aware of the undercurrents in her tone. "Miss Whitlock, I was hoping you could shed some light on what exactly we're celebrating here."

Eleanor's gaze held him like a vice. "The harvest, Professor. We give thanks for the bounty of the land. And the land, in turn, requires our... devotion."

A shiver ran down Thomas's spine, the word 'devotion' hanging between them like an unspoken threat.

Meanwhile, Sarah's attention was caught by a group that strayed from the crowd, slipping away toward the old Whitlock barn on the edge of the field. Without a thought, she followed, drawn by the same curiosity that had her poring over ancient newspapers the night before.

Inside the barn, the dim light filtered through the cracks in the weathered wood, casting long shadows. Sarah watched as the group formed a circle, their faces obscured by the dimness, their voices low but charged with an urgent intensity.

At the center of the circle stood a makeshift altar, and upon it, an assortment of items that made Sarah's heart race—an old corn doll, adorned with red ribbons that looked too much like drying blood; a collection of bones from various animals, arranged in a pattern that made her stomach churn; and a knife with a handle carved from antler, its blade glinting dully in the scant light.

The ritual was nothing like the sanitized version of Thanksgiving she had known. There was a primitive earnestness to their chants, and the air felt charged with a palpable energy.

A part of her screamed to run, to grab her father and flee this madness, but another part, a deeper, darker part, was entranced, needing to know how deep the roots of this horror went.

Thomas, searching for Sarah, noticed her absence and felt panic rise like bile. His gaze darted through the crowd, finally resting on the old barn. He moved toward it, each step heavy with a father's dread.

The chant inside the barn crescendoed as Thomas stepped in, and the participants' voices became a cacophony that seemed to claw at the very walls. His eyes met Sarah's, wide with horror, as the group parted to reveal the true horror of their offering—a young woman, her face pale with terror, bound with ropes that were intertwined with the same red ribbons as the corn doll.

"No, this isn't—" Thomas began, but his voice was swallowed by the roar of the crowd.

"We offer what the land requires, Professor," Eleanor's voice cut through the chaos, suddenly behind him in the barn. "A soul for the soil. It's the covenant that must be fulfilled."

The revelation hit Thomas with the force of a physical blow. The Wicker Man wasn't just a symbol; it was a vessel, and they intended to fill it with life—a human life. Sarah's eyes, full of tears and terror, met his. And he knew, with a clarity that shook him, that they were caught in a web woven long before they had come to Harvest Cove, entangled in a history soaked with blood and belief.

As the chanting reached a fevered pitch, Thomas and Sarah realized the true nature of the Feast of the Wicker Man, and the darkness that lay at the heart of Harvest Cove. But before they could react further, the crowd surged forward, the ritual reaching its climax, and the barn doors slammed shut behind them, shrouding them all in an expectant gloom.

In the oppressive darkness of the barn, Thomas's breath came in shallow gasps, the sound absurdly loud in his ears. The fervent energy of the crowd pressed against him, a physical force that seemed to push him towards a precipice he could neither see nor understand. Sarah's hand found his, her grip like a lifeline as they stood amidst the madness.

The bound woman on the altar wept silently, her despair a tangible shroud that fell over the onlookers. Thomas's mind raced, each thought a disjointed fragment of disbelief and rising terror.

"We have to do something," Sarah whispered fiercely, her voice a thin thread of sound in the tumult.

Thomas shook his head minutely, a gesture more of confusion than negation. "We don't even understand—"

But Sarah was already moving, pulling him with her, edging around the periphery of the circle towards the trembling form on the altar. The crowd's chants crescendoed, the words foreign, yet each syllable a dark echo of dread. Eleanor's eyes followed them, her expression an inscrutable mask.

They reached the altar, and Thomas's hesitation dissipated in the face of the victim's silent pleading. He reached for the knife with the antler handle, its presence on the altar a silent permission for what he was about to do. As his fingers closed around it, a hush fell upon the barn, the crowd's anticipation tangible in the sudden quiet.

The ropes gave way under the keen blade, and the woman's quiet thanks were drowned by a thunderous roar from the crowd. Sarah pulled the woman to her feet, urging her towards the barn doors that had slammed shut.

Thomas turned to confront Eleanor, the blade still in his hand. "Why?" The word was torn from him, a father's fear and a scholar's demand for understanding.

Eleanor's gaze didn't waver. "To preserve. To thrive. The land demands, and we obey," she said, her voice laced with a conviction that chilled him to the core.

The roar of the crowd built again, their anger a palpable force. They had been denied their offering, their ritual left uncompleted. As the tension mounted, a crack of light splintered the darkness; Sheriff Ava Collins had forced the doors open, her presence a sudden beacon of sanity.

"Enough!" Her command cut through the frenzy. "This ends now."

The crowd, emboldened by tradition and the promise of the harvest, hesitated. In that moment of uncertainty, Thomas, Sarah, and the released woman slipped through the throng, escaping into the chill of the Thanksgiving day.

Outside, the world seemed unnaturally still, the frenzy of the barn a dissonant memory against the quiet town. They didn't stop to catch their breath until they reached the safety of the town's archives, the old brick building a stoic sentinel amidst the chaos.

Thomas's hands were steady as he began to rifle through the ancient texts, the musty smell of old paper and forgotten lore thick in the air.

Sarah stood guard at the door, her eyes scanning the street for any sign of pursuit.

Page by page, the grim history of Harvest Cove unfurled before them. Journal entries, town records, newspaper clippings—all telling a tale of blood-soaked soil and harvests bought with the price of a human life.

"It's all here," Thomas muttered, his voice hollow. "Every Thanksgiving... they believe it ensures the prosperity of the town for the coming year."

Sarah's face was pale as she came to stand beside him, reading over his shoulder. "But it's... it's murder."

"In their eyes, it's survival," Thomas replied grimly. "A sacrifice to something they don't understand, or maybe something they understand all too well."

They found it then, the origin of the feast, a tale of desperation and dark pacts. A creature of legend, a deity of the earth that demanded tribute through the cycle of the seasons. The Wicker Man was its sentinel, its conduit, a vessel to carry the sacrifice into the embrace of the earth.

As the afternoon light waned outside, the truth lay bare on the table between them. An ancient entity, a deity as old as the land itself, had been awakened in Harvest Cove's earliest days, and it hungered for a harvest of a different kind.

"What are we going to do?" Sarah's voice broke the silence, her eyes wide with the realization of the horror they faced.

Thomas looked at his daughter, at the fear and resolve etched in her features, and felt a fierce surge of protectiveness. "We're going to end it," he said, though he knew the path would be fraught with peril.

"But how?" she asked, the shadows of the archive room gathering around them as if listening.

"We expose it," Thomas said with a determination that belied his inner turmoil. "We show the town the cost of their prosperity. We break the cycle."

Sarah nodded, and together they turned back to the archives, to piece together a plan from the fragments of history that lay scattered before them. They had until nightfall, until the Wicker Man was to be lit, to change the course of Harvest Cove's history.

But outside, as the sky darkened and the townspeople prepared for the evening's grim festivities, the land itself seemed to stir, as if anticipating the feast to come. And in the growing shadows, something old and hungry watched, waiting for its tribute.

The twilight stretched its grim fingers across Harvest Cove as the townsfolk congregated in the square, a sea of shadows pooling around the towering silhouette of the Wicker Man. The effigy, woven from the very crops it was meant to bless, stood like a pagan deity, its hollow eyes gazing down upon the assembly with a god's indifference to mortal fear.

Thomas and Sarah had merged with the crowd, their plan a fragile shard of hope against the tapestry of impending doom. Their eyes, restless and alert, scanned the faces illuminated by the flickering torchlight, each one etched with the fervor of the ritual.

Sheriff Ava Collins stood at the fringe, her posture rigid, the weight of her newfound knowledge a visible burden. She watched with a complex blend of duty and dread as Peter Granger stepped forward, the torch in his hand a beacon of madness. His voice, raw with passion, sliced through the evening chill.

"We gather, as our forebears did, to give thanks and to ensure the continuation of our prosperity. The land has given us its bounty, and now we return the favor. Let the Feast of the Wicker Man commence!"

The crowd answered with a fervor that rattled the heavens, their chant a single organism, a living, breathing, crying entity that vibrated with ancient rhythms. Ava felt the tightness in her chest grow as Peter approached the Wicker Man, his silhouette merging with the outline of the effigy in a hellish embrace.

As the torch touched the base of the Wicker Man, fire greedily licked its way upward, consuming the dry wicker with a ravenous hunger. The crowd surged with a wild roar, their voices melding with the crackle of flames, the heat scorching the night air.

Ava's hand instinctively reached for the pistol at her hip, the metal cold and grounding. Her eyes locked with Thomas's across the flames, a silent pact between them. No more. This had to end.

As the Wicker Man blazed, its shape becoming an inferno of dancing demons, Ava fought her way through the crowd, her deputy's badge a small shield against the tide of bodies. She pushed forward, her voice firm, a counter-chant to the madness.

"Back away! This is no longer a sanctioned event—"

Her words were swept away by the roar of the fire and the cries of the townsfolk, their tradition a force she could no longer contain.

"Collins!" The voice was a lifeline, and she turned to see Peter, his face a twisted mask of devotion and fury. "You cannot stop what has been ordained!"

Ava squared her shoulders, the orange firelight casting deep shadows across her face. "Watch me."

The two faced off, the fire a flickering witness to their confrontation, the heat intensifying as if to match the burning intensity of their wills.

Meanwhile, Thomas and Sarah had edged closer to the archives, the knowledge they'd unearthed their only weapon against the dark history of Harvest Cove. But the land was awakening, and as the fire soared, so too did the air grow thick with a palpable hunger, an ancient appetite stirred from the soil itself.

"It's feeding," Sarah gasped, her words barely audible over the din.

Thomas turned to her, his eyes reflecting the inferno. "The fire, the chants—they're not just for show. They're a part of it. The entity... it's here, Sarah. It's always been here."

In that moment, Ava made her choice. With a swift movement, she drew her weapon and fired into the air. The report of the gunshot cleaved the night, and the chanting stumbled, the crowd's frenzy breaking as they turned towards the unexpected defiance.

"The feast is over!" Ava's voice was iron, her stance unyielding as the townspeople wavered, the spell momentarily broken.

The Wicker Man continued to burn, the flames now a monstrous pillar reaching for the sky, a beacon for something that lurked in the shadows of Harvest Cove's history. And as the fire blazed, something in the earth below responded, a rumble that felt like the growl of a giant beast.

Sheriff Collins, Thomas, and Sarah stood together, an island of resistance as the tide of tradition and terror swirled around them. The truth about previous feasts, the fate of the "offerings," clawed at the edges of the night, desperate to be revealed.

But the fire raged on, the heart of Harvest Cove's horror beating with heat and flame, its appetite unsated, the feast just beginning to ignite.

The ground beneath them trembled, a subterranean thrum that sent a wave of alarm through the crowd. Eyes that had been fixed on the blazing Wicker Man now darted to the earth, to their neighbors, to the armed sheriff who stood as if she were the only sane person left in the world.

Thomas felt it, a resonance in his bones, a call that seemed to beckon him to look deeper, beyond the fire, beyond the terror. Beside him, Sarah clutched his arm, her own fear a tangible thing, but her determination was just as strong. She was her father's daughter, after all.

The entity was awake, and its hunger was palpable, a psychic maw that yawned wide beneath the foundations of Harvest Cove.

"It's now or never," Thomas whispered to Sarah, his voice hoarse with smoke and realisation. They had to act before the entity's grip tightened any further.

But Eleanor Whitlock was already moving through the crowd, her presence commanding even as panic began to take hold. "Do not falter!" she cried, her voice cutting through the chaos with the sharpness of a bell. "The Great One stirs! We must give it what it craves!"

Her eyes found Ava's, then Thomas's, and within them was the gleam of fanaticism, the unshakeable belief that their course was righteous, that the sacrifice would bring salvation.

A shudder passed through the throng as from the ground where the Wicker Man's embers fell, the earth began to split, a dark chasm yawning wide, its edges glowing with the same fierce heat as the effigy above.

"Sarah, with me!" Thomas shouted, pulling her away from the crevice that threatened to swallow them whole. They made a dash for the archives, for the truth needed to confront the entity, to break the cycle.

Peter Granger stood his ground, his eyes alight with the reflection of the flames. "It demands a vessel!" he roared, pointing towards the chasm. "The earth must be sated, or we will all perish!"

Ava's gun, still in her hand, seemed suddenly insignificant against the primeval forces at play. Yet, she brandished it with unwavering resolve, her stance firm despite the tremors that threatened to knock her off her feet.

The crowd, caught in a frenzy of fear and belief, turned their eyes toward the chasm, toward the woman who had led them, toward the sheriff who opposed them.

A figure stepped forward, shrouded in the night, face obscured by the glow of the fire. It was a young man, his eyes wide with the fervor of the devout or the madness of the damned. He moved towards the chasm, his arms spread wide, a willing offering to the gaping maw.

"No!" Sarah screamed, breaking from her father's grasp.

Thomas grabbed her, holding her back. "We need to get to the archives!" he insisted, his voice strained with urgency.

But Sarah's gaze was fixed on the young man, on the all-consuming hunger of the earth. "He doesn't know what he's doing!"

Ava, between her duty to protect and her horror at the scene unfolding, hesitated only for a moment before she charged forward, her deputy's badge forgotten, her humanity now her only authority.

"Stop!" she commanded, but her voice was swallowed by the roar of the flames and the cries of the crowd.

The Wicker Man's structure began to collapse, sending sparks and embers swirling into the night, the heat an oppressive wave that pushed them back.

And as the fire consumed the last of the effigy, the chasm pulsed, the glow from within throbbing with an unholy light, and the earth groaned with hunger, a sound that echoed through the very souls of those gathered.

Thomas, Sarah, and Ava stood as if on the edge of the world, staring into the abyss that beckoned with a terror and a truth too dark to fully comprehend. The story of Harvest Cove, of the Feast of the Wicker Man, was unraveling before them, a tale written in fire and blood, its end not yet written, its horror not yet fully revealed.

The aftermath was immediate, the air thick with the scent of char and the low murmurs of a crowd turned silent. Ash fluttered down like grim snowflakes, coating the ground with the grey remains of the Wicker Man. Thomas, Sarah, and Ava, caught in a tableau of shock, could only watch as the young man approached the chasm, his steps almost beatific as he headed toward what they could only perceive as his doom.

Ava regained her composure first, breaking the trance. "Back, everyone get back!" she yelled, though her command was more plea than order. The townsfolk, locked in a spell of their own, seemed not to hear, their eyes glassy, reflecting the fire's death throes and the dark promise of the gaping earth.

Thomas, his heart hammering against his chest, his mind a whirlwind of fear and anger, felt a sharp tug at his arm. Sarah was pointing toward the town hall, toward the sanctuary of records and lore that might hold the key to ending this nightmare. He nodded, and together they began to push through the crowd, which seemed to part, not for them, but for the spectral anticipation of the sacrifice.

The young man was now at the edge, speaking words lost in the crackling of fire and the shifting of the earth. His words were for the entity, an intimate and ancient dialogue between mortal and whatever lay beneath.

But Ava was not swayed by ancient pacts or the fervor of sacrifice. She reached the young man, grabbing him by the shoulder, her other hand still gripping the gun. "You don't want to do this," she said, her voice steady but her eyes betraying her terror.

The young man turned to her, his face illuminated by the chasm's glow, his smile serene, deranged. "But I do, Sheriff. We all do, whether we know it or not," he whispered, then stepped back, slipping like a shadow into the maw's embrace.

The crowd gasped, some crying out, others silent, but all were motionless, as if the young man's final act had robbed them of their will.

In the archives, Thomas and Sarah began to search frantically, throwing open ancient books and unrolling yellowed scrolls. The knowledge they sought was hidden within allegory and cautionary tales, the true history of Harvest Cove bound in obfuscation.

"What are we even looking for?" Sarah's voice was edged with desperation, her eyes scanning over the texts with frenetic energy.

"Anything that tells us what it wants, how to appease it without..." Thomas's voice trailed off, unable to finish the thought.

As they searched, the earth continued to rumble, an ominous soundtrack to their frantic quest. Outside, the townspeople remained in a collective stupor, their silence a stark contrast to the carnage they had witnessed.

Eleanor Whitlock moved through the crowd, her eyes now hollow, the steel in her voice melted away to something soft, something afraid. "We must rebuild," she murmured, more to herself than to anyone else. "We must prepare for next year."

But Ava, standing at the edge of the abyss, her skin prickling with the residual heat, knew there would be no next year. The pact was broken, the tradition unmet. The entity beneath Harvest Cove would not slumber again, sated by smoke and symbol. It had tasted something more, something alive.

And in that moment, Sheriff Ava Collins made a decision. If the town was to survive, if the past was not to be prologue to a future written in ash and atonement, then she would have to break the cycle for good. She would have to find a way to sever the town's tie to the entity, to starve it, to render the tradition impotent.

The chapter of the Wicker Man's feast had closed, its embers dying in the cool night air. But the story of Harvest Cove was far from over. In the hallowed halls of its archives, in the empty eyes of its matriarch, and in the defiant stance of its sheriff, the seeds of a new chapter were being sown—a chapter of resistance, of reckoning, of reclamation.

And as the dawn threatened to rise on a town no longer bound by the fetters of the past, it was clear that the true feast was only just beginning. The feast of knowledge, of truth, and perhaps, of survival.

Months had passed since the chilling events of Thanksgiving, since the flames that devoured the Wicker Man had also consumed the innocence of Harvest Cove. Autumn had come again, with its crisp air and shorter days, a reminder of the cyclic nature of time—and perhaps, of terror.

Thomas Wakefield, whose skepticism had been burned away like mist over the fields at sunrise, stood at the edge of his property, overlooking the scarred earth where the Wicker Man had stood. He thought he could still see a faint outline of the structure that had brought so much horror, but then again, it could have been his imagination, the mind's relentless play with the eyes when confronting memories best left buried.

Beside him, Sarah, a year older and countless years wiser, her rebelliousness now tempered with the kind of understanding that only comes from facing the darkness head-on, watched in silence. Her father's transformation had been a catalyst for her own. Where once there was defiance, now there was a purposeful quietude.

"They're going to try again, aren't they?" she finally asked, her voice carrying the weight of unspoken fears.

Thomas took a moment before answering, his gaze never leaving the fallow field. "Eleanor Whitlock is gathering the town's elders tonight. They believe they can reinstate the old ways, make things right with... whatever it is that lies beneath."

"And can they?" Her green eyes sought his, searching for the steadfast certainty that used to define him.

"No," Thomas said firmly. "Because they don't understand. It wasn't the adherence to tradition that saved us, if anything, we were saved in spite of it."

A gust of wind brought the scent of turning leaves and a faint whisper from the town below, where the townsfolk, resilient as they were, had begun to rebuild what had been destroyed. New structures were rising, but the old fears, the whispers of what had transpired, were as sturdy as the ancient oak that stood sentinel at the town's border.

At the rebuilt town square, Sheriff Ava Collins walked among her people with a new purpose. Where once her stride was that of law and order, it now carried the urgency of a guardian. She nodded to the passing faces, faces that had seen the same horror she had, faces that, despite everything, were trying to recapture a semblance of normalcy.

Peter Granger, the disturbed carpenter whose hands had once weaved the fate of Harvest Cove into the sinews of the Wicker Man, now turned his skill to crafting cradles and cabinets, a silent vow to no longer be the architect of fear. His eyes, though, carried the shadow of his former belief, and some whispered that the fire of fanaticism was not so easily quenched.

As evening descended upon Harvest Cove, the community gathered, not at the behest of tradition, but out of a shared need to feel whole again. Old Eleanor Whitlock stood atop the steps of the town hall, her steel hair now streaked with white, her voice less commanding, more pleading.

"We must remember," she started, the tremor in her voice uncharacteristic of the matriarch the town knew. "But not to repeat, to learn. We have been given a second chance, and we must—"

Her words were cut short by a sudden chill that swept through the crowd. It was not the bite of an autumn breeze, but something deeper, a coldness that seemed to rise from the earth itself.

In the fields beyond, where crops had begun to timidly sprout again, a low mist gathered. It was thin, hardly noticeable if not for the last rays of the setting sun that caught and seemed to curl around it, like fingers stroking the air.

There, at the edge of perception, a shape seemed to form—a hint of something that lingered, patient and watchful. It was not malevolent, not exactly, but it was not benign. It was as though the land remembered, as though the very soil held the memory of old pacts and rituals, waiting for the right moment to remind its people of their place within the ancient and ever-turning wheel of the year.

Thanksgiving was approaching, and with it, a whisper of a question—had the Feast of the Wicker Man been a closing chapter, or merely a prelude? As the darkness settled, and the first stars pierced the evening sky, Harvest Cove found itself in the grip of a wary vigilance, a community standing on the threshold of an answer they both feared and desired.

The embers of the old ways had been scattered to the winds, but embers, by their nature, hold the potential of fire. The story of Harvest Cove was far from over, and the dance between the shadows of the past and the light of the future was about to begin anew.

The end.

Thanks-taking

The roads were empty as Daniel Harrow's Jeep cut through the November chill, the bare branches of New England trees clawing at a sallow moon. Inside the car, the laughter and chatter of his four friends warred with the sound of the wind outside.

"You're sure this is the place, Danny-boy?" Jack's voice carried over the sound of the engine, laced with a jesting undertone that failed to conceal an edge of apprehension.

"Whittaker Farmhouse should be just beyond these woods," Daniel replied, eyes on the road, his voice the very model of academic detachment he was known for. "And yes, I'm sure."

Emma sat close to him, nursing a can of soda between her hands, the green of her eyes catching the dash lights as she glanced at him. "This isn't your usual idea of a date, you know," she teased, trying to stoke the fires of normalcy with her words.

"It's not a date, it's a dare," Lila chimed in from the backseat, her petite form hunched over her camera. "A dare to outdo all those mundane Thanksgivings."

"Right," Jack snorted. "Because nothing says 'Thanksgiving' like spending the night in a haunted hellhole."

Daniel's lips twitched into a half-smile. "Haunted hellhole is a bit dramatic, don't you think?"

They were all acquainted with the stories: The Whittaker Farmhouse, where it was said the Thanksgiving of 1919 had never ended. The Whittaker family had sat down for their holiday dinner and, if the tales were believed, never got up again. A feast that continued beyond time, where the courses got progressively more... inventive.

As the vehicle broke free of the woods, the Whittaker Farmhouse loomed into view, a silhouette that seemed to absorb the faint moonlight rather than reflect it. Emma's comforting tone faltered as she muttered, "It's just stories, right?"

"Just stories," Daniel echoed, though his intense brown eyes were fixed on the structure as they drew nearer.

Jack killed the levity entirely when he said, "I heard they never found the Whittakers' bodies. Just an endless set of dishes on the table and the remains of a meal that looked like it had been served up from hell's own kitchen."

Lila's voice was quieter than usual, a note of seriousness tainting her usual assertiveness. "My last piece on haunted Massachusetts barely scratched the surface of this place. They say the house feeds on the fears of its guests, twists their desires. It's the perfect story."

Jack snorted, "Feeds on fear, huh? What does it do for dessert? Suck out your soul?"

The Jeep rolled to a stop, gravel crunching beneath its tires. Daniel turned off the engine, and for a heartbeat, they sat in silence, the farmhouse's oppressive presence filling the air around them.

"Well, let's not disappoint the house then," Daniel said, mustering the same tone of reason he used when presenting a paper on cultural anthropology. He opened the door and stepped out into the cold, followed by a chorus of car doors slamming shut.

They approached the front door, the porch creaking under their weight, the house watching them with its dark, windowed eyes. Jack was the one who pushed the door open, the sound a shrill complaint in the stillness.

The entryway opened into darkness, like the maw of some ancient beast. They entered, each step seeming to echo into infinity. The dim outlines of a long dining table emerged in the faint light that filtered through the boarded windows, the wood groaning as if resenting their intrusion.

As they ventured further, the air grew colder, dense with the must of decay and the faint, cloying scent of rotted meat. Emma stayed close to Daniel, her hand finding his in the dark.

Jack let out a low whistle. "This is some next-level creep factor," he murmured, his attempt at humor falling flat in the thick atmosphere.

Lila's camera clicked, the flash a sudden burst that painted everything in stark relief for a fleeting second. "Did you guys see that?" she asked, her voice a soft, urgent hiss.

"See what?" Emma whispered.

"Faces," Lila breathed. "In the flash. For a moment, it looked like..."

"Like the Whittakers were still seated at the table," Daniel finished for her, a chill that had nothing to do with the cold sliding down his spine.

Jack let out a nervous laugh, but it was cut short by a sound from the depths of the house—the faint scratch of silverware against china.

"Someone's idea of a practical joke?" Emma suggested, but her voice betrayed her fear.

Daniel took a step forward, his skeptic's heart battling with the undeniable dread that clawed at his reason. "There's got to be a logical explanation for all of this," he said, more to himself than to the others.

But as the house seemed to breathe around them, the air thick with the anticipation of the feast to come, logic was the first course to be stripped away. They were about to learn that in the Whittaker Farmhouse, fear was the main ingredient... and terror the only guarantee.

And with that first nightmarish loop of dinner chimes echoing through the halls, their Thanksgiving dare began.

The chimes carried on like a funeral dirge, calling them to the table. With trepidation etched on their faces, the group converged around the ancient dining setup, where tarnished silverware lay beside porcelain plates that bore the fine cracks and the stains of time. Dust particles danced in the beams of light cast from their flashlights, creating an illusion of movement as if unseen guests shuffled into their seats.

"Is it just me, or is it getting colder?" Emma's teeth chattered, her knuckles white as they gripped Daniel's arm.

"It's not you," Daniel admitted, eyeing the head of the table where a large, empty chair sat like a throne of shadows. "It's like we've stepped into the house's past, or it's seeping into our present."

Jack had always been the one to break the tension, but now his jokes were swallowed by the thick air, his usual smirk replaced by a line of concentration. "Okay, so we sit, we wait for nothing to happen, we check off the box for the dare, and we get the hell out, deal?"

They all nodded, the decision unanimous, and pulled out the chairs. The wooden legs scraped against the floorboards with a shriek that seemed to protest their presence.

Lila set her camera down, letting the strap fall around her neck as she sat. "We should document this," she said, her voice steady but tinged with an edge that hinted at her own fear. "Just in case..."

"In case of what?" Jack interrupted, but he fell silent as the others turned to look at him, their expressions a mirror of his own trepidation.

As they settled into the seats, the air grew thick, almost palpable with dread. A wind whistled through cracks in the walls, carrying with it whispers that sounded too much like distant laughter, or sobs, Daniel couldn't tell which.

Then, with no one to serve it, the feast began to appear. It started as a low hum, like the buzz of a fly, but grew into a cacophony of sounds—the clink of glass, the rustle of movement, the creak of laden platters materializing upon the table.

First came the appetizers: dishes filled with wriggling things that might once have been olives or stuffed peppers, but now looked like eyes and fingers, twitching in their bowls.

"Jesus," Emma breathed, pushing her plate away, her face pale in the flashlight's beam.

Lila reached out tentatively, her journalistic instincts wrestling with revulsion. She touched what looked like a shrimp cocktail, only for the shrimp to coil around her finger with a life of its own. She retracted her hand quickly, a gasp escaping her lips.

Jack stood abruptly, knocking his chair over. "This is insane. This isn't happening."

But it was. The main course followed: a turkey that seemed to breathe under its garnish, the stuffing writhing with a nest of insects that buzzed angrily as they were exposed.

Daniel, his scholar's mind reeling, tried to stand, to rally the others, to insist on leaving, but his body refused to obey. He was transfixed, his gaze locked on the grotesque parody of food before him.

"Don't," he managed to choke out when Jack made to touch the silverware. "We shouldn't... we can't..."

The air shivered with silent laughter now, the house delighting in their horror.

The side dishes were no kinder—a cranberry sauce that pulsed with a sickly rhythm, sweet potatoes that seemed to sweat a foul, dark oil. And the pie, oh the pie, its crust crawled with what looked like maggots spinning silk.

"It's a test," Lila whispered, her voice breaking. "It's trying to see what scares us..."

"And it's winning," Jack added, his humor nowhere to be found.

Emma's nurturing nature was nowhere in sight now, replaced by a raw survival instinct. "We need to go," she said, but it was a plea, not a declaration.

Before they could move, the chimes sounded again, louder, closer, a clear signal that the first feast was not over. Something was coming, something that would make the horrors on the table seem trivial. The anticipation was almost worse than the sight of the macabre meal.

Daniel's heart hammered against his ribs like a thing desperate to escape. The meal may have been false, but the fear? That was painfully real. As he exchanged looks with his friends, he saw in their eyes a reflection of his own terror.

The feast was just beginning, and the house was hungry for more than their bodies—it craved their sanity, their souls. It had ensnared them in its ghastly tradition, a tradition where gratitude was devoured, and only the ravenous remained.

The shadows of the Whittaker Farmhouse seemed to pulse and breathe around them, closing in with suffocating intimacy as the chimes faded into a stifling silence. The horror on the table lay still for a moment, but their dread was far from over. It was Emma who first noticed the peculiarity of the windows – they seemed dimmer, almost opaque, as if twilight had smeared itself against the glass.

"We should leave, now," she said, her voice a hollow shell of the comfort it usually carried.

Daniel nodded, his body finally obeying his desperate commands. They pushed back from the table, the chairs screeching a chorus of unrest. With a shared, silent agreement, they moved towards the door they'd entered through, the door that should have led to the moonlit fields and the path to their abandoned car.

Jack reached it first, his hand grasping the cold doorknob, twisting and pulling. The door swung open with a groan – not to the freedom of the outside world, but to an impossible view of the farmhouse's interior, a dusty, decrepit foyer that mirrored the one they had stepped through hours earlier.

"What the—" Jack's voice trailed off as he stepped through the threshold, only to reappear from the doorway on the opposite side of the dining room. He whirled around, disbelief etching his features.

"Some funhouse trick," he muttered, but his eyes were wide with the first real seeds of panic.

Daniel's thoughts raced. He'd read about spatial loops, psychological effects, but this was no illusion or trick of the mind. The house was bending reality, warping it.

Lila's voice pierced the confusion, "Try the windows!"

They rushed to the nearest one, their movements frantic. Emma and Daniel pried at the frame, but when they managed to shove it open, it revealed not the expected cool night but another room of the house – the kitchen, with its hanging pots and pans clanging softly as if caught in a non-existent breeze.

The realization that they were trapped settled over them like a shroud. Emma's fingers clenched the windowsill, her nurse's training offering no remedy to the insanity before them. "This can't be happening," she said, a mantra against the impossibility.

"We need to stay calm," Daniel said, though his own heart raced traitorously. "There's got to be a logical explanation."

Jack snorted. "Logic left this place a long time ago, buddy."

Lila's dark eyes flicked from window to door to the relentless darkness that seemed to claw at the corners of the room. "It's like the house is alive," she whispered, voicing the dread that had taken root in each of them.

The wind's whisper became a mocking imitation of their earlier conversations, and time began to stretch and compress in unnatural ways. One moment it seemed like seconds were stretching into hours, the next, hours seemed to pass in the blink of an eye. Their watches became useless, hands spinning wildly or stopping altogether.

Daniel felt his skepticism crumbling as he watched the candlelight flicker, its dance too erratic, too intentional. "It's toying with us," he murmured, his voice strained with the effort to maintain a semblance of control.

"Yeah, well, it can toy all it wants. I'm not playing," Jack said, his attempt at bravado unconvincing. He headed for the stairs that led to the second floor, but as he climbed, he seemed to get nowhere, his movements taking him on an endless loop of ascent.

"Jack, stop, it's useless!" Lila called out, her voice sharpened with fear.

He ignored her, determination fueling his steps until he finally stopped, panting, looking down at them from the top step – only to be standing at the bottom again. "I don't understand," he said, his voice breaking, the joker now a man undone.

The house seemed to breathe around them, the walls contracting slightly, the ceiling pressing down. Emma, with her green eyes wide and shimmering with unshed tears, clung to Daniel. "What does it want from us?" Her voice was a whisper of terror.

"Not what, Emma. Who," Daniel said softly, the truth dawning on him with chilling clarity. The house wasn't just playing with them; it was choosing them, savoring them.

They huddled together, their minds grappling with the relentless horror of their situation. The feast had been an overture, and the night promised a symphony of terrors. And above all, the farmhouse hungered, a silent predator in the endless night, waiting to strike again.

As if in response to Daniel's realization, the room trembled, a low growl emanating from deep within the bowels of the farmhouse, vibrating the fine china on the table. And then, almost imperceptibly at first, the table itself began to change.

The remains of the first course – a mockery of Thanksgiving fare – writhed and squirmed, decomposing before their eyes, giving way to the second course. The air filled with a sickly sweet stench as new platters appeared, materializing from the ether as if by some dark culinary magic.

Jack, whose humor had been a comforting constant, staggered back, his face ashen. "I'm not hungry," he choked out, but his voice was swallowed by the room's acoustics, which seemed to mock them with a hollowness.

Lila, her breaths shallow, raised her camera, her hands shaking. The lens captured the ghastly feast: meats that pulsed with an inner life, vegetables that twisted into grotesque shapes, and gravies that bubbled with a life of their own.

"Don't record it," Emma gasped, her eyes fixed on the shifting shapes of the food. "It's like it wants us to remember, to relive..."

Daniel reached out, not to touch the food but to halt Lila's hands. "This is what it wants," he said, his voice threadbare with stress. "To feed on our reactions, our horror."

But the meal wasn't done with them. The second course had a perverse intelligence to it, a malicious intent that sought to invade more than just their sight and smell.

Emma felt it first, a creeping sensation at the back of her mind, like fingers rifling through her thoughts. Her nurturing nature, her compassion and care, began to turn inward, festering. Images flashed before her eyes: patients from the ER, their faces contorted not in pain, but in accusation, their wounds speaking of her failures, not their injuries.

"No, stop," she whimpered, squeezing her eyes shut, but the images were behind her eyelids, etched in her mind.

Lila dropped the camera with a clatter as her own terror took shape. The farmhouse forced upon her an insidious documentary, each friend's face a byline in a narrative of nightmare. The house whispered stories of those who had sat at this very table, of madness and despair, of endings with no escape.

Jack's laughter had always been his fortress, but now it was a cell. The sounds of merriment he'd once brought forth were now twisted into a cacophony of manic, mocking echoes that filled the dining room, the laughter of friends turned into a taunting chorus that seemed to come from the very walls.

Daniel felt the farmhouse probing, testing his skepticism, confronting him with phenomena defying logic and reason. The room spun with impossible geometry, walls angling inwards, corners stretching into infinity. His world was a paradox, and with each breath, his rationality was squeezed from him like juice from a fruit.

They were caught in an intimate web, the house drawing out their innermost fears, feeding on them. Daniel managed to pull his gaze from the impossible sights and turned to his friends, his voice a desperate rasp, "We have to resist it. Don't let it inside you."

"How?" Emma's voice was almost a sob, the resilience of the caregiver consumed by the house's corruption.

Jack, staring at the laughter-turned-screams that seemed to echo from his own mouth, struggled to speak. "By not giving in," he said, but the platitude sounded empty in the face of such relentless dread.

"We document it," Lila said, her voice regaining some of its lost assertiveness as she retrieved her camera. "We bear witness, not just for ourselves, but for those it has taken, for those it might yet consume."

Their resolve was a flickering flame in the oppressive darkness of the farmhouse's design. It was then that the feast began to shift again, the second course not content with just mental torment. The plates in front of them began to fill with new horrors, tailored to each, a mirror to their souls and the fears that lurked within.

The room grew colder, the air thick with the scent of decay and the sound of their quickening breaths. The Whittaker Farmhouse was feeding, and they were the main course.

The walls seemed to pulse with a hungry rhythm, absorbing the echoes of their distress. Emma's hands were trembling, her nursing instincts now a cruel jest as the table presented its new ordeal. The centerpiece had transformed, an abomination of intertwined limbs and gaping mouths that begged for her care with voices stolen from those she could not save.

"Help us, Emma," the voices pleaded, in a discordant chorus that sounded like twisted imitations of past patients. "Ease our pain."

Her stomach churned, her nurturing soul recoiling at the perverse request. "This isn't real," she whispered, but doubt gnawed at her, the farmhouse's influence insidious and intimate.

Jack's eyes darted to Emma, his usual banter dying on his lips. "What do we do? We can't... We can't just sit here."

But it was Daniel who moved first, his hand grasping Emma's. "It's a trap," he said, his gaze locked with hers, a lifeline amidst the madness. "Your compassion is a weapon to it, not a weakness. Remember that."

Lila's hands were steadier now as she aimed her camera at the monstrous centerpiece. "We document," she reiterated, her voice firm. "We show the world its ugliness, its falsehood."

The farmhouse groaned around them, displeased with their resistance. A draft slithered across the floor like a living thing, and the food on the plates began to writhe, each dish a tailored terror. For Jack, the meats twitched and flexed, as if each muscle came from a car engine that he couldn't repair, that he couldn't understand.

His face pale, Jack pushed back from the table, his chair scraping harshly against the floor. "I fix things. That's what I do. But I can't... I can't fix this."

"And you're not meant to," Daniel replied, a thread of anger weaving through his fear. "This... feast wants us broken. But we're not going to break."

For Lila, the vegetables had turned to eyeballs, staring at her accusingly, each blink a shutter capturing another frame of their nightmare. She could feel the weight of untold stories, the despair of subjects she couldn't bring to light, but she held the camera steady, recording every horror.

Emma felt a sob clawing its way up her throat, not for her own fear, but for her friends. The house seemed to know exactly how to fray the edges of their sanity, to peel back their defenses.

"It's eating at us," she said, her voice breaking. "Not with teeth, but with... with this."

The dining room faded for a moment, the atmosphere thick with the echo of their fears, and in its place, they saw glimpses of others who had sat at this table, their faces etched with despair. They were all part of the farmhouse's tapestry now, threads in a macabre design of endless Thanksgiving.

"We can't let it," Daniel said, squeezing Emma's hand tighter. "We're stronger than this."

But the farmhouse seemed to laugh at their defiance, the air curdling with its mirth. The next course was laid bare before them, a grotesque parody of dessert, a final insult. It was not food that lay on the platters, but memories, each one a bitter morsel of past regrets and guilt, coated in a glaze of helplessness.

Daniel watched as Emma recoiled, her psyche barraged by the torturous feast. "Look at me," he urged, his own fear warring with the need to protect her. "Don't look at it. It's lies, all of it."

But the lies were convincing, tailored by an entity that knew them better than they knew themselves. Emma's breath hitched, each ragged inhalation a battle.

The farmhouse fed on the tension, the fractures within the group. Accusations hovered on the edge of their tongues, suspicion blooming like a vile weed. They knew they should not succumb to it, that it was what the house wanted, yet the strain was palpable, drawing forth the darkest parts of themselves they had hoped never to confront.

Jack finally let out a hollow laugh, devoid of any true humor. "So this is it, huh? This is how we go out?"

"No," Lila said, snapping her camera shut with a finality that echoed in the tense air. "We're going out fighting."

They stood together, a fragile unity forming once again. Yet the farmhouse, undeterred, seemed to be only biding its time, waiting for the fractures to deepen. It whispered of secrets yet to come, of divisions yet to be sown, and of an appetite that was far from sated.

In the gathering gloom, their shadows stretched across the floor, twisting and contorting, as if trying to pull away from their owners. The friends held each other's gaze, each silently vowing to endure, even as the house promised them there was much more to endure.

The feast was not over. It was never over. And as the shadows danced, the true horror of Thanks-taking was yet to be served.

The parlor of the Whittaker Farmhouse wore the past like a second skin, the wallpaper peeling back to reveal layers of bygone eras, each pattern more grotesque than the last. It was here, amidst the must and decay, that they found the first clue—a yellowed newspaper clipping pinned to the mantle, the headline screaming about a Thanksgiving tragedy decades old.

Daniel, his brow furrowed, leaned in closer, the words blurring as he read aloud. "'Family Found Dead—Foul Play Suspected at Local Farmhouse.'" The date was from the 1930s, the faces in the grainy photo below the headline mirroring the fear that now gnawed at their insides. "This could be it—the origin of the curse."

Emma huddled close, her hand gripping Daniel's as if to anchor herself in the present. "There are more clippings," she observed, her voice a shadow of its usual warmth. "It's like... like a timeline of horror."

The fragments of articles formed a chilling mosaic. Each Thanksgiving, another incident, another family lost, the details growing more harrowing as the years bled on. Lila, camera abandoned for the moment, began to frantically assemble the pieces, her fingers tracing the lines of text.

"Guys, look at this," she said, her tone urgent. "Each of these... massacres. They're all linked by—"

"Despair," Jack cut in, his voice rough. "Every last one of these people, they were at their breaking point before they even set foot in the house."

Daniel's mind raced, trying to weave reason through the madness. "So the house doesn't just feed on fear; it's like it... harvests it."

As if stirred by their discovery, the farmhouse shuddered, a deep moan vibrating through the foundation. The air grew colder, their breaths misting before them in quivering plumes.

Jack's eyes flicked to the windows, where the twilight had curdled into an oppressive darkness that pressed against the glass like a physical force. "We're on its damn menu, and it doesn't like us poking around its kitchen."

"It means we're onto something," Emma said, her voice steadying. "If understanding its past is a threat, then we have to keep digging."

The next clue lay within a locked drawer of a dust-laden bureau. The key, a rusted piece of metal heavy with age, had been clutched in the hand of a wooden doll, its painted eyes worn away to nothing. It took all of Jack's resolve to prise the key free, the doll's other hand snapping at him with a life of its own, barely missing his flesh.

With a trembling hand, Lila turned the key in the lock, the drawer creaking open to reveal a diary bound in leather that was cracked and faded. She leafed through the pages, the handwriting a spider's dance of ink and fear.

"It belonged to Abigail Whittaker," Lila read, her voice a murmur. "The last of the Whittakers. She writes about... rituals, and a hunger that couldn't be sated. Oh God..."

"What is it?" Daniel asked, peering over her shoulder.

"The last entry," she said, her voice breaking. "She talks about 'giving back to the earth', about an offering... She sacrificed her own family, hoping the land would be fertile again."

The revelation hung in the air like a shroud. Emma's eyes met Daniel's, a silent understanding passing between them. This wasn't just about survival anymore; it was about ending the cycle of Thanks-taking that Abigail had begun.

"We have to finish this," Emma said, steel lacing her words. "For everyone that the farmhouse has consumed."

The house seemed to wail in response, the floors buckling, sending a spray of splinters into the air. A cacophony of whispers swelled, rising and falling in a macabre rhythm. The walls pulsed more fiercely now, the heartbeat of the house quickening.

They stood amidst the chaos, the echoes of the past screaming for release, their own fear mingling with those of the souls long lost. The true horror of the Whittaker Farmhouse was unfolding, the layers peeling back to reveal the rot at its core.

And as they braced themselves, knowing that the darkness was far from spent, the whispers coalesced into a singular, bone-chilling promise: "You cannot give what has already been taken."

The feast was only beginning, and the past was just the first course.

Jack's laughter had always been the light in any darkness, but in the belly of the Whittaker Farmhouse, it twisted into something unrecognizable—a manic symphony that clashed with the whispers from the walls.

"Would you look at this? A real-life funhouse, folks," Jack barked out a laugh that spiraled into a delirious giggle. His shadow, cast by the flickering light of the oil lamp, danced grotesquely against the peeling wallpaper.

Lila clutched her notebook to her chest, a futile shield against the creeping terror. "Jack, this is no time for jokes," she said, but her voice was drowned in the rising tide of his madness.

Daniel glanced at Emma, catching the terror in her eyes as they watched Jack pace back and forth, muttering to himself. The dining table that they had left behind, laden with its gruesome feast, seemed to be a nexus of the house's power, a fact they couldn't ignore any longer.

"Jack, you need to focus, man. We have to think," Daniel tried to steady his voice, to pierce the fog that had enveloped Jack's mind.

"Think?" Jack's face contorted in mock thought. "Oh, I'm the king of this castle, Dan-o. And the king doesn't think—the king just is."

The floorboards groaned beneath them, and the house seemed to lean in, eager to hear Jack's deranged proclamations.

"We need to stick together, Jack. We're stronger that way," Emma pleaded, her hands outstretched, her nurse's instinct to soothe the afflicted kicking in despite the dread that coated every syllable.

But Jack's eyes were glassy, reflecting not the room, but some inner vision that seemed to hold him captive. "Together?" he snickered, "Oh, we're together, alright. We're a regular Norman Rockwell painting, aren't we?"

Lila's breath hitched as she whispered to Daniel, "The house—it's doing something to him. It's feeding off his fear and...and twisting it."

Jack suddenly stopped pacing and turned his gaze to the group, his eyes narrowing. "Don't you see it?" he hissed, "The more we fear, the more it grows. It's hungry, and we're the damn turkey!"

A cold draft swept through the room, carrying with it the scent of decay and the remnants of anguished screams. The very air felt thick with the misery that the farmhouse had consumed over decades, over countless Thanksgiving horrors.

Daniel took a step forward, his mind a tempest of fear and resolve. "So we starve it," he said, more to himself than the others. "We starve the house of its feast."

"Starve it?" Jack's voice cracked as he spun toward Daniel. "And how do you propose we do that, Einstein? Tell it we're on a diet?"

Lila's camera lay forgotten, her journalistic drive smothered by the oppressive force of the house. "We need to understand the rituals. Abigail's diary," she said, her gaze locked on the leather-bound book. "There has to be a way to reverse what she started."

They formed a tight circle, the diary in the center like a talisman. The words within were cryptic, the scrawls of a mind lost to a mania not unlike Jack's. Emma leaned in, her fingers tracing the arcane symbols sketched in the margins. "It speaks of balance," she murmured, "of something taken, something given."

"And what do we have left to give?" Jack's question was a spear, and in his eyes, the spark of lucidity flickered, fighting the encroaching darkness.

"We have ourselves," Daniel said, his voice steady despite the panic clawing at his insides. "Our will, our refusal to succumb to the madness."

The house groaned, a lullaby of creaks and sighs, as if it laughed at their defiance.

"We need to find the heart of this place," Lila said, standing up, her small frame rigid with newfound purpose. "The ritual started somewhere. There's a source."

"And we're going to find it," Daniel declared, his scholar's mind clinging to the notion of a solution, to a pattern beneath the chaos.

Emma nodded, her nurse's compassion now a steel-hard resolve. "For all those who were taken, we owe it to them."

Jack's laughter had receded, a curtain falling on the act of a mind fraying at the edges. He looked at his friends, a flicker of the old Jack—a plea for help or perhaps forgiveness—in his hollow gaze.

The house seemed to draw a breath, the shadows leaning in hungrily. The whispers were back, a chorus of the damned that swelled until words were indistinguishable from the wails of the wind outside.

They were but morsels in a feast that had spanned ages, and the house hungered for more. The feast of Thanks-taking was far from over. There was no end to the courses in this banquet of terror, only the mounting dread of what was to come.

The boards of the floor moaned a requiem as the quintet inched forward, their silhouettes stretched and warped like dark, contorted odes upon the farmhouse's grim walls. Daniel led with a lantern quivering in his hand, its feeble light casting monstrous shadows that seemed to writhe in delight. Each footfall was a heartbeat, each creak a breath drawn by the malevolence that ensnared them.

They moved through the hallway, a gullet of peeling wallpaper and warped wood, following the sour thread of rot that beckoned them deeper into the farmhouse's core. The house whispered secrets in a tongue not spoken by the living, a cadence that crept beneath skin and skull, promising truths too malignant for the mortal mind.

Daniel's voice was the first to slice the silence, a scalpel through the thick curtain of dread. "We can't let it break us," he said, his words as much for himself as for his friends. "We're here, and we're together. This thing, this... entity. It feeds on isolation, on the erosion of who we are."

But the house was a masterful predator. It sensed the taut threads of their resolve and, with a creak of floorboard or the flicker of a shadow, plucked them one by one. A portrait hung askew on the wall, its subject's eyes following them, the gaze filled with a sorrow so profound it bordered on madness.

Emma's hand found Daniel's, her grip tight enough to send her pulse skittering into him. "We're losing ourselves, Daniel," she whispered, her voice a thread unraveling fast. "I can feel it... taking pieces of me, feasting on the scraps."

Lila, camera hanging limply by her side, echoed Emma's dread with a sharp inhale as she surveyed the corridor, a stretch of abyss that seemed to both beckon and mock. "Every step is a step into its stomach," she murmured. "We're walking down its throat."

Jack's once booming laugh was now a hollow thing that scuttled behind them like a forlorn ghost. "Feasting on despair, huh?" His whisper barely carried over the house's rumbling chuckle. "Well, ain't that a mouthful."

It was then, as they descended the final stair that spiraled down like a coil of a rotten apple, they encountered the aberration—the grotesque mimicry of a Thanksgiving feast, but this time the chairs held twisted versions of themselves. Spectral doppelgangers, contorted in ghastly revelry, their mouths agape in silent laughter as they tore at translucent morsels of anguish.

Daniel's breath hitched, a strangled sound of disbelief. His doppelganger turned to him, its eyes pits of void that seemed to pull at his very essence, stripping away the layers of skepticism until all that was left was primal fear. "No," he gasped, "this isn't real."

But the scent was real—the copper tang of blood mixed with the sweetness of decay. It was a pungency that clung to the back of the throat, a flavor that stained the soul.

The doppelgangers paused, their feasting interrupted, and turned as one to the group, their movements a grotesque pantomime. Their eyes, if they could be called that, were endless wells of sorrow, draining the hope from their living counterparts.

Emma's double, a perversion of her kindness, gestured with a crooked finger, beckoning her to join the grim banquet. Emma's scream was a thing ripped from her, raw and jagged. "No! You're not me!"

Jack's double belched out a cacophony of broken laughter, a sound that seemed to fracture the very air around them. "Come, Jack. Sit," it mocked, its voice a twisted echo. "Dine on the hilarity of hopelessness."

Lila's doppelganger was the quietest, its eyes fixed upon her with an intensity that whispered of untold stories—tales that ended in nothingness. Lila's own eyes reflected the void before her, and she murmured, as if entranced, "It's writing my end..."

The farmhouse rumbled with glee, its timbers creaking in anticipation of the feast to come. It was a symphony of horror played upon the instruments of their psyches, a crescendo building toward an inexorable end.

"We have to break this cycle," Daniel managed to choke out, his voice a flimsy thing against the deafening silence of the doppelgangers. "We can't let it consume us—our fears, our pain. That's its power. We have to starve it. Starve it of us!"

But the house had already set its table, and in the eyes of their twisted selves, they saw the reflection of their own terror, a mirror held up to the soul, revealing not the surface but the depths—the darkness that lurked within, waiting to be fed.

The feast of Thanks-taking was just beginning, and the house was patient. It had all the time in the world to savor each bite.

The lantern's glow flickered as Daniel's declaration hung in the air, a fragile challenge to the house's sprawling darkness. For a moment, there was silence—both the living and the not-quite-dead seemed to hold their breath.

"We starve it," Daniel repeated, firmer now, the scholar within him clawing up from the depths of terror. "This... tradition it's created, it's a mockery. A trap for us to feed it willingly."

Emma's hands were no longer trembling when she released Daniel's. Her nurse's instincts, suppressed by the house's perverse feast, surged to the forefront. "He's right," she said, the tremor in her voice now a blade. "It's a parasite. It wants us to be thankful for our own damnation."

The grotesque figures at the table tilted their heads, a mockery of curiosity, their silence more taunting than any words.

Jack, whose humor had been twisted into a lifeline, now felt it fray. "So, we just... what?" he asked, eyes narrowed as he regarded his own grotesque reflection. "Turn our backs on it?"

"Exactly," Lila interjected, her voice steadying as she raised her camera, a shield between her and the abyss. "We document this—expose it, refuse it. We don't participate in this... charade."

Their resolve was a shared flame, now burning brighter against the encroaching dark. They turned away from the table, from the specters of themselves who sat feasting upon nothingness.

The house did not take kindly to their rebellion. The walls began to shudder, the very air thickening with malice. A chorus of whispers erupted, as if the house itself were admonishing them.

"You can't ignore me," it hissed through the wheezing wind, the voice not one but many, a tapestry of every scream ever uttered within its confines.

Daniel's shadow, long and distorted against the wall, seemed to stand taller. "We reject your feast," he said loudly, each word a hammer against the foundation of the house's power.

The doppelgangers stood now, their chairs scraping back in unison, a grotesque imitation of etiquette. They didn't advance, but their stillness was a threat, their silence a challenge.

Emma, eyes wide with a clarity born from the brink of insanity, began to recite something under her breath—a litany of things she was truly grateful for, her family, her health, the love she bore for Daniel, each word a note in a symphony opposite to the house's discordant tune.

Jack laughed, the sound bitter but defiant. "Yeah, and I'm thankful for real food, not whatever horror you've got plated up there!"

Lila's fingers moved over her camera with purpose, each click a testament to their resistance. "And I'm thankful for the truth, no matter how ugly," she added, her resolve transforming fear into something fiercer.

The farmhouse groaned, its timbers twisting as the temperature dropped, frost creeping like dead ivy over the windows. The doppelgangers' mouths opened, and the sound that spilled forth was a dire wailing, the lamentations of past victims who had succumbed to the feast.

Yet, the living quintet stood firm, a bulwark against the tidal wave of despair. Daniel, the skeptic, who demanded evidence, found the greatest proof not in the tangible but in the intangible will to resist.

Emma's recitations became louder, a mantra that filled the room, a light against the encroaching shadows. "We won't be part of your cycle," she declared, her words stitching a tapestry of gratitude genuine enough to rival the house's fabrications.

The house's retaliation was swift—a cacophony of groans and shrieks, the lights flickering as if it were trying to regain control, to reassert the narrative it had woven for so long.

But the friends had planted their feet, and in that moment, they were an unmovable force, a rebellion against an ancient eater of joy. There would be no feast this Thanksgiving, not of the kind the house craved. They had decided, with the power of their defiance, that the menu would change.

The doppelgangers, robbed of their purpose, began to falter, their forms flickering like faulty projections. The feast of Thanks-taking was beginning to crumble, the table setting itself for a conclusion that had been a century in the making.

The house shivered around them, the celebration of sorrow it had so carefully curated peeling away in tattered shreds, revealing beneath it something new—a glimmer of an ending, or perhaps, a new beginning. But it was not yet complete; the chapter of their escape, of their triumph, still awaited its final, harrowing lines.

The windows rattled as if bones in a giant's throat, the panes vibrating with the frequency of the damned. Emma's litany grew into a crescendo, cutting through the cacophony of the house's rage. Each window became a tableau of their worst fears, but they held their ground, unyielding, refusing to partake in the ghastly visions.

Daniel could feel the air pulsate with desperation as the entity realized its nourishment was slipping away. The scenes in the windows grew more frenetic, their contents spilling into the room. A grotesque turkey with flesh that pulsed and writhed crawled onto the table, its stuffing a squirming mass of unnameable things. But Daniel, Emma, Jack, and Lila turned their eyes away, sealing their sight from the horror.

"You can't do this," the house groaned, a petulant titan denied. Its voice was a rusted blade over their nerves, each word an attempt to slice into their resolve.

Jack's laughter had become a mantra, and now he boomed it out, a roar of defiance. "Oh, but we can! And we are!"

The chandeliers swayed as if caught in a tempest, their crystals clinking together to form a discordant lullaby. From the shadows stepped out the forms of pilgrims and natives, their faces void of eyes, their hands reaching out not in unity, but in accusation, a spectral reenactment of history twisted and wrong.

Lila's camera captured it all, the flash from the lens searing the images into nothingness. "Lies!" she shouted. "Your truths are lies!"

Emma clasped Daniel's hand, her fingers cold yet firm. "This house, it's a liar, a thief of joy. But we see it now, don't we? We see!"

Daniel nodded, his own voice a low rumble of agreement. "We do. We see through the veil."

The farmhouse shuddered, a creaking, wailing creature as its illusions began to shatter, the fabric of its malice tearing like old cloth. The Thanksgiving spread decayed before their eyes, mold overrunning the once enticing dishes, a visual echo of their rejection.

The specters of the dinner party, those haunting mimics of mirth and gratitude, dissipated like mist, their essence unspooling into the ether. The house moaned its sorrow, a low, keening wail that vibrated through floorboard and beam.

Then, as if the universe itself had recoiled in disgust, the very essence of the feast began to recoil from the friends. The walls bled shadows that retreated like a low tide, the ceiling lifted, and the air itself seemed to sigh with relief.

But it was not over. Not yet. The farmhouse had one last card to play, one final hand to force them to fold. The floor beneath them became unsteady, boards bending upwards, forming a maw that threatened to swallow them whole.

"We can't let up," Daniel yelled, pulling Emma closer to him as the floor heaved like the sea.

Lila swung her camera in a wide arc, her face set in grim determination. "Then we won't! This ends now!"

The house seemed to gather itself, its malevolence focusing into a single, terrible point. And from that point emerged the very core of the house's darkness, a maelstrom of loss and hunger. It was the essence of the Thanks-taking, the spirit of consumption without end.

They could see it now, a swirling vortex of shadow and light, a physical manifestation of the house's greed and despair. It was beautiful in its horror, terrible in its allure.

Jack, ever the warrior clad in jest, raised his fists. "Come on, you bastard. We're not done yet!"

The house's lament became a scream, a siren call to their primal fears. But they were a phalanx, a unit bound by more than friendship—by survival, by defiance, by an awakened awareness that some traditions were meant to be broken.

As the vortex swirled, as the house threw its last desperate illusion at them, they did not waver. Instead, they stepped forward, together, into the eye of the abomination, where the truth awaited, where the Final Course would be served, but not devoured.

The feast was ending, the guests were revolting, and the house... the house was learning the bitter taste of its own medicine.

The vortex swirled with increasing ferocity, a whirlpool of insatiable appetite that threatened to drag them into oblivion. But within this chaos, within the eye of the malevolent storm, they found clarity.

"It's feeding on us," Emma realized, her voice cutting through the din. "On our fears, our desperation."

Daniel, his eyes locked on the swirling darkness, nodded. "Then we starve it. We give it nothing."

"How?" Lila's voice was almost lost, a wisp of sound in the maw of darkness.

"By giving it everything," Jack said, an edge of madness in his voice. "We stuff it 'til it chokes!"

Their eyes met, each pair reflecting the same fierce resolution. They began to throw whatever they could grab into the vortex—chairs, silverware, pieces of the rotting feast, each item laden with their revulsion and refusal to be consumed. With every throw, they shouted out their defiance, their words talismans against the encroaching doom.

The farmhouse creaked and groaned, its foundations trembling as the vortex grew bloated with the offerings. The entity, gorged yet unsatisfied, wailed in confusion and rage, its cries echoing through the walls as if the building itself were in its death throes.

"We're not your feast!" Emma screamed, tearing a curtain from its rod and hurling it into the void.

"Not your victims!" Lila added, smashing her camera into the ground before kicking the pieces into the gaping maw.

"Not your entertainment!" Daniel declared, flinging a book from the shelf into the heart of the darkness.

"And sure as hell not your playthings!" Jack finished, tossing in the last of the shattered dinnerware.

The entity, bloated beyond measure, began to convulse and quake, the house shuddering with each spasm. Cracks snaked along the walls, and the ceiling splintered as the creature that was the farmhouse tried to regurgitate the excess, to rid itself of the poison that was their rebellion.

The very air turned heavy, a tangible pressure that seemed to press down upon them, suffocating and relentless. But they stood firm, their circle unbroken.

"It's too much!" Emma gasped, her eyes wide with terror and awe as the entity writhed.

"Keep going!" Daniel urged, his voice barely audible over the roar of the collapsing house.

The vortex faltered, its spirals losing cohesion, becoming erratic. The house's lament turned into a gargle, the sound of a glutton choking on its own greed.

"Leave something behind?" Jack panted, his eyes gleaming with a fierce light. "How about a piece of its own damn self?"

The friends, drained and pushed to the brink of their own sanity, did not hesitate. They understood now what the house demanded—their essence, their very souls.

With a final, collective shout, they took the last of their deepest fears, the darkest corners of their hearts, and flung them into the consuming whirlwind. Their shadows, their echoes, the imprints of their presence, all were cast into the gaping mouth of the farmhouse.

As these offerings tumbled into the abyss, the friends felt a pull, a tugging at the very core of their beings. They clung to each other, a lifeline against the riptide that sought to claim a part of their souls.

The entity that was the farmhouse convulsed once more, its form blurring, the boundary between the physical and the spectral crumbling. The vortex, engorged on the feast of their darkest selves, recoiled upon itself with a screech that pierced the veil of realms.

For a moment, all was silent, the friends locked in an embrace, the entity still, as if the world held its breath. And in that silence, in that stillness, the farmhouse began to implode, the gluttony it embodied now a force of self-destruction.

The friends felt the release, the severing of the entity's hold on them. They stumbled back, their eyes locked on the center of the room where the vortex had been. Now there was only emptiness, a void where the heart of the house had beaten with voracious hunger.

They knew it was not over; they could feel the parts of themselves they had left behind, the essence given up to the maw of Thanks-taking. But in its consumption, the entity had devoured itself, a snake eating its own tail.

As the house crumbled around them, the path to freedom lay exposed, a narrow passage of reality amidst the ruins of nightmares.

"Move!" Lila cried out, her voice hoarse but commanding, and they ran, half-falling, half-sprinting toward the promise of escape.

Behind them, the Whittaker Farmhouse collapsed into silence and dust, a monument to gluttony and despair that had finally, fatally, gorged on the one feast it could not withstand—the indomitable human spirit.

The relentless November chill had a bite that seemed personal, a gnawing reminder that the air outside the Whittaker Farmhouse was free to tear into them, much like the horrors that had feasted upon their innermost fears. The remnants of the house lay like a carcass, picked clean by the voracity of its own hunger. They stood there, the survivors, on the outskirts of the ruin, the sun a weak witness to the morning after.

Daniel's breath misted before him as he watched the sunrise with an intensity that bordered on the devout. Emma leaned into him, her body still trembling intermittently as if she might shudder apart. Jack's arm was around Lila, her camera now just a memory buried under the rubble of the house. They were silent, a silence borne not from a lack of words but from an excess of them, each too raw, too sharp for speech.

Daniel finally broke the silence. "It's really over, isn't it?"

Emma looked up at him, her green eyes a mirror to the desolation around them. "Is it ever? I can still feel it, Daniel. Inside." Her voice was a hoarse whisper, the remnants of screams that would echo in her nightmares.

"We gave it everything," Jack said, his usual levity a shipwreck in his tone. He gazed at his hands as though they were foreign to him, stained not with blood but with the intangible taint of the farmhouse.

Lila's camera had been her third eye, and now, without it, she seemed lost. "We documented nothing... and yet it's written in us. Every moment."

Their car, parked along the old dirt road, was a mute promise of return to normalcy. They moved towards it as if they were walking through molasses, the weight of survival heavy on their shoulders. Once inside, Daniel turned the key in the ignition, the engine's familiar growl a lullaby after the cacophony of the house's death throes.

As they drove away, the farmhouse in the rearview mirror was a dwindling specter, its presence fading but never truly gone. The towns they passed through were waking up, the scent of pumpkin pie and roasted turkey drifting from windows, a stark contrast to the feast they had endured.

"We should be thankful we're alive," Emma murmured, her gaze fixed on the passing scenery, a blur of mundane life that felt alien now.

"Yeah," Jack agreed, his voice empty. "Thankful." But the word seemed like an ill-fitting suit, something borrowed and never meant for them.

They reached Daniel's place first. He stood at the door, keys in hand, a hesitation gripping him. Would his home welcome him back or would the walls whisper of his absence? Emma's hand on his back was steady, a testament that some things remained unchanged.

At Emma's apartment, she paused at the threshold, turning to them. "Come in for coffee," she offered, but they declined. They shared a look, an understanding that solitude was a necessary step towards healing.

Jack dropped Lila off with a promise to call, a promise they all knew he would keep, not out of duty but out of necessity. They were bound now, not just by friendship but by shared survival.

Finally alone, Jack sat in his quiet apartment, a beer in hand at 9 a.m. It wasn't even Thanksgiving yet, the actual day still a calendar page away. He toasted to an empty room, to the echoes of a feast that would never leave him.

Lila sat at her desk, her fingers poised above the keyboard, but the words wouldn't come. How could she write of what had happened? Who would believe it? And yet, the story clawed at her from the inside, a tale desperate to be told.

Daniel and Emma found themselves in the kitchen, mechanically making coffee. They sat at the table, not touching their mugs, just staring at them, as if expecting the liquid to solidify into another grotesque meal.

"We'll have to talk about it, you know," Daniel said, his voice a stranger's in the quiet apartment.

Emma nodded. "Not yet though. For now, let's just..." She trailed off, unable to finish.

"Live," Daniel said, finishing for her. "For now, we just live."

The farmhouse stood in ruin, but its appetite felt undiminished, lurking in the rubble, waiting. It had tasted the essence of its invaders, the flavors of their spirits infused into its broken beams and shattered walls.

Thanksgiving would come again. The feast fades, but hunger... hunger is eternal. And in the forgotten corner of Massachusetts, a foundation hungry for repair, for revival, awaited its next helping of souls brave or foolish enough to challenge the legends.

The end.

Don't miss out!

Visit the website below and you can sign up to receive emails whenever S.B. Fates publishes a new book. There's no charge and no obligation.

https://books2read.com/r/B-A-EFGAB-CLJQC

BOOKS 2 READ

Connecting independent readers to independent writers.

Did you love *Harvest of Bones: A Thanksgiving Horror Anthology*?
Then you should read *Eclipsed Virtues: Tales of the Damned
Superhuman*[1] by S.B. Fates!

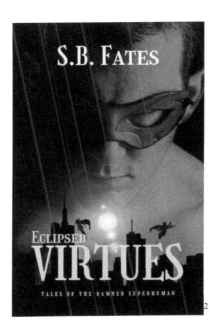

²

Dive into a realm where superpowers reign supreme but come at a dire
cost in S.B. Fates' enthralling anthology, "Eclipsed Virtues: Tales of the
Damned Superhuman." This collection of dark fantasy stories explores
the blurred lines between heroism and villainy, unearthing the chilling
consequences of superhuman capabilities.

"Shadowed Justice" reveals the Night Whisperer, a vigilante with a
haunting ability to trap souls in an eternal torment, finding pleasure in
their endless screams."The Haunting of Hero's Hill" uncovers an
invisible force preying on superheroes, stripping them of their powers
and memories, leaving nothing but an empty shell."Crimson Savior"

1. https://books2read.com/u/bPeYx7

2. https://books2read.com/u/bPeYx7

delves into the life of Lumina, a beloved hero with a dark secret: her healing powers require a terrible sacrifice."Voices in the Static" explores the mind of Resonance, a telepath who hears whispers from beyond, pushing him towards atrocities in exchange for power."Eyes of the Abyss" follows Gaze, a hero tormented by visions of his own descent into madness, questioning if his foresight is a gift or a curse."The Parasite Paradox" deals with a hero who absorbs others' powers and, with them, their darkest desires, leading to a chaotic and terrifying identity crisis."Frozen in Fear" presents a time-stopping heroine trapped in a loop of witnessing horrific murders, questioning her reality and her role in these events."Pandora's Mask" tells of a hero seduced by a mask offering immeasurable power, only to find his identity consumed by an ancient malevolent spirit."Echoes of the Damned" explores a superhuman's ability to raise the dead and the eerie prophecies and pleas for rest that follow."Infinite Descent" delves into the nightmare of a flyer drawn into the night sky, facing unspeakable horrors and an eternal detachment from earth.

"Eclipsed Virtues" delves into the dark side of power, presenting stories filled with psychological horror, moral ambiguity, and tragic heroes. Fates masterfully weaves tales of twisted powers, ethical dilemmas, and chilling narratives, reminding us that our greatest enemies might just be the powers that dwell within. Step into a world of supernatural abilities and unraveling madness, and discover the thin line between savior and damned.

Also by S.B. Fates

Dark Corners: Tales from the Shadow Realms
The Shadows We Cast: Tales of the Uncanny
Shadows of the Multiverse
Echoes in the Void
Shadows of Malice: Chilling Chronicles of All Hallows' Eve
Eclipsed Virtues: Tales of the Damned Superhuman
Harvest of Bones: A Thanksgiving Horror Anthology

Milton Keynes UK
Ingram Content Group UK Ltd.
UKHW041822211123
432980UK00001BB/134